The
Chestnut
House

Can the truth finally set them both free?

Anna
Valencia

The Book Guild Ltd

First published in Great Britain in 2022 by
The Book Guild Ltd
Unit E2, Airfield Business Park
Harrison Road, Market Harborough
Leicestershire, LE16 7UL
Freephone: 0800 999 2982
www.bookguild.co.uk
Email: info@bookguild.co.uk
Twitter: @bookguild

This work is entirely fictitious and bears no resemblance to any persons living or dead.

Typeset in 11pt Minion Pro

Printed on FSC accredited paper
Printed and bound in Great Britain by 4edge Limited

ISBN 978 1913913 854

British Library Cataloguing in Publication Data.
A catalogue record for this book is available from the British Library.

For my father Robert and my mother Paula

1

Emma

2017

Stazzana. I don't recognise the name, and yet as the lawyer speaks the air around me shifts slightly, the song of it echoing through my mind. I catch the faint scent of tomatoes and I'm back in the garden with my nonno Giovanni. I see his sprightly figure bent over weeding, and I remember how lovingly he tended to his plants. He and my nonna Assunta ran an ice-cream parlour, but he was happiest in the garden, with the earth between his fingers and the sky above his head. He'd learnt to work with the Scottish weather and seasons, he told me, so different to his native Italy. Pushing my nose into the roses and breathing them in, filling a basket with beans and sweet peas, picking mint and rubbing its perfume over my hands; these were my favourite times with him. It was where he seemed to relax and would on occasion reminisce a little about Tuscany.

He'd tell me about the mountains and their queen, a rocky peak he called *La Pania*. From there, he said, you could see the world. The glittering blue sea and all the villages of the

Garfagnana, tiny dots in the swathes of chestnut-clad slopes. He'd talk about a childhood marked by the rhythms and rituals of the year, the *vendemmia*, the grape harvest, the olive picking, the chestnut collection. He'd forget I was there sometimes, his voice soft with nostalgia, his soul back in Italy. I treasured those confidences, those moments I caught a glimpse of another side of my grandfather, another world. A world where lemons grew on trees and wolves ran wild.

I alight on the memory I am looking for, a summer's evening sitting with Nonno watching the flames of a bonfire lick the sky. Usually we worked in companionable silence; my grandfather was never one for chatter. That evening he brought me a small glass of his elderflower wine, a nod to my new teenage status. As we gazed into the crimson flames I could see he was far away, his eyes misted with memory. I waited patiently, feeling grown-up with my glass of wine. It tasted of spring, light and full of promise.

"You should have seen the fires we had at Stazzana, *cara* Emma," he murmured, so quietly I almost missed it. Intrigued to finally learn something about my grandparents' life before they emigrated to Scotland I kept still, praying he would continue uninterrupted. "If the frost returned in the spring we'd light fires between the rows of vines, to keep the plants warm. We'd do the same for the apple trees in the orchard at night, and it would be like another world, full of smoke and shadows. My father could tell, of an evening, whether the cold would return. He said he could smell it in the air, feel it in his bones. He said I would learn to do the same, when the farm was mine." He trails off, and I hear the regret in his voice, the pain he carries. "It was a magical place," he continues, the words slipping out into the dusky night air. "A place that now exists only in memory, a way of life that is no more." There was so much I wanted to ask him, but before I had a chance my grandmother's voice came barking out from the house, shattering the beauty of the moment and breaking our connection. My grandfather stiffened, as if reminded of a rule he was breaking. He mumbled an excuse and limped back towards the house, leaning on his walnut walking stick...

"Emma? Are you OK?" Sam is pressing my arm, a concerned look on his face. I'm brought back to the present moment, to the wet April day in Edinburgh, to our meeting with William, the family lawyer.

"Yes." I nod, not yet ready to share the precious memory I have recovered, unsure what any of this means yet.

William clears his throat and continues, "The house and its terrain, inherited by your mother from your late grandparents, I believe. Located in northern Tuscany." He has the deeds, which are hand-written and look ancient, and a map. I press him for more information, but he knows no more, and I sense our time is up. He offers to put us in touch with a lawyer in Italy, and again offers his condolences. In a daze we leave the office and emerge onto the streets of Edinburgh, where the world is rain-stained shades of grey, from the slick slate streets to the ashen skies. Sam drives us home, and we pick the girls up from my best friend Cat en route.

As we drive my thoughts drift back to my grandparents, and the house in Italy where my nonno grew up. This house that my mother inherited following their deaths, and never visited to my knowledge. My grandparents passed away while I was studying to become a teacher at university, first my grandfather and then my grandmother half a year later. For her, life had been inconceivable without 'l'altra metà della sua mela', the other half of her apple, her soulmate. I remember crying, missing them, but the natural order of things was respected, and I was so wrapped up with my new life that to tell the truth I had no time to grieve for long. I was giddy with the first flush of freedom, the joy of being young and alive in a world full of possibility. I had friends from all over the world, a hot whirl of a social life and that naïve conviction that our generation could really make a difference.

So young, so foolish, we were playing at life, believing ourselves with our youth and our long words to be safely distanced from the rawness of our subject matter.

Two decades have now passed, I am a mother myself and one month ago all that distance was ripped away when my parents were killed in a car accident. Since then I am living on the precipice, constantly peering into the void, squinting through the hazy fog of grief. The odd thing about grief is that you do not, as you might imagine, feel distraught all the time. It's as if our brains can't accept the enormity of it all at once, and so in small doses our sorrow seeps in. One moment I can laugh with my two small daughters, I can kiss my husband, I can sing along to the radio, and then I remember. Sometimes remembrance sneaks in uninvited and I am left sobbing on the floor, gasping for breath, praying for respite. Sometimes I am driving and out of nowhere tears are silently spilling down my cheeks, a bottomless well of salty sadness. Sometimes denial stamps his foot angrily and I rant at life, and sometimes a grey melancholy stains everything, and I can no longer see the colours.

We collect the girls from Cat, and she hugs me tight. I return her embrace weakly; I have no friendship to give. I am empty. Our eldest, Aria, chatters away about the day they have had, and I try to give her my attention, to return from the past to the present moment. I play a role with them, determined not to let the despair inside me leach into their world but terrified it will anyway. I hear the forced jollity in my voice and wince at the falsity of it all. They don't appear to notice, or if they do, they forgive me instantly. Aria is five, and her beauty sometimes takes my breath away. My perfect creation. Her little sister Luna is two and her mirror image, although very different by nature. Aria is made of golden fire; she burns brightly, like the sun. Luna is her counterpart: the moon, serene and wise beyond her years. An old soul, my mother always said. Aria puts her hot little hands around my neck, presses kisses onto my cheeks, sobs with me when she remembers her nonni. Luna watches me with those knowing green eyes and seems to read my every thought. They are sleepy from their long day and soon we have two nodding blonde heads in the back of the car. I carry Luna up to her bed, breathing in the warmth and the reassurance of her solid little body. I lay her carefully down in her cot bed, and she snuggles up to her bear. For a moment I watch her breathing, and kiss her cheek, soft as pink satin. I head downstairs and find Sam in the kitchen.

"Vino?" he asks, wrapping his arms around me. My rock. I melt into his chest, feeling the love and support I need surrounding me. I nod and head over to the lounge, sinking deep into the sofa, rubbing my aching neck. We peer at the copy of the deeds to the house William has given us. "They never mentioned it?" Sam asks. "Your grandparents, your mum? Did your mum ever go there?" I shake my head slowly, searching my memories from the time after my grandparents had died. Yes, there it is, a conversation with my mother.

"My mother did tell me," I say, looking up at Sam. "It's the farm my grandfather inherited when his parents passed away. They'd been in Scotland many years by then and had never gone back. My grandmother tried to sell it, but apparently it was a wreck and no-one was ever interested. She told her it was a bad place, that it was cursed, but she would never talk any more about it." I sip my wine, gratefully feeling it coat my dry throat and numb a little of the pain in my chest that always accompanies remembering my mother. "I was away at uni at the time, then I was off with my first job, getting married, having the girls. I never really thought about it to be honest. Life got in the way." I realise vaguely this is the first time since the accident that my mind has been preoccupied, that underneath the emptiness there is a seed of something. Hope? Interest? A real-life mystery? My parents cannot come back, but perhaps I can find out more about our family, find other surviving relations in Italy. I know this is sudden and I am not thinking clearly, but one thought crystallises above all the noise and I know what we need to do. "Sam," I say, breaking the silence. He looks over at me, this blue-eyed husband of mine, who has promised to stand by my side no matter what. "We need to go to Italy." I don't know the details yet – there is the house to think of, Sam's job, the girls – but I know we will find a way. If he agrees. This feels like a crossroad in our lives; we may be about to take the road less travelled. He pauses, but only briefly. In that pause all the possible permutations of our lives crackle in the air, in a metaphysical dance of chance. He nods and smiles at me. My soulmate.

"When shall we go?" he asks, taking my hand. As is my way now, tears rise to my eyes, blurring my vision. But this time they lack the bitterness of despair; they wash away some of the pain, and Italy beckons.

2

Giuliana

2017

I have spent a lifetime trying to forget, and now I am nearing the end, memories are flooding in uninvited. I am worn and creased, ninety years old, and I no longer have the strength to resist them. I find that all my years of suppressing them have in fact achieved the reverse. They are bottled, sharp, preserved in time. There is a bittersweet taste to their return; the pleasure is spiked with pain. I ran from them for so many years; now I can stop and let the years fall away. I can go home.

My mind takes me back to the last *vendemmia* of my childhood, the year before war broke out and life as we knew it changed forever. It was the end of summer, long days of playing outside and exploring the mountains once our morning chores were done. Looking back it was an innocent time, an idyllic way of life. When the mountains were ours alone, and freedom was our birthright. The annual *vendemmia* was usually in the month of October, when the earth was still baked with memories of summer, before the wheel of the year started to creak into action once again. The grapes hung heavily on the vines, their violet skins bursting with juice. The eldest and wisest nonni decided when the time was right for the harvest to begin, and it heralded the start of weeks of hard work, as each family helped others in the village. My own nonno would listen for the *Tramontana*, the wind that came over the Apennines. He'd tell me how it whispered to him of the blue-cold winter on its way, stories of ice and snow from the northern lands.

I remember the last day of the *vendemmia* at Stazzana, a farm on the edge of our village down in the valley. It was the home of my best friend Matteo, and I had always thought it a magical place, hidden away from the rest of the world. Protected by acres of forest and chestnut-covered hills, the farmhouse emerged in the centre of a clearing, surrounded by several acres of sloping fields. A river ran along the bottom of the valley and during the summer months we spent afternoons in the shade of the trees, splashing in the icy water where trout flashed in silver streaks across the shallow pools.

That day we rose at dawn and trekked down to Stazzana along the old mule track, carrying baskets full of bread, *salame*, cheese and wine for our lunch. From the village of Montaltissimo the track descended through the woods and ran parallel to the river. We passed first the *mulino*, the mill, and then the *metato*, the chestnut house, where just a few weeks later we would be carrying sacks full of chestnuts, ready for them to be dried over the fire and ground into flour. I haven't tasted a chestnut in decades, but I recall so clearly the aroma of them roasting on the fire, the cloying taste of the polenta that saw us through the mountain winters, the comforting *tullore* that my mother made by cooking them in milk, adding a few bay leaves for flavour.

We were a merry party, laughing and chatting as we walked. Our mood was light knowing it was the last day of the grape harvest, and that the day's work would be followed by the traditional festa, eating, drinking and dancing into the night. I walked with my mother and father, my two sisters Margherita and Rosa, both older than I, and my little brother Luciano. My sisters were typical teenagers, always whispering amongst themselves and making eyes at boys, and as a rule I left them to it. Luciano was a sweet child, always desperate to tag along with Matteo and I on our adventures. Sometimes we let him and would make allowances, but I'm ashamed to recall that often we would escape on our own, leaving him crying with frustration in Mother's arms.

We left the shade of the woods and started to climb the meadow towards the farmhouse, where Matteo and his family were already out in the vineyards lining the terraces above the house. His two Maremma sheepdog puppies came bounding across the field barking a warning, only to collapse wriggling on the grass when they recognised us. I stroked their tummies, soft as white clouds, and they licked my hands and face. When Matteo was ten they had been gifted to the family by a shepherd who herded his flock from the high mountains in summer to the lower hills in winter where he sought shelter for them. Tiny balls of fluff, they made us laugh with their puppy antics and constant play, and they'd grown at an alarming rate. Each week they seemed to have doubled and their rough play could easily send a child flying. Their inky, soulful eyes could be full of naughtiness one moment as they leapt upon a passer-by, and tug at the heartstrings the next as they lay on the grass and looked up at you, begging your forgiveness for their latest misdemeanour. Highly protective, their main purpose was to protect the livestock, a job they took very seriously. Their protection also extended to their family and our little group of friends, and they were always on the look-out, watching for wolves, wild boars or snakes.

I broke away from the others and ran ahead up to the farmhouse. Stazzana has always been a welcome sight for me, and not only because of my friendship with Matteo. She was built by Matteo's great-grandfather, and she is both typical of many farmhouses in the area and completely unique in all the world. Her stones are held together with *muratura povera*, little more than mud, and the colour of the earth lends a warmth that makes her glow in the sunlight. There is something special about Stazzana, as if she remembers every soul who has breathed between her walls, lived and died under her beams. As if she is listening, protecting, caring. The laughter of ages trapped within her eaves; the love that has been shared there soaked into the stones that once lay in the river. I always greet her in my mind as I approach, and I sense her welcome. Oddly, I have always felt more at home at Stazzana than in the house I was born in.

I rushed past the house that morning, eager to find Matteo before the others arrived, to confirm our plans for later that night. I scrambled up the terraces, pushing through the vines until I reached the row I'd seen Matteo working on, but as I stepped out I found it to be empty. Breathing fast from my uphill exertion I looked around, my senses alerting me to an ambush. Sure enough Matteo sprang out from a leafy vine, knocking me to the ground and pinning me there, laughing at having caught me off guard. He was framed against the sea-blue sky, his black curls falling towards me, tickling my face. His eyes shone darkly, alive with mischief. His face was bronzed after a summer working in the Tuscan sun, and his broad smile melted away any anger I felt at his trick. I struggled to free myself and realised with some surprise how strong he'd become over the summer. I knew I must use cunning if I could not use force. The smile fell from my face and I stared at the vine, hissing, "Snake!" Matteo reacted instantly, rolling me away to the side and jumping to his feet. I hooted with triumph and fled down the row of vines, with Matteo just a pace behind me.

"Giuliana!" came a disapproving voice, and our games were curtailed by the arrival of my family. We settled down to work and began picking the plump clusters of grapes, dropping them into the chestnut barrels that sat at the end of each terrace. We stopped at midday for our lunch, sitting in the shade of the apple trees in the orchard. The sun was still strong, but I sensed it would not be many days before the autumn storms arrived.

After lunch I stretched out on the grass, soaking up the last warm rays of the year. Matteo sat with his parents and his two brothers, Francesco and Giovanni, both older than he. With them sat his mother's sister, Giulia, her husband Renzo and their four children, Fiorlindo, Canzio, Rosina and Antonietta. They lived up above Stazzana in the hamlet of Sassi, where they farmed their steep terraced land. I sensed someone seeking my attention and glanced towards where Matteo sat. Instead I saw his cousin Fiorlindo studying me from his reclined pose, his gaze unfaltering even when my eyes met his. I looked away, flushing, seized with a sudden desire to disappear. There was no smile, no friendly wave, just a cold scrutiny that made me aware of my changing body in a way that made me uncomfortable. Matteo's cousins had always been part of our gang of children, meeting for yearly rituals like the harvest, playing in the piazza after Mass, attending lessons at the small school in Sassi. Fiorlindo had been a sly child, quick to charm the schoolteacher, slippery as a trout when it came to getting out of trouble. He showed little inclination to take over the family farm despite being the eldest, and Matteo and I were instinctively wary of him.

After lunch we continued picking the last of the grapes, and as the sun started to sink towards La Pania, Matteo's father declared our work complete, to great cheers from the workers. The men carried the laden barrels down to the meadow, and we children stripped off our shoes in excitement, ready for our favourite part of the *vendemmia*. Slipping and sliding we jumped on the grapes as their skins burst and the juice flowed, while our families sang traditional harvest songs which rang out across the valley. Sticky and flushed we finally clambered out of the barrels and marched along to the spring that emerged from the rocks up above the farmhouse. The spring cascaded down into a branch of the river and we all washed off, joking and splashing each other with the freezing water as we did so. When we returned in dry clothes the long table was laid in the orchard, lit by candles and a thousand stars starting to appear in the dusky sky. The last day of the harvest usually coincided with the full moon, and that year the moon was already rising above Montaltissimo, a gilded lantern hanging heavily in the night sky. We knew it would be a memorable evening of feasting, drinking the last of the previous year's wine, storytelling by the fire and dancing until midnight.

As I walked up to the table my mouth watered at the sight of so many of my favourite dishes, prepared by the womenfolk of the village. I spotted *tordelli con ragù*, parcels of pasta filled with pork and cheese, drizzled with a meat sauce and piled high on a dish. Next to them was a mountain of chestnut polenta, and a steaming bowl of *zuppa di farro*, spelt soup. There were various types of *salame* and prosciutto, and matured *pecorino* cheese made with sheep milk. There was chestnut bread, sweet and crumbly, and plenty of last year's olive oil to mop it up. There was *castagnaccio* for dessert, a cake made with chestnut flour, olive oil, rosemary and walnuts. I had helped my mother to prepare one the day before, cooking it in the communal bread oven we all shared up in the village. We feasted and drank and laughed, and the celebrations resonated through the still night air.

Matteo was sitting further down the table, and when he caught my eye I knew exactly what he was thinking. I slipped away from the table unnoticed, disappearing into the inky night away from the candlelight. Matteo grasped my hand in the darkness, and silently we started to climb upwards through the trees, heading for the summit above the farmhouse. For years Matteo and I had been exploring the hills and mountains around us, studying the plants and wildlife we came across. Always curious, we were natural explorers, lost in a world of a magic older than the mountains themselves. Out in the wilderness we always felt completely at home, free to be ourselves. While other children shied away from the dark forests and the beasts who lived there, Matteo and I were in our element. The mountains ranged for thousands of miles, and had we ever become lost or injured the chances of finding us would have been slim, but we never felt we were in any danger in the hills. We trusted each other with our lives. Matteo was as much a part of me as the mountains were. We were inseparable, and I imagined that was how it would always be. The most dangerous part about our escapades was usually returning home, clothes ripped and faces filthy, to the wrath of our parents and grandparents.

That night we were on a mission, and the festivities and the full moon provided us with the perfect opportunity. We knew all the tracks by heart and the two of us were born hunters, able to move without sound through the woods, our bodies bent low to the ground. On the steep ascent we spread our weight between our feet and hands, grasping familiar trees on the way, safe in our knowledge of their age and strength. Away from the festa the woods were silent; there was only the sound of our beating hearts. The moonshine threw dark shadows around us, creating illusions and shifting shapes, but we were relying on senses other than sight. The touch of bark under our fingertips, the scents on the breeze, the silence of the birds and beasts that told us a predator was near. There was another sense too, something deeper, the instinct that only truly came alive in the wilderness. At the top of the hill we emerged into a clearing lined with old oaks and we quickly climbed our favourite, a tree with generous, well-spaced limbs. There was a spot high up on a thick branch with space for two, and from there we gazed out over the surrounding hills. The valley dipped down sharply below us, and rose equally steeply on the other side, up where the Lost Barn was. We'd named it that when we were children, in our world of make-believe it was beyond the map, off limits to all but the bravest warriors, the only way to find it was by following your heart. We lived in a land where myth and reality existed side by side, where the caves were full of fairies and the mountains were slumbering giants.

We settled onto our branch and turned ourselves around so that we were looking down at the glade beneath the oak trees. Now the moon was high it was so bright we could see every stalk of *nepitella*, the wild mint that grows so abundantly in the warmer months. We could see the bones we had left in the centre of the clearing, our bait was laid out, but would the hunters come? We had no patience in the school room and were constantly in trouble, but in the woods Matteo and I could wait for hours on end, never moving a muscle. From the edge of the clearing I thought I saw a shadow stretch, and then retreat. Matteo had also spotted the movement, and we stared, amazed, as a shape slunk out from the darkness. We held our breath and Matteo squeezed my hand tight; this was the moment we had been waiting for.

For months we'd been tracking a wolf pack, finding their scat and paw prints, and occasionally the remnants of a wild boar or a deer that had been their dinner. We'd come to know their routes, how often they passed by Stazzana, and this evening we'd set our trap, hoping but not really expecting to see them. The first wolf to brave the opening was large, clearly a male. We could read his wary body language: ears down, every sense alert to danger. The moonlight glinted off his coat, and we could see shades of grey, darker around his neck, marking his status within the pack. He sniffed the air, raised his head and stared straight at us in our tree hide-out. Time seemed to freeze as the connection was made, our triangle of humans and wolf drawn. His eyes glowed yellow, completely fearless. I recognised in them something that lived inside me, the wildest and most joyful part of myself. The part I shared only with Matteo and the mountains. I didn't know it at the time but looking back now I think it was freedom – the freedom to be your whole self. He must have decided we were no threat as he lowered his head and took a bone. Some signal undetected by us must have been given as more shadows crept out of the undergrowth, and the rest of the pack joined him. They feasted on the pig bones just as we had feasted earlier in the evening ourselves, and it was our greatest privilege to watch them. Relaxed and at ease we could observe and admire them, and I still remember that night as one of the best of my life. Watching these magnificent creatures, the heads of the food chain, the hunters who took only what they needed.

Towards midnight they left, melting back into the darkness and disappearing into the woods. Matteo and I hurried back down to Stazzana where the festa was still going, though the flames had turned to embers and the dancing had given way to storytelling. We took our places by the fire and sat listening to the tales of old, not really hearing them but reliving the wondrous events of our evening in the woods. Matteo and I grinned at each other in the firelight, united by our experience. We were one being, we shared everything, and I believed that was how it would always be. It was the last festa of the summer, and little did we know it, the last festa many of us would ever attend.

3

Emma

2017

We land at Pisa a month later, and my first impression is the light. The brightness is blinding, and I grope about in my rucksack for sunglasses. The sky is not the cornflower blue of a British sky, but a stronger, braver shade. The heat shimmers off the runway and through it we spot the mountains in the distance. Like a mirage they beckon us; what will we find there?

We left the Scottish countryside at dawn, with mist lingering in the valleys, green smudges of hedges and trees lining the fields. It was cool for June and we are clad in shirts, jeans and jumpers – now unbearable in the heat that envelops us. As we leave the airport I catch the scent of jasmine, the flowers trailing above the entrance and the aroma of freshly ground coffee from a nearby bar. I turn my face to the sun and gratefully breathe in the warmth. The colours dazzle; it seems like a filter has been applied to everything and we are in a new world.

In what feels like serendipity there was a house for rent in the hamlet of Montaltissimo, very close to where Stazzana is located. Apparently there are lots of empty properties in the mountain villages, as younger generations chose the lure of the city or life abroad over the countryside. I have been in touch with the owner, Pietro, and they are expecting us.

In the end it was surprisingly easy to extricate ourselves from the UK. We become so entrenched in our daily lives that we come to see them as part of our identity, but now we have unwoven some of those ties and flown away I see them fall to the wayside, mere accessories. Our core, our essential being, is so much more, and translates wherever we go. I decided to leave my teaching job, unwilling to make the school wait any longer for my return. Sam is self-employed with his carpentry work and is hoping he'll be able to pick it back up when we return. Our little house has been rented out to a friend, who conveniently was looking for somewhere at just the time we left. My friend Cat was worried when I told her about our trip, concerned that without my support network I'll be unable to cope.

"It's too soon, Emma," she protested on the evening I told her. "Who will you turn to? You don't know a soul out there." She's right, and I know she worries I will lose myself, unravel the few strands that are still holding me together. But I am already lost, and I can't explain it to her, but I am hoping to find something in Italy.

"I'll have Sam, and the girls," I reply, and she gives me a knowing look. Sam has been my rock, looking after the children, taking care of everything. But he won't talk about the accident, or my parents. He can't find the words to ask me how I'm feeling, and the distance between us is growing. Our conversation feels stilted, meaningless. The silence between words hangs between us, and I don't know how to cross the divide. Worse still, I lack the inclination to try. I barely recognise myself these days, so Sam must feel he's married to a stranger. I'm sure he wants the old days back as much as I do, the old Emma who sang in the shower and cooked the girls' favourite pancakes every morning. Perhaps he is hoping to find her in Italy.

As we leave Pisa and head north I gaze out of the window at the olive trees, the vineyards, the houses in warm shades of yellow, orange and ochre. Everything seems so different, and yet strangely familiar. Sam is driving, concentrating on the road and remembering to stay on the right, adjusting to the Italian rules of the road. The girls are both asleep in the back of our hire car, fair curls clinging damply to their necks, cheeks flushed with the heat. We pass the ancient fortified town of Lucca, skirting around the city walls, and the scenery becomes more rural. We enter a long rocky tunnel and emerge to find ourselves in the mountains. I've read a little about the area we are heading to, the Garfagnana. Tuscany is well known for its classic beauty, the fields of sunflowers and olive trees, the patchwork slopes of the Chianti region. The wonder of Florence and Siena, the fame of Cortona and San Gimignano. The Garfagnana seems to be off the map, generally unmentioned in tourist guidebooks. It's where the Apennines and the Apuan Alps meet in a rugged landscape, a hidden world that has remained thus for centuries. A part of Italy shrouded in mystery, rich with legends. As we wind our way up the valley our guide is the river Serchio, its green-blue water glistening alongside us.

"Look!" I say to Sam, and up ahead is a bridge that looks like it is straight out of a fairytale. I recognise it from a photo on Pinterest, the Ponte del Diavolo, the Devil's Bridge. Its narrow stone arches over the river unevenly, appearing to be a trick of the eye. Legend says that the man building it ran out of time, and in his despair struck a deal with the devil: he would finish it in exchange for the first soul to cross the bridge. With the help of the local priest the man outwitted the devil and sent a dog across for him to claim. Mad with rage the devil dove into the river, creating a white whirlpool of fury, and was never seen again. The bridge does have an unearthly feel, and I keep my eye on it as it fades out of view in my mirror.

We pass tiny hilltop villages overlooking the valley, always dominated by a church. Small patches of the hillside have been planted with rows of olives and vines, but most of the mountainside is wild. I'm reminded of my childhood conversations with my grandfather in his garden, his tales of wolves running free. I imagine they could roam for miles here without coming into contact with civilisation, and I wonder if they still live here, or whether they have been hunted down like in so many parts of Europe.

At a town called Gallicano we turn off the main road and start to climb up a narrow lane, whose sharp hairpin bends make me glad I haven't eaten recently. The wayside is dotted with red poppies, and grass as high as the car ripples as we pass. The *pianura*, the valley floor, falls away below us as we drive ever higher, passing little farmsteads along the way. The temperature has dropped five degrees since Pisa and we wind down the windows, breathing in the sweet air with a hint of wildflowers on the breeze. As we drive I wonder when this road was built – I imagine after my grandparents left in the forties. Did they travel from the house down to Gallicano the way we are driving? Did they have a mule to ride, or would they have been on foot? The way is steep, and the return journey must have been difficult. Memories of them in Scotland drift back, of their house, their possessions. They had little from their old life here – I remember an effigy of the Madonna that was precious to them, my grandmother's first embroidery, a family bible. I think of them, always so dedicated to my mother and me. *Family is everything*, my grandmother used to tell me. Is my mother with them now? I hope so; it comforts me to think of them reunited. My vision starts to mist up with tears and I hastily blink them away – I don't want to miss anything about our arrival. I'm sure we must be close now, and as I gaze out over the hills to my left, I have a sudden sense of homecoming, of recognition. Something about the valley with the little village tucked into the hill above it, something about the lay of the land, the shape of the trees. I shiver despite the heat, and the feeling passes as quickly as it came.

Around the next corner there is a road sign for Montaltissimo, and we've arrived. A little piazza is on our left, edged with stone cottages, all decorated with red-and-pink trailing geraniums. On the far side of the piazza is a rendered church with wooden doors wide open, and a stone church tower housing a large bell. Our satnav tells us to turn up a lane next to the church, and as we pass a tiny walled cemetery I get a glimpse of graves splashed with brightly coloured flowers. We follow the lane past rows of grape vines, their heavy leaves waving a lazy welcome. We approach a collection of old stone houses leaning into one another, with doors and windows scattered in an apparently random fashion. It's hard to tell which house is which, and several of them appear to be abandoned, with missing roof tiles and peeling shutters, their eyes long closed. Two dogs sleeping in the courtyard shade wake from their doze and spring into action, surrounding our car and barking madly at us. They sound quite ferocious, but I notice their tails are wagging, and we seem to pass some test as they allow us to get out and stretch our legs. Pietro comes to greet us, all smiles and vigorous handshakes. I like him immediately and find that I can, to my relief, understand his Italian fairly well.

The girls wake up, and in their sleepy state cling to us as we introduce them. From the safety of our arms they glance around curiously and are soon wriggling to be set free. They trot off and Sam follows them as they run along to an orchard full of apple trees. Pietro shows me to the house, explaining that it has stood empty for several years. The house is the end cottage on a row of diminutive dwellings, and I have to duck as I enter the front door. I think of Sam, all six foot four of him, and wonder how he will cope. Clearly, these houses weren't designed for Nordic giants. The house has been cleaned but a musty smell lingers, bringing to mind lavender and moths. The sunlight flooding in through the newly opened shutters catches the dust particles floating in the air, caught in their slow dance. The cottage is simple and rustic, but there is everything we will need. As we look around I'm drawn to the view from each window, each different and more spectacular than the last. From the first floor we look out over the valley, right across to the Apennines. The view stretches for miles and I can see tiny hamlets scattered across the mountains. On the horizon there lingers a low cloud, blurring the line between mountain and sky. This must be the sort of view that birds of prey have, gliding on thermals on days like this. Pietro seems amused that I keep falling into raptures and agrees,

"*Si, molto bella la vista, è normale, non?*" and I muse that yes, for those who live here this is everyday stuff. It strikes me as the prettiest place I have ever been.

I open one of the windows upstairs, first opening the internal wooden shutters and then swivelling the handle upside down to open the two windows. I look across to the orchard, where I see Sam and the girls bent over – examining some insect, I imagine – and their voices float up to us. It's lunchtime, and I gather from Pietro that most of our neighbours are having their siesta after lunch, a sacred tradition. He leaves us to settle in and have a late lunch made from *pane* his wife has made, some local cheese and honey, and some *salame*. He's also left a bottle of dark-red wine, made from the vines we've just passed. The girls dash about their new home and are happy playing as we start to unpack after lunch. Their giggles fill the air and the house slowly starts to wake up, fresh air streaming in to replace the air that has sat here growing stale, heavy with memories of the previous inhabitants.

At about three o'clock we venture out to explore the surroundings, and we meet many of our neighbours. An elderly couple who live next to us embrace us warmly, and press a loaf of bread and a bowl of strawberries onto us. I thank them, my

Italian slowly returning to me, and introduce the family. They nod, yes, they know who we are. I imagine the village grapevine must have been buzzing with news of our arrival. They know I am the *nipote*, granddaughter, of Assunta and Giovanni. I gage that they must be in their seventies so they would not have known my grandparents, and I realise with some disappointment that my chances of meeting many people who remember them are slim. My grandparents were in their early twenties when they left Italy, so anyone who knew them would be in their nineties now. Perhaps a younger relative or family friend could be mid-eighties. I remember reading that life expectancy in Italy is very high thanks to the Mediterranean diet, so perhaps I will find someone after all, and the thought cheers me somewhat.

Throughout the afternoon more people drop by to meet us. Gifts of early cherry tomatoes, salad, jam, bread, wine and biscuits are brought, and we feel quite overwhelmed by the welcome. Families from neighbouring farms come to greet us and we try to remember names, but there are too many. We feel a bit like celebrities, and the girls are universally admired and cooed over. I glance at Sam, towering over the locals, flashing the beautiful big smile I first fell in love with. I realise I've barely looked at him for weeks now, and it's with faint surprise that I register how handsome he is and how much he stands out here. He doesn't speak much Italian yet, but he is nodding and trying his best, acting out what looks like being on an aeroplane and it being cold in Scotland. I smile as I see him miming flying and hugging himself, shivering. It feels like a surreal game of charades, like we used to play at Christmas.

"*Cosi bionde!*" "So blonde!" the villagers exclaim, pressing kisses upon the girls' cheeks. Our eldest, Aria, catches my eye and scowls; my little wildcat. My mother Giovanna was dark-haired like her parents, and I remember my grandmother dying her hair to hide the white roots. I inherited my looks from my father's side of my family, the Scots. My dad, Duncan, was tall and fair; we always joked that the Celt had been stronger than the Roman with me. I am half of the north, of my father's land, but half of me is from here, I remind myself. The side of me I am yet to discover. The connection to my past, to my grandparents and to my mother's ancestry. This is such a beautiful place; these seem like such friendly people – *why did they leave?* The question hovers all around me, growing stronger with every passing minute. I know the reasons I was told as a child: that times were hard in Italy post-war, and they sought their fortune elsewhere. But why not come back to visit? Did they stay in touch with anyone here? I don't even know if they had siblings, perhaps still here? I must find out, do some family-tree research.

Once the girls are asleep Sam and I sit out on the balcony in the heat of the June night. Our first evening here in Montaltissimo. Our heads are buzzing from all the people we have met, all the sensations of our first day. Strange to think that this morning we were back home, chilly in the early-morning mist, and here we are sitting out under the stars, the air still balmy on our bare skin. Millions of stars stretch overhead, and in the valley below us lights from the villages start to twinkle. It's hard to know where sky ends and mountain begins. *As above, so below.* A new moon hangs in the sky above the Apennines, a sliver of silver. In the orchard we see lights that start to flash and move, and we stare, wondering if the local wine is much stronger than we suspected.

"Fireflies!" Sam whispers, entranced. We sit and watch the fireflies, the first I have ever seen, while the air is filled with the song of crickets. We have travelled far today, and more questions have been raised than answered. But inexplicably, I feel completely at home.

4

Giuliana

1940

The arrival of war in 1940 and the departure of our fathers and older siblings changed everything. Where before there was lightness and joy, slowly, increasingly, it was replaced with heaviness and worry. Overnight Matteo found himself to be the man of the house at Stazzana, working long hours on the farm. When my own father left for North Africa I had to take over the care of our animals, including the morning milking. The school we all attended in the village of Sassi closed, and it had felt as though life had become a serious affair. News was a precious commodity to be traded, and everyone was now political, with some opinion to express about Il Duce, Mussolini and the war. It was an abrupt end to an idyllic childhood, and the sense of loss mingled with the strange and sometimes exciting realisation that if not quite fully-fledged adults then we were no longer children either. I was acutely aware of this change when I was with Matteo. The same understanding existed between us when our eyes met, but there was an awkwardness to our conversations, a formality where before it had been effortless.

The night he told me he had signed up for the army was one I will never forget. We met down by the river in our old meeting spot by the chestnut house, halfway between Stazzana and the village. It was a late summer evening, the sun had set over La Pania and the earth beneath our feet still glowed with the warmth of the day. A dusky half-light lit the way, and the moon was already climbing over the Apennines. Matteo was buzzing with excited energy to be leaving the farm, going to fight for his country. To join his father and brothers, to become a real man. His face was flushed with anticipation, and he spoke of a new world, advancement, ideals. Not just about winning the war but also changing the system, creating a fairer world. I didn't recognise this new side of him; it sounded like his head had been filled with noise, noise I couldn't understand. I felt anger coursing through my veins as I realised that in all his eagerness for change there was no thought of me, no sadness to be leaving this place, our world. He was my other half, I realised, but was I his? Was I so easily forgotten, left behind? All my life others had overlooked me for being a girl, for being young, for being too headstrong. I could hear my mother remonstrating with me for being unladylike, my teacher urging me to achieve more 'grace' in my demeanour, but Matteo had always seen me as I really was and accepted me. Was I now so readily put by for the thrill of war, of faraway lands? As I stared at his face in the fading evening light, his features lit with animation, his curly dark hair tousled and his eyes dancing with spirit, it hit me how much I cared. No, not cared, that I loved him. That I had always loved him and assumed my life and his would be spent together. No other option had ever been conceivable. This revelation only served to increase my rage, at the war, at myself, but mostly at Matteo, the cause of my turmoil. I slapped him hard, right across the face, and both he and the forest fell silent. He looked at me, and I felt like he was seeing me for the first time that evening. With no words standing between us something else took over, and time slowed as he stepped towards me, took my face in his hands and kissed me. Lost in the sensation of his lips on mine, my entire body responded to his touch. I was aware only of him – his hands in my hair, the heat of his chest – and yet I felt an acute awareness of the natural world around us. It seemed to me I could count every drop of the passing stream, hear every leaf dancing in the gentle breeze. Some strange magic was at work, for with our union we were truly one with the forest, one with the star-studded sky. I was spell-bound, dazed, more alive than I had ever been. Even now, seventy years later, I can feel that thrill of first love. A force that can move mountains. We crossed a boundary that night, from childhood into adulthood – from friends to something more.

The next day he was gone. I had no idea where, and my whole body ached heavily with his loss. Mother fretted that I was ill, so pale and compliant was I, my spirit elsewhere. Everyone had their cross to bear in those days, and my misery went unnoticed by most. My brother Luciano, always a sensitive child, tried to cheer me up in small and thoughtful ways. I was aware of Luci's presence and grateful for his concern, but I was a girl in love for the first time, a soul obsessed. In the selfish fashion of first love, little else existed for me. He would bring bread and cheese out to the barn where I would sit listening to the heavy autumn rain, pining for Matteo. He quietly helped when I neglected my own chores, for there was much to be done in those days. Wood to collect and chop for the ever-hungry fire, bread to knead, prove and bake in the bread oven. Animals to feed, eggs to collect, the cow to milk. Icy spring water to collect from the pump, not only to drink but also for washing and cooking. My favourite tasks were always those done outside, and my sisters were only too happy to let me volunteer for those. They feared the feisty boar that roamed the hills snuffling up the ground with their snouts, and the wolf packs who were rarely seen but occasionally stole a sheep or a goat from the villages. Once a village boy had been chased by a boar, protective of her piglets, and gored in the leg. He'd managed to climb a tree, but she'd waited underneath it, and it was only later that evening when his father had come to look for him along with his pack of hunting dogs that she had left her post.

In autumn there were the chestnuts to collect, and we would need many sacks collected to keep us in bread for the following year. More than ever that year I sought solace in the woods, taking pleasure in finding the copper treasures in their armoured shells, which started out so soft and gentle on the trees and hardened into a fierce shield as harvest time came around. In the mornings when the household jobs were done and Mother was satisfied she would give me her permission to go out and collect kindling for the fire. Quick as a flash I would be off out the door, never looking back. I would gulp great lungfuls of mountain air, a contrast to the smoke-filled house, heavy with gossip and the women's worries about the war. What I would have given to be a man off fighting for my country, seeing the world at Matteo's side!

Autumn turned into winter, and the dark days that seemed to last an eternity finally stretched into spring. One morning in spring 1943 I remember I was especially glad to be free of the house. That morning I received a letter for the first time in my life. A letter that made the long journey from Russia, a place I could not even imagine. After all these long months at last there was word from Matteo. I needed to reach a quiet place, a special place, to read it. I ran down the mule track past the small houses and barns of the village; I flew past the rows of olive trees and vines on the terraced slopes leading down to the fields where the goats and cows grazed. I remember stopping to catch my breath, gazing out over the hills to the high mountains beyond, still snow-capped up above the tree line. There was a little mist in the valley, and some of the first blossom of spring was coming out on the apple trees in the orchard. Up above the valley on the other side of the hill the villages of Eglio and Sassi nestled into the hillside, the rock fortress that was the Church of San Frediano protecting them as it had since the middle ages. Farmhouses, barns and chestnut houses were scattered among the slopes, and I knew that down in the hollow, just past the river, lay Stazzana. The light was growing each day and the birds had returned, their singsong waking me early in the morning. Every day and night thoughts of Matteo consumed me. Where was he? Was he safe? Was he alive? I wondered briefly if he would still be the boy I had known, carefree and quick to laugh, with his dark curly hair that I longed to run my fingers through. His skin burnished to a golden hue from all the work on the family farm through the summer, his arms strong from the manual work. Now I had some answers in my pocket, and I was both elated and terrified to read what they said.

I followed the track down into the woods until I came to a little clearing. The spring grasses were coming through and I caught a faint perfume of wild mint. This clearing was the only spot where Stazzana could be seen from, Matteo's family farm, and scene of many of the happiest moments of our childhood. I sat down in the little meadow and gazed at Stazzana, the house framed by the trees in the foreground, the mountains rising up around her on all sides. I muttered a fervent prayer for good news, and almost guiltily, I added on a prayer for my father.

Mia carissima Giuliana,

It's been many months now since I left you, and it feels like a lifetime. We were children, happy and free, in those sunny days. Now all is dark, our country is ripped apart, and I have seen so much death and blood I feel like I am a hundred years old. The only light left in my life is you, my love. The angel who protects me. How I long to see your face, to kiss your soft skin. In your arms, back in the hills where we belong, perhaps I could be redeemed. Does it really still exist, that place where the eagles soar and the wolves run free? Where you can walk for days with only the wind for company and never see a soul? Does the church bell still ring at midday, and Don Franco still sing Mass on a Saturday? I dream of you, of Stazzana, of our lives there. I dream of our future, raising children of our own in those fields, teaching them how to hunt, to fish, to grow crops in the fields.

By day we are busy, obeying orders, staying alive. But at night when I see the stars above and all is quiet my soul flies south to you in the mountains and finds itself again. I hope you are all well, and there is enough to eat? Stay safe, my love, stay quiet. If trouble should come head to the hills, my darling, hide out until the storm has passed. Never underestimate our enemy, I have seen what man is capable of. The enemy can also lurk in unexpected places – do not trust even those closer to home.

I must go now, my love, dawn is coming. I kiss you and hold you tight. My love as ever,

    Your own Matteo

5

Luciano

2017

I am an old man, and I had thought life held no more surprises for me. I was working in the field, *a seggare*, scything grass for hay the old-fashioned way, when she fell into my life. It was warm, and I am no longer young. The June sun was strong, and it was nearly time to head in for lunch. I remember wondering what Maria was preparing for lunch, hoping it would be my favourite *tordelli con ragù*. I glanced up, and through the hazy heat rising from the field I fancied I saw an *angelo* coming towards me. Dressed in white, golden hair dancing around her shoulders, she had a faraway look in her eyes. The long grass dotted with wildflowers gave the illusion that instead of walking she was floating, and the thought flashed through my mind that this was it: my time had come. I did not protest; as I say I have lived long, much longer than most. Then the spell was broken, as the angel tripped and fell. I heard some foreign words – I gathered from the tone of voice that they weren't the politest of words – and I hurried over to help. She looked up at me, and I had my second shock. Those eyes, an unusual shade of green fringed with black lashes, they looked straight into my soul, and my heart paused in my old chest. Eyes I haven't seen in a lifetime. Confused, shaken, I offered her my hand and helped her up. She smiled, and spoke to me in accented Italian: "*Grazie, Signore.*" I asked if she could walk and she winced as she tried to put weight on her ankle. I offered my arm, and helped her across the field to the farmhouse, where I knew my wife would help. She paused and fixed me with those green eyes, direct and questioning. She told me her name was Emma, and she was the granddaughter of Assunta and Giovanni. But I had known straight away who she was, and I had never thought to meet her. She noted my recognition and asked if I knew her grandparents.

"Yes," I replied simply, "I was sorry to hear they had passed away."

"Thank you," she murmured, her eyes welling up with tears. She hesitated, then blurted out, "Not only them – also my parents." I inhaled sharply, painfully, and the sky above me spun; the horizon blurred. I had heard, years ago, about the passing of Assunta and Giovanni. But Giovanna, their daughter, taken so young. I struggled to take it in, and my heart went out to this young girl, their granddaughter, now an orphan. I have never been terribly good with emotions. Never a very romantic husband to my wife, Maria, never very demonstrative with our children, or my grandchildren. But with this young woman, who had somehow returned to us, after so long, I just knew what to do. Without thinking I took her in my arms, this stranger who was one of us, and a great cry escaped her. Long held in, I thought. She felt like a child in my arms, her body wracked with sobs, and we stood like that for a long time in the field, with the bees buzzing around us quietly. When her breathing settled finally she pulled away, looked at me with her tear-stained face and smiled. We needed no words, and we carried on to the farmhouse, where Maria saw to her ankle and fussed around her with home-made *torta* and some of last year's vino to ease the pain. I busied myself with Maria's commands and thought of the past, returned to us in the present today. Not only her eyes, but also her smile, the way she moved her hands; it all reminded me so much of her grandmother. I wondered if she had already been to Stazzana, how much she knew. I wondered why she was here, and how long she would stay. I drank her in, this part of our lives that had long been missing. Raised in foreign lands, places I have never been, cannot even imagine. I remembered the questions present in her eyes when she told me who she was, watching for a reaction. I wanted to be her friend here, but I felt a pang of unease as I wondered how I would answer her. I am not a liar; I have never lied. But the past compromised us all – made us live different versions of the truth. For the best reasons – for family, for the future, for our children; we all have our secrets. I pushed this to one side; for now I would enjoy this moment. This unexpected joy, this ray of sunshine. This prodigal granddaughter, who had, two generations later, found her way home.

As the sun started to set over La Pania I drove Emma home, dropping her up the hill above the piazza, where she and her family are renting a house from Pietro. I hadn't been up this far for years; we have become so isolated, Maria and I, keeping to ourselves. I drove home and sat in the field, watching the darkness fall, trying to take in the events of the day. The shock of seeing those green eyes, eyes I hadn't seen since the end of the war. Two generations later, and in a different form, she had returned to the mountains. I was just a child when the war began, and by the time it ended I felt much older than my thirteen years. There was so much to do, in those post-war years. Life was harder than ever before. A certain innocence was gone, never to return. The silence, the absence of the missing, was incongruous with the joy we were supposed to feel to have peace. There was so much to re-build, and no money to do it. Bridges blown up, railways annihilated, churches and schools destroyed. Times were hard, and children continued to starve. When the war ended people returned to their family homes to find nothing – no furniture, no clothes, no belongings. My family left the chestnut house down at Stazzana, our refuge during the occupation, and returned to the village to our house. We found an empty shell, but at least it was still standing. Many found no home at all, destroyed by the thousands of bombs that rained down on our beautiful land. Our village church in the piazza had been bombed and lay in ruins, the holy site where we had all been baptised, where our parents had married. Slowly, painfully, we made new lives. Our families re-grouped, but the rifts in the communities remained. There was suspicion where there once was friendship. So many families from these villages were torn apart, some by death or illness, some by different allegiances. Brothers who were *fascisti*, brothers who were *partigiani*. Civil war tore apart our villages, our communities. I should know, for it ripped my own family apart, leaving wounds that have scabbed over but never healed.

And so the years passed, and our once-prosperous land is for the most part abandoned, un-farmed, unloved. I saw it all, and was helpless to stop it. The real destruction of our communities was not the war but the changes that came in the following years. The world opened up, promising a better way of life, sullying the old ways. Younger generations left for the cities, ashamed to be *contadini*, peasant farmers, as they say now. No longer happy to live from the land, to trade for what they need; the lure of money called them away, to work for others instead of themselves. To lock themselves away working every hour God gives them, so that one day they may retire and buy some land and lemon trees. They shun our old dialect, words passed down through the generations, a language which is shaped by us, part of us. They tell us it is *brutto*, and that we should learn proper Italian. They live in modern apartments with straight walls; they have machines to make it warmer, machines to make it colder.

They fill their lives with noise, with movement; there is no time to stop and see the world around them. They have forgotten the old ways. A choice, this forgetting, a collective choice.

My own children left as soon as they could, and took what was left of my heart with them. Elena to Florence, to work in a museum; Antonio to the coast, to work in tourism. They talk of history, of our beautiful region, but they are blind to the magic of the Garfagnana. Perhaps it is my fault. Perhaps I drove them away. Perhaps this is the punishment I so richly deserve. As small children they loved me, would spend hours in the fields, marvelling at the wonders all around us. We roamed the world of imagination together and for a while I had my sister back, my childhood back. They were the best years, before they started to outgrow me, to leave me behind, again. As they became teenagers, did well at school, started to go on school trips, I slowly lost them. Each year we had less to talk about, and I could no longer understand much of what they talked about. Travel, technology, career plans. I was proud of them, so proud, but we could no longer see each other, the real essence of who we are. To me they were glazed with modernity, belonging to another generation, a generation who has lost touch with the mountains. They see them as somewhere to visit, to holiday but not to live. I should have tried harder to reach them, to adapt, but the old ways die hard. I retreated into myself, becoming a grumpy old man, and I can see when they visit me it is from duty. They have children of their own now, children who arrive at the farm with their gadgets and headphones, children who struggle to understand our dialect, who stare at our old farmhouse as if it was a dungeon. I know Maria blames me for letting them go, for driving them away, rarely to return. For leaving her alone so much, out working on the land every hour I could. For keeping my hands occupied, my mind busy, so I would not have to remember, to venture into the shadows of the past. For never taking her on a holiday, never going to visit the children when we could still have done. Now we are old and worn, fit only for the grave. I remember the love I once bore for these mountains, glimpses of a previous life. But time has worn us down, tricked us into forgetting; we have lost our faith. I have not been the husband or father I would have liked to be; perhaps I never really believed I deserved it. The land has healed, but the young have left. What will remain, once we old ones have gone? Just memories, crumbling ruins of farms that were once family homes. Like the chestnut houses that litter the hillsides, returning to the earth.

I was ready to return to the earth, when I fancied I saw an angel coming for me. Tired with carrying this burden that has been mine for so many years, for a lifetime. Ready to give up, to lay down my scythe and go with her. But angels come in different forms, and it strikes me that this one needs my help. She is lost, cut off from her roots, struggling to deal with her grief. Perhaps I can help her, and there is the smallest chance that I might be able to make amends, before it is too late. I am aware of the wheel turning, of the cycle coming full circle, and I must muster the courage to face it as best I can. I failed her last time; I pray to God this time I can do better.

6

Emma

2017

Like climbing a mountain I allowed myself to acclimatise slowly. At first just being near Stazzana was enough. My gaze would drift across the valley, from Montaltissimo to the villages of Eglio and Sassi, and my mind would try to impose the old maps I had seen, black and white crisscross parcels of land, upon the green hills that faced me. I found myself dreaming of Stazzana, this last link to my mother, my grandparents, my family history. Half of me longed to run down there, to greet the old house, to call out to whatever ghosts lingered there. The other half of me was terrified of finding no link to the past, no feeling of connection, of it being just another abandoned old farmhouse like so many in the Italian countryside. Remnants of a bygone era, crumbling back into the land beneath them. The seeds of fear had been planted a generation ago with my mother, the horror of what had forced my grandparents to leave. The unspoken terrors, the curse my grandmother had warned us of, the thinly veiled threats. In usual circumstances I would never have dared venture there, but since my parents died I am already living in hell, and I have no space left for fear. There's something else as well, something I struggle to articulate. A feeling that a change has occurred, that the time has come to reclaim my birthright, to lay the ghosts to rest.

Our first day was spent shopping for supplies at the little village shop, greeting more neighbours and unpacking our belongings. The girls enjoyed exploring the local area, and Sam and I were happy to stay close to home. The next morning I wake at dawn and the whisper has become an insistent voice: *It is time.* From my window I see the first blush of sunlight staining the horizon. Dawn is a magical moment when the mountains, dark and slumbering, get those first rays of pink and gold washed over them. It starts up in the high mountain, rocky and bald, spreads slowly down the tree-clad slopes, and eventually reaches the villages of the *pianura*, the valley floor. I slip out of bed, leaving Sam and the girls curled up together. Since the accident we all sleep together in one huge bed. If the girls are in another room I wake from nightmares gasping with the desperate fear I have lost them, trapped in the black fog of panic, and I spend the entire night leaving the room to check on them. The nightmares still come, reaching for me through the night with their cruel fingers, but when I wake I am soothed by their breathing, the warmth of their little bodies, the soft curve of their cheeks. Over the other side of them I see the outline of Sam with his tousled bed hair, his arm curled protectively around the girls.

I dress quietly and pad downstairs in the silence of the early morning. I make myself a coffee, enjoying the ritual of preparing my stove-top percolator. When it bubbles away and the rich aroma fills the air I take my milky coffee out to the balcony and sit watching the sun rise over the mountains. One by one the hilltop villages are illuminated, blessed with a new day. The light changes by the second, and I hear the world waking up. Birds singing, neighbours stirring in the village, dogs barking in the distance. I feel like I am on top of world, gazing down at creation. When Sam and the girls make it downstairs, I've already decided.

"Let's go to Stazzana," I say to Sam, trying to sound more confident that I feel. "Today." He nods, meeting my gaze enquiringly. We breakfast and dress the children, and head off in the early-morning sun, down the old mule track we have been told will lead us to Stazzana. The well-kept countryside of the village gives way to a wilder, more ancient forest, long since abandoned by man. Patches of sunlight dance ahead of us, leading the way, but most of the light is blocked by the trees encroaching on the track. Acacias reach out to scratch us with their thorny tentacles, and birds screech warnings as we disturb their sanctuary. Creepers hang, snake-like, from the taller trees and ivy covers many of them, slowly suffocating its hosts. I try to picture my grandparents as young people, on foot or perhaps on a mule, treading this same track. On the way to market, or to neighbouring Molazzana. I glance down the hill, over the ferns and bushes, and my stomach turns as I see a steep drop down into the ravine, with only a few spindly trees to break the fall. The ground is bare, scarred, and we deduce there has been a landslide, perhaps during the winter storms when the rain floods down the hillsides, taking any weaker trees and half the soil down with it. My thoughts flicker back to Scotland, and our neat little semi-detached house there – the tarmac road leading up to it, the allocated parking spaces. I smile to myself; the contrast could hardly be greater.

We have finished our descent now, and we cross a little stone bridge with rotten fencing hanging precariously over the edge. I grab the girls' hands, fear flickering through me, and I wonder whether it was wise to bring them. The voice of warning – my grandmother's voice, I realise – tells me this is a bad idea, that I am selfishly putting the children in danger. The voice gets louder as we descend the track, a note of red panic entering it. I focus on the countryside around me, and the quiet conviction that I need to do this. The track follows the curve of the river, up to another bridge. The riverbed is rocky and wide, with only a trickle of mountain water running through it. The water saunters from pool to pool, and the dappled light through the trees illuminates them. I see tiny insects fluttering above the water, their wings backlit, and Aria tells me delightedly that they are water nymphs. We cross the river again and emerge into the daylight, a meadow stretching out to our right, following the river, and up above us my eyes are immediately drawn to the house. I stop and stare, seeing her for the first time, and I am overwhelmed by a sense of familiarity. A sense of reawakening, a distant memory from many years ago. Perhaps a lifetime ago. My head spins and I reach for Sam's arm to steady me. A wave of impressions, sensations, stories, are flooding through me. I won't say memories, as they're not that specific; I see no faces, know no dates. It's vaguer than that, but also more powerful. Not a sense of déjà vu, more a sense of homecoming. A connection. An *energy*. Is my family's history written into this place? I've heard of places situated on ley lines, where compasses behave peculiarly and the usual rules of science do not apply. Is Stazzana such a place? I had been expecting a wreck, after so many years of being abandoned, but at first glance I could almost believe the house is inhabited. The walls are stone, varying shades of sandy grey, not blackened with mould or fire as many I have seen. The roof, darkened with age, sits squarely on the house's shoulders. How has the house resisted the storms so well all these years?

We start walking along the track that leads us through the lower field, up past the woods, and back around on itself to approach the house. From this angle the house seems much smaller, almost a cottage. I realise the house is built into the hillside; from this side the cantina, the cellar level, is hidden from sight. Up close I can see the glass from the windows is mostly missing, the rotten wooden windows and their shutters hanging from their frames. The eaves of the house are damp and dark, and the guttering is dangling precariously on one side. There are rough stone paving slabs all around the house, overgrown with weeds, and I see half of the barn next to the house is swamped with ivy. I'm reminded of *Sleeping Beauty*: everything silent and still while nature slowly reclaims its kingdom. These inhabitants aren't asleep, though, I remind myself; they are all long dead and gone. My grandfather, Giovanni, was born here, as I believe his father was before him. The eldest, Giovanni, inherited the house when his own father passed away. I don't know when this was, although I imagine I could find his grave in his little cemetery in Montaltissimo. I don't imagine they had much money for repairs after the war, or even much manpower, after so many young men were killed or seriously wounded. It must have been such a blow, I reflect, to have a healthy son survive the war, only to lose him to a foreign country. Never to return, never to bring his own child to see them. Had they got on well? My grandfather spoke only very occasionally of his parents, of life on the farm, but all the memories had seemed like happy ones. I remember an old black and white photo of his mother, Benedetta, that he kept on his bedside table. A strong woman, he'd said, a fierce mother. Two sons lost in the war, and another lost after the war, to the North. What could have caused such a rift?

My grandmother, Assunta, was from the neighbouring village of Sassi. She and Giovanni married just before the war: a small-town love story was how she always described it. Stolen kisses after festas in the shadow of a tree, or in one of the narrow streets off the piazza. Scribbled notes passed at Mass, shy glances across the pews. Giovanni had been wounded in the war, fighting in North Africa, and after a long spell in hospital had been one of the lucky ones who made it home. He walked with a slight limp, and I always knew him with his wooden walking stick, carved by himself. He had several, made from different types of wood, so he could choose the one which suited his outfit best.

As I child I loved to stroke the smooth wood, imagining the tree it had been, the life it had lived. Not long after the war ended they left the mountains of the Garfagnana for the mountains of Scotland. Many young people left then, apparently, unable to see a future for themselves after the war.

We stand in front of the house – Sam, the girls and I – staring up at her. This house we have put our lives on pause for, travelled across Europe to come and see. Aria and Luna are uncharacteristically still as they too gaze up at the house, aware that this is a big moment. Perhaps memory deceives me, perhaps it was the sun, but we all feel it. A flush of warmth, a stirring in the trees around the house. A *welcome.*

We agree that Sam will take the girls to play near the house, and I will explore on my own to check if the house is safe. I find I am standing in front of the door, and I turn nervously to Sam.

"Can I go in?" I ask, not quite daring to touch the rusty brass handle.

His face breaks into a slow smile, as he tells me, "Emma, it's your house!"

I smile back, feeling his encouragement, and turn the stiff door handle. I still don't quite believe it. It doesn't feel like my house. I may be the legal owner, but I am not the one who built this house, stone by stone, who made it a home, who farmed these fields. I was not born here; I have not woken up to this view every day of my life. This house belongs firmly to the past.

I have to push quite hard to open the double wooden doors, and they slowly shudder open. I cross the threshold, and my eyes gradually adjust to the gloomy light. The air is stale and musty, and I wonder who the last person here was. I see a fireplace, blackened with smoke and with a large iron hook above it – for cooking on, I imagine. There is a stone sink and a tap in the corner of the room, and I try to imagine my great-grandmother here preparing meals. The chairs are rotten through and have collapsed, but there are some large pieces of chestnut furniture which have withstood the test of time. I see a large *madia*, a chest divided in two; I have seen these in some of our neighbours' kitchens. One half was for grain, the other half for the chestnut flour. There is a large table, still standing strong, and I run my hand over its dusty surface, trying to imagine the trees it was made from, and the hands that milled it. I open the windows that are still intact, the shutters creaking as they move, allowing the sunlight to flood in. The house seems to shift in its sleep, heavy with the slumber of ages. I move from room to room, as if in a dream. I reach out to touch the walls and the plaster crumbles under my fingers. What must be enormous chestnut beams support the ceiling, but I cannot see them; they are boxed in with some sort of mouldy cardboard-like material. How ironic, I muse, today people pay a fortune for original beams with all their character and charm, but my ancestors clearly wanted to hide them from sight.

I start to climb the steep narrow stairs, praying they will hold as I do so. I emerge onto a large landing, and ahead of me a ray of light from an unshuttered window shines upon a face, looking straight at me with a serene, wise expression. *La Madonna.* The only decoration on the plain plastered walls, faded and stained; the wall-hanging of Mother Mary smiles down on me as I approach her. How long has she waited here, without visitors? Was it she who protected the house from the storms? From the bombs?

I wander from room to room, wondering who last slept in these beds. The frames are made from iron and have rusted over the years, but little details inset into the headboard catch my eye. Some tiny mother of pearls glimmer in the half-light. The mattresses rustle under my touch, and I learn later that they are stuffed with maize leaves. There are wardrobes and drawers, but I don't dare open anything on this first visit. I feel like an intruder, like I need to introduce myself. I face the Madonna, with her all-knowing gaze and her faded beauty, and bring my hands together in what I hope will pass for reverence. My parents were lazy Catholics – agnostics, really – and I am sadly lacking in the correct protocol to address the Virgin Mother. My grandmother would have been horrified. Instead, I speak from my heart, hoping she will appreciate honesty. Silently I thank her for protecting the house, for keeping it safe for me. I tell her who I am, that I am the granddaughter of Giovanni, who was born here. My mind wanders a little, and I wonder which room he was born in. The screams and pains of labour are hard to imagine in this heavy silence. Was the Madonna hanging here, even then? I pray for all my departed ancestors that I never knew, and I pray for my grandparents. With a deep breath I also pray for my parents, Giovanna and Duncan. The atmosphere around me seems to change subtly, a wave of shock rippling through the fabric of the house. My own disbelief mirrored around me. The Madonna swims before my eyes, through sudden tears, and I ask her to give them my love. In the peace and silence of the house I feel held, comforted. I am not aware of any specific presence, and there is nothing that alarms me; the overall impression that I remembered later was feeling supported, like floating in the sea and being weightless.

Eventually I emerge out into the brilliant sunshine and rest my hand on the stone wall. I am drawn to the house, the feeling of peace within her walls, the connection I feel for the first time to my Italian roots. I look around at the green hills that surround the house: the fertile fields, the orchard full of apple trees. With a shock I realise this must be where my grandfather meant when he spoke to me of lighting the fires to keep the trees warm when a late frost came. The memory that returned to me in the lawyer's office in Edinburgh, prompted by the mention of Stazzana. The only time in all my childhood I remember him speaking of it. It's hard for me to reconcile the memory of him in Scotland with this place, the place where he was born. It seems like a paradise, an unspoilt Eden. *Why would you ever want to leave here?* I wonder.

Laughter drifts across the meadow and I follow it, looking for Sam and the girls. I glance back at the house, one more time, and feel a strange reluctance to leave. There are stories to hear, tales to be told, and I hope she holds some of the answers I am looking for. But for now, for today, I am happy. This is enough: to have seen her, touched her stone walls, gazed at the view that greeted my grandfather every morning. To be in this spot that my ancestors chose to build the house, to found our family. This special place that has seen centuries come and go, survived two wars, and been neglected for more than sixty years. All this time, she has waited. *For me*, I realise, with a shiver of excitement.

7

Emma

2017

It's strange how quickly a new life can envelop you, how your old life can drift into the past. I remember our first day here, how loud the flies, crickets and cicadas seemed, and now I don't even hear them. The heat was a constant presence on my skin, making me glow with it. I was aware of my clothes clinging to my body, the dampness at the back of my neck. The desperate search through my wardrobe for the coolest yet still respectable clothes I owned. The heat has intensified if anything since our arrival, and we live according to it. We rise at dawn when the air is cool and fresh, and our neighbours in the village are already out in the fields, tending to their vegetable gardens, picking fruit, having bonfires. Doing all the strenuous work before the land heats up and we must all retire inside for siesta time. There are potatoes to cook and mash for the *pane* to be made in the communal oven, the fire itself to tend to and get up to temperature for cooking. The *sugo*, the meat sauce, to prepare early and leave to simmer, ready for lunch. These traditions and ways of working the land that we are learning from our neighbours are ancient, and are repeated week after week, month after month. The thousand daily tasks of the contadino to do before the heat of the day ramps up.

We sleep at night with our windows open, desperate for a night breeze to soothe our sweltry skin. We are cocooned in white mosquito nets hung around our beds, safe in a world of our own. Dawn is always a time of great possibility, and the villagers seem to spring into action immediately. I never need my watch as, like clockwork, Gian Piero the shepherd sets off to see to his goats at half past six on his three-wheeler. As he leaves the scent of freshly brewed coffee mixes momentarily with the whiff of two-stroke, and now immediately brings him to my mind. I love the peace of the mornings before the girls wake up and the usual chaos of the morning routine ensues. A moment of sun-christened fresh air, clarity of mind. These days I find I need these moments more than ever to pause, to think. To try to start to process what happened to my parents, but it still feels too huge. An insurmountable mountain. I can almost believe I am here on holiday, and they are safe at home in Scotland. Living their usual lives, walking along the beach, having tea in the garden. When one of the girls reaches a new milestone, a new tooth, a new word, I feel an unbearable urge to call my mother. The realisation I can't brings the reality crashing down upon me once again. I struggle to breathe with the enormity, the finality of it. There are a million things I miss: my mum's blackberry and apple pie with cinnamon, sprinkled with brown sugar; the way her eyes danced and crinkled at the corners. My dad's ability to fix anything, the sweet aroma of smoke from his pipe.

It was always the three of us. With no brothers or sisters my parents were everything: my playmates, my confidantes, my best friends. That they would always be there was something I took for granted, like the sun rising in the east, and spring following winter. Without them my world is unrecognisable, strange to me.

Part of my confidence as a mother came from their presence in my life, to support me, guide me. Their absence in my daughters' lives only deepens my sorrow, the loss increased threefold. And so my days are filled with highs and lows. Life is still beautiful and there are moments of joy, of lightness. But death is always lurking in the shadows, waiting to claim my thoughts and then my heart, again and again.

The day I met Luciano I was particularly lost. Even the girls' cuddles and kisses and little gifts of foraged flowers could not lift my mood, and I set off on a walk to try to find some peace. I have become an expert at hiding my grief, playing the role of happy wife and mother when I am crying inside. I have learnt to breathe through the shooting pain, blink back tears and force a jolly voice when playing or reading bedtime stories. Anything can trigger it: a photo in a book, a little note from my mum, one of millions over the years. Off to a sleepover, off to university, off to get married. The sight of a *nonna* holding hands with a grandchild, a Father's Day card in a shop. It's a whole new world of grief that I now realise is inhabited by thousands of people all around us, putting out a semblance of normality but bleeding on the inside. Dozens of small wounds, reminders of what they have lost.

I left the house and headed downhill to the piazza, and then across the fields. I didn't want to encounter any friendly villagers; I knew I needed solitude. The grass was long and was dotted with wildflowers of many hues. I inhaled sweet perfumes of wild mint and lemon balm rising up, released by my movement through the field. The sun was hot on my skin, and I abandoned myself to the sensations all around with sweet relief. I wandered, unaware of where I was headed. Just away, away from the pain, from the pretence of being fine, from loss.

My reverie was interrupted by a sharp pain in my ankle, and I fell to the ground. Cursing, I struggled to get up, and to my surprise found I was no longer alone. An old man, a farmer with twinkly chestnut eyes, was offering me his arm, and gratefully I took it. His skin was the colour of a ripe hazelnut, baked from years of toil in the Tuscan sun, but he seemed to pale as I met his eyes, even to recoil slightly. Perhaps I imagined it, as moments later he was recovered and offering his assistance to the farmhouse, where his wife would attend to my injury. He wore corduroy trousers, a long-sleeved shirt rolled up to the elbows, braces, and from his belt hung a machete tied on with string. When he smiled I sensed a humour in him, a youthfulness that belied his age. How strange I must have seemed, this foreigner from what was as good as outer space to him, limping across the field he was cutting for hay. I told him who I was, and I could see that my name meant something to him, that he had known of my existence. Who had told him, I wonder, who had my grandparents been in touch with? I could tell from his reaction that he already knew of my grandparents' deaths, and he offered his condolences. I wondered again how he had heard of them, who had told him. My mother? I found it hard to believe she could have known about this other world and not shared any of it with me. No, I felt sure there was more to it, much more. He told me his name was Luciano, and he shook my hand courteously, a perfect gentleman. Then, and I am not sure where it came from, I blurted out in my faulty Italian about my parents' accident. It hit him hard, clearly, and I saw the blood drain from his face again. For a moment he staggered, his balance lost, the axis that his world turned on shifting beneath his boots. He regained control quickly, caught himself in time to catch me, unstable as I was on my sore ankle. I had no idea why I told him, this stranger, of my deepest injury, my most painful secret. Once the words were out I cringed inwardly, seeing myself as the stereotypical westerner, oversharing their life story with someone who is patently not interested. Why would he be? But for some reason how this man reacts becomes of vital importance to me and I wait, breathless, for his response. He didn't offer any of the platitudes I have had from many people, while I stand awkwardly by with no response to offer, my usual habit of looking for the positive failing me completely. There are no words, really, in any language. He just took me in his arms, this old man I'd just met in a field in Italy, and something inside me broke open. The dam I had so carefully constructed burst, the floodgates to my grief opened and a great sob escaped me. The sound was alien to me, as though coming from somewhere else, someone else. I cried out the pain, the shock and the hurt inside me, and when it finally abated and my breathing became more regular, I felt lighter, freer. I became aware once more of the field around us, the drone of the bees, the butterflies dancing through the late afternoon sky.

I pulled gently back from Luciano, wiping my eyes, and we shared a smile, a smile that turned into laughter, laughter all the more precious for being completely without a reason. He wiped his own eyes with a cotton handkerchief and offered me one of my own which I happily accepted. I took the arm that he offered, and we made our way across the field towards the farmhouse.

We arrived at an old stone farmhouse, set at the end of a jut of land that then fell steeply away. The land below was terraced and each terrace was lined with vines, verdant and leafy in the summer sun. The farmhouse itself was typical of many in the area, with chestnut shutters and terracotta roof tiles. On the patio outside the front of the house sat several lemon trees, each laden with fruit, plump and bright. There was a small orchard filled with apple and fig trees, and two persimmon trees. I would later learn that many farmhouses in Italy had a persimmon tree next to them, following a decree of Mussolini's during the Second World War. The persimmon fruits, or kaki, as they are known as here, are extremely high in sugar, providing valuable energy in difficult times. The fruit comes very late in the year, when many other fruits have finished, the harvest past.

Luciano's wife Maria came scuttling out of the farmhouse shouting at her husband, and when she saw me she exclaimed loudly and proceeded to bustle me into the cool of the darkened sitting room. She sat me down on an armchair next to the fireplace, raised my ankle on a stool and set about mixing up some herbs to pack around it. I've always been interested in using herbs as medicine, though I've never made a study of it. I watched, fascinated, as she ground the dried plants together with a pestle and mortar, made from an olive tree, she told me. I was able to recognise calendula, chamomile, rosemary and lavender, and the perfume as they combined with the olive oil was intoxicating. Throughout the whole process she continued to yell orders out to Luciano, and to berate him for allowing a guest to fall in his field. Luciano obeyed meekly, shooting me a conspiratorial smile as he passed. I was issued with a glass of last year's wine, red and fruity, and a slice of Maria's home-made *torta squisita*, a tart with crumbly pastry and filled with their own ricotta and dark chocolate drops. I remember sitting there, enjoying the sensation of feeling cared for, being fussed over. Inexplicably I felt as though I was with family, even though I had just met this eccentric old couple. Once I was fed and my ankle bandaged up with the herb poultice applied, Maria relaxed back in a chair herself, and the proper introductions were made. Maria proudly showed me the photos of their children and grandchildren, but explained to me that they lived far away, in the city of Florence and by the coast. Luciano grunted in the background when she told me this, and I sensed this was a painful subject. Like our neighbours in the village they spoke with a local dialect, the dialect I recognised from my grandparents' Italian, although I believe that in the many years they were away from Italy it had been somewhat diluted. They were obliged to learn the 'official Italian' that was standardised after the Second World War, since their neighbours in Scotland were from other parts of Italy and their dialects were mutually incomprehensible. Without having learnt it from my grandparents I would struggle to understand anyone here, even were my Italian perfect. It seems to be the case that the older and more rural a person is, the stronger the dialect becomes, and Luciano and Maria's language is a real test for my abilities. It takes some time and a glass of wine to tune into their frequency, and when I do I find I can understand their meaning, even if each individual word remains a mystery to me. My ankle recovered with the help of Maria's potent herbs, and I felt strong enough to limp around the *orto*, the vegetable garden, and admire the crops growing there. Luciano showed me his lemon trees with the pride of a new father, and I could see how tenderly he cared for them. He told me how in winter he moves them inside out of the cold and wraps them in blankets. How they are brought out once he is sure the last frost has passed, how he positions them carefully to get enough sunshine but not too much, shaded by the farmhouse for the latter part of the day. I smile to myself, honoured to be allowed to see the softer side of this old farmer.

That was the day our friendship began, born of grief and loneliness and with time blossoming into real affection. We often walk down to the farmhouse now, Sam, the girls and I. Maria is always waiting to press home-made biscotti on us all; she kisses the girls emphatically and dances around the kitchen with them. She can be heard screeching, "*Mie bambine d'oro!*" "My golden girls!" as we approach, and Luciano tells us she is ten years younger when we are there, and he doesn't get scolded as much as usual. They have taken us into their home and their hearts, this elderly couple. Perhaps they see the family that have left, abandoned the mountains for the lure of the city, for a different life. Perhaps they appreciate our interest in the old ways, enjoy having company, having the lightness of children back in the house. For whatever reason, they seem to enjoy our company as much as we enjoy theirs, and it feels like fate that I met Luciano that day. I sense that he holds some of the answers that I am looking for, that he may be able to help me in my search. I need to be patient, but I sense that beneath the gruff exterior there is a kind heart. I see it in the way he works the land, in the way he cares for his lemon trees.

8

Giuliana

1944

I remember the day they came like it was yesterday; every detail is etched onto my memory. It started like any other day, at dawn, with floors to sweep and bread to make. It was early autumn and still golden during the day, but the mornings had a nip in the air that spoke of cold days ahead. I recall pulling the shawl my mother knitted me tight around my shoulders when I first went out to collect water from the pump, sensing the change in the seasons. We were all tense, as we had been for weeks now, with the war rumbling closer to us by the day. Rumours were flying around the village like wildfire, catching alight and spreading from house to house. These days information is so easy to access, but back then we relied purely on word of mouth, and we knew so little.

The day they came started as any other. Looking back, none of us really believed anyone could be interested in our little village, high in the mountains. We'd just finished the morning's jobs and the sun was rising, warming the earth with its lazy latent heat. Mama was preparing coffee and the bread had come out of the oven, filling the house with its tantalising aroma, making my stomach rumble. Without warning the peace of the morning was shattered by machine-gun fire, louder than it had ever been before. It kept up for several minutes, biting through the air, echoing around the hills. The dread realisation that the enemy was close spread slowly throughout my body, and I clutched my mother, who was shaking with fear. It sounded like the shots were coming from the neighbouring village of Molazzana, and as they died down our neighbours all gathered out by the water pump, talking nervously and glancing down the track. I remembered Matteo's warnings in his letter, and felt fear, cold and grey, coursing through my veins. *Germans.* Real ones this time, not the fictional figures from my nightmares. I felt a flash of remorse at how often I had wished for change, for action, for relief from my boredom. *Not this way*, I begged silently.

Presently there was the sound of hooves approaching, and I dashed out to see my brother Luciano riding fast towards us. He slipped from his mule, red-faced and urgent, and had to breathe for a few minutes before he could blurt out the news. I held his hand and pressed some calm into him, inhaling and exhaling, until he was able to talk. He spoke with a stutter when he was nervous, and he was shaking with fear. Finally he managed, "*T-t-t-tedeschi*, at M-M-Molazzana, coming here." We ran to tell our mother, and news quickly passed through the village.

"Surely they won't hurt us," I recall our neighbour Marta saying, "women and children?" My mother was pale with fright, her jaw tight with strain. I could see she was thinking of us, her daughters and her son, Luciano. He was underage but could he be taken, deported even? Made to fight? Words from Matteo's letter floated into my mind and I could almost hear his voice. *If trouble should come head into the hills, my darling, hide out until the storm has passed. Never underestimate our enemy.*

"Mama," I said, looking straight into her eyes. "We must

leave. Now." She nodded, accepting the necessity of the decision. We gathered what belongings we could take in haste and packed them onto the small cart that could be pulled by the mule. We had no idea how long we would be gone, what would happen to the house, and we had no time to prepare. Our packing was panicked, hasty, and we forgot many items that later we would long for. Mother packed what little money we had, the family Bible, her religious icons. Some clothes, some food, some blankets. I managed to remember to include a knife, and the precious mother yeast we kept alive for bread-making. We took a couple of chickens, shoved into a wicker cage, and we decided to take our cow, Renata. Luciano was still in shock, trying to help where he could but completely unequipped for the situation. The pressure of being the only male left in the family, the man of the house, weighed heavily on his young shoulders. Never a natural leader, he looked to me now to make the decisions. My sisters were of no help, huddled by the fire, clutching each other's hands.

"Must we really go?" Margherita asked, grabbing me as I passed, interrupting my feverish preparations. "Where are we going, Giu?" I stopped and nearly laughed at the absurdity of the fact that I had no idea. I had to think fast. It needed to be somewhere out of the way, off the route the Germans would take. Somewhere we could hide out, away from potential crossfire and bombings. Somewhere we could hide Luciano, who could be taken and made to fight for the *fascisti*. Suddenly Stazzana sprung to mind, not the farmhouse where Matteo's mother still was but the *metato* by the river. The chestnut house, where each autumn the chestnuts were dried out. It was small but well hidden, and not too far a ride from here. I was sure Matteo's family would be happy with us being there until the Germans had gone and we could return home.

"Stazzana," I told my sisters, "the *metato*. It's small, but we'll be safe there. Just for a short while." Margherita and Rosa nodded palely, flinching as the gunfire resumed, ricocheting up and down the valley, a sickening chorus of metal birdsong. Like a nightmare it seemed to be getting louder, closing in on us.

In the end I think we only just made it in time. Our little procession was slow, Mother driving the cart and mule, her face tight with terror, her shoulders hunched. Luci, Margherita and Rosa followed, laden with belongings and food, bags of grain we'd put by for the winter. I came last, leading our precious Renata. We knew she would be requisitioned for milk or end up as meat for the enemy if we left her. Besides, she was part of the family too, a gentle animal whose soft sides I loved to press up against whilst milking her in the winter, warm and sweet-smelling. We descended the track down to the church, and past the piazza. Many of the houses were already empty; the piazza was ominously quiet. We passed some neighbours similarly laden who were heading the other way, towards Castelnuovo di Garfagnana, where they had family up above the town. We had no idea how many of us would become *sfollati*, displaced, during those long months. Many of us moving not just to one place, but again and again, as the enemy penetrated further into the mountains and grew more familiar with the terrain. The danger of our journey was that we were heading directly towards Molazzana, from whence the *Nazisti* were coming. We risked meeting them on the track and being confronted, perhaps even shot at. If we had been a lighter party, without the cart and the animals, we could have travelled cross-country, down into the valley and through the woods as we did for the *vendemmia*, but without the animals and our foodstuffs our chances of survival would have been seriously reduced, even in peacetime. It was a calculated risk, and luckily this time it paid off. As we turned off the main track onto a smaller unmarked track we all breathed a little easier.

We continued to descend until we ran alongside the river, a mere trickle after the summer, and eventually came to the bridge that crossed over into Stazzana territory. I glanced up at the house above us, imagining Matteo's mother to be on the lookout having heard the shooting echoing around the higher villages. Stazzana was relatively low down compared with most dwellings in the area, and by virtue of this was hidden from view. My mother and the other villagers often referred to it as '*il buco*', the hole, as in the stormy season it filled with mist and cloud and disappeared from view. True, it did not enjoy the mountain views that the hilltop villages did, but I'd always loved Stazzana, and wished I lived there. Most villagers love the community around them, with neighbours continually popping in and out of each other's houses, borrowing an egg, some flour, some milk.

"Who would want to live there?" they would say amongst themselves. "Down in *il buco*, alone with the wolves and the boar?" To me, it sounded like paradise. No-one to sit and gossip by the fire all day, no-one to disturb me when I wanted to be alone with my thoughts. No-one to comment on my torn dress, or my dirty nails. *Well*, I thought drily, *here's my chance.*

I knew Matteo's family would not have heard any news by this point and would be anxious. We made our way up to the house, weaving along the lower meadow and up through the edge of the woods before the main approach to the house. I always greet Stazzana in my mind as I make my approach, but today something felt different. I shivered, aware of a cold gaze upon me, and I saw a face at the upstairs window, pale and still. The glass was hand-blown in those days, and not smooth but rippled, blurring the face within. But the enmity I felt directed towards me was enough to tell me who it was. I groaned, remembering that Assunta had married Matteo's older brother Giovanni just before the war. Assunta was a few years older than I, but we had been at school together. The perfect student, never a hair out of place, her dislike and disapproval of me was palpable from my very first day. We lived in different worlds, and there was little crossover. I breathed adventure, longed to run wild in the mountains, loved to laugh and play rough with the boys in the yard, Assunta was the model Catholic Fascist. Always demure, devout, on time, in the right. She would never raise her voice at me, never speak out of turn, but her criticism was constant; her gaze noted every one of my failings, of which I admit there were many. My soul was made of fire, and hers of ice. I'd never understood quite why she hated me so, but both Matteo and I had been horrified to hear she was to marry his brother. Giovanni had grown into a young man, ready to shoulder his responsibility as the elder son and carry on farming the land at Stazzana. He worked hard and was always ready to help anyone. He lacked Matteo's spirit, his courage, his energy, but they got on well, and I was very fond of him. What he saw in Assunta we couldn't imagine.

As we approached the farmhouse the two dogs came rushing out, barking furiously. The Maremma sheepdogs had grown up with us and were like family. They quickly recognised me, wiggling sheepishly, apologising with their licks for having mistaken me for a foe. Fully grown, the pair were more like polar bears than dogs, with enormous rounded heads, shaggy white coats and long, curled tails. I gave them a quick stroke and we pressed on towards the farmhouse.

Matteo's mother Benedetta rushed out to meet us, and embraced my mother, who began to cry. My sisters were also greeted and ushered into the house to sit by the fire, blurting out the story as best they could. Luci and I saw to the animals, putting them in the barn next to the house, and seeing they had hay and water. When we returned to the house we were met by quite a crowd. The house was filling up with *sfollati*, displaced family members who had lost their own homes. Benedetta's sister Giulia was also staying there after losing her own home, fortunately when she and the children had all been out in the fields. Matteo's female cousins were there too, Rosina and Antonietta. The boys Fiorlindo and Mario were away at war, fighting in Greece, Giulia believed. A house full of women, all desperate to hear what had happened in Montaltissimo. Before we spoke Benedetta placed hot *polenta con sugo* on the table, polenta with her home-made sauce, made from the tomatoes of late summer. I can still remember how the fragrance filled the room, how my stomach grumbled, how I suddenly felt weak from the day's events. We ate hungrily, aware already of the need to keep our strength up, unsure of what now lay ahead. The unthinkable had happened, the enemy we so feared, our former ally, was now in our village, perhaps even now already in our homes. Surely invasions like this were for Rome, Lucca, Florence? Cities that had been conquered and fought over for centuries, strategic strongholds? If they were here, were they indeed everywhere? Was the whole country invaded? Were we safe even here?

After the meal it was agreed we would indeed move into the *metato*, as I had suggested. It was well-hidden in the forest by the river, not on any main tracks, and the Germans were unlikely to discover it and take Luciano away. Emboldened by the meal and the glass of wine he now expanded on what he had heard in Molazzana, and we all listened, horrified. He'd been on his way to Molazzana on the mule, carrying milk from our cow. We sold the excess to the mayor and his family. They were already gone, suspiciously. Luciano had encountered a distant relative of ours and her daughter, shaken and weak, carrying their paltry belongings on their backs, wending their way down the mountain to Cascio where they had relatives. They told him the story, their faces shocked and tearful, pressing him to warn the village. Molazzana had been taken by surprise, early in the morning. The villagers were in their beds, unaware of the threat creeping up the mountain in the darkness. They woke to shooting and shouting, guns and unfamiliar uniforms, rounded up like beasts in the piazza. Doors kicked down, tables overturned as the town was raided. Centuries of peace, living in the clouds, brought to an abrupt end. A couple of brave boys tried to resist and were left bloodied and beaten as an example to the rest. *Do not resist us.* Gentle mountain folk, never exposed to any violence worse than a brawl outside the bar after one too many glasses after the *vendemmia.* Their world shattered one September morning. The villagers were rounded up, the men taken away down to Gallicano, the women and children made to wait for hours in the piazza. They were eventually released and advised to leave the village since would likely be fire from Barga where the *Alleati,* the Allies, were stationed. We were the lucky ones, at Montaltissimo, to have a warning. To have a messenger, in the form of my brother. Aware of the danger and the fact that the Germans could already be on their way to Montaltissimo, Luciano had raced home to warn us.

Our village, as the name suggest, is situated high up on the mountain, overlooking the valley. If Molazzana had been taken, we knew Montaltissimo would be next. We all listened to his story in silence, my sisters weeping, thinking of their friends and sweethearts in the village. We were all acutely aware that although we were currently safe and well-fed, sitting by the fire, the land we called home was now in enemy hands and no-one was safe. I thought of those still away from home: my father, Matteo, his brothers. All our group of friends and cousins who had grown up together in these hills. Where would they go, if their home was occupied? What if they returned to Montaltissimo, and found our home destroyed, or worse still walked straight into another prison?

Looking back now that day seemed to stretch into eternity. Had it really only been that morning we had been waking up in peace, going about our morning routines? Time had stretched into a vacuum, an endless and unreal day. As we sat there dazed, I noticed the sun had started to drop lower in the sky, and I knew we had to get moving again. We needed to be settled, as much as we could be, by dusk. Once the sun set the darkness would be absolute down in the woods.

Luciano tacked up the mule again, I put the harness on Renata and we set off back down the track to the lower field. There we veered off into the undergrowth, on the track that lead to the *metato*. It ran alongside the river; we knew it well from countless fishing trips as children. Trout hid in the deeper pools and we would wait, statue-still, until we lunged to spear one with a sharpened stick, giving our war cries and splashing about wildly in the icy water. It seemed like a lifetime away now, those childish games. We had entered the very adult world of war and survival.

Further along the track the greenery thickened around us, and the mule and cart only just pushed through. Renata was snorting in alarm, her black eyes pools of fear. We all knew this was an oft-used wolf track; we had seen the imprints many times in the mud and sometimes the snow. When we emerged into the light again, we were at the chestnut house. The river that ran in front of it was a trickle after the summer droughts, and we easily crossed over. A hill rose up steeply behind the chestnut house, and the two branches of the river met in front of it, joining their forces to head down the valley together. The molten gold rays of the late sun filtered through the remaining leaves and cast a welcoming glow upon the little barn. *Our sanctuary.* It had always been one of my favourite spots, the sort of place I believed the faeries of the forest danced by the moonlight, coming out of the old oaks to dance and feast on mossy rocks by the water's edge. I'm not sure my sisters were as enamoured of it as I was; their faces registered no relief at our arrival, but disbelief and disgust. I laughed at their reaction, asking them if they would prefer cohabiting with the Germans? They made Luciano and I go in first, to check for snakes and scorpions. The chestnut house had been deserted since last autumn, and it would take some work to make it habitable. My heart sank a little as I saw how many dried leaves had blown in and how damp the earth floor was. It would soon become a mud bath with five people living there. There was no glass in the small top window of course, as that was where the smoke from the fire to roast the chestnuts escaped. At night I knew the cold wind would drive in, bringing the rain with it. We brought our belongings in but were at a loss to know where to put anything. There were no tables, no furniture, nothing but the forest floor beneath our feet. Being next to the river and in the valley bottom it was also much damper than we were used to, and despite how early in the cold season it was the chill penetrated our clothes. *It's only September*, I thought with dismay, *what will winter be like?* We couldn't light a fire that night, with no dry wood ready and no fireplace. Benedetta had kindly given us some sacks full of dried maize leaves and we arranged them at one end of the barn, with our blankets over them. By the light of a single candle Mother read a passage from the Bible, and we lay there in the darkness, huddled together for warmth, exhausted from the day's events. It was then that the birds stopped singing, and Mother paused. The sound of machine-gun fire bit through the air, sudden and terrible. It cracked like a grey metal whip and echoed its threat all around the mountains. And I knew, deep in my soul, that as cold, damp and disheartened as might be, we were in the right place. Nothing would be right for a long time, perhaps ever again. But I resolved to do whatever it took to keep my family safe. I screwed my eyes shut and started to silently recite the same prayers I said every night. *Madonna, please keep him safe. Please bring him back to me.*

I don't know what my brother, sisters or mother were praying for. I was so wrapped up in my thoughts, my concern for Matteo, that I only thought of myself. I'm sure they were terrified; everything they had ever known had been ripped away from them in one day. The gunfire stopped abruptly: an empty village held no threat. Montaltissimo fell quickly, with no defence.

The seeds of my rebellion were sown that night. *One day*, I vowed, as rage coursed through my veins, *one day, they will pay.* Slowly, I heard my siblings' breathing settle, as weariness overcame their fear. My mother's Bible slipped from her grip, and the heat from our bodies warmed our bedding. Eventually I too felt myself sinking down towards sleep. That was our first night in the chestnut house, the first of many.

9

Emma

2017

Our first few weeks in the mountains pass in a bright blur of new discoveries. Slowly, we start to connect names with faces, and draw the family trees that are growing all around us. Everyone is related somehow, and it thrills me to know that we too are part of this forest. In some ways we feel like foreigners, with our height and our fairness, our northern language echoing around the streets, but we are warmly welcomed by the locals. Everyone we meet seems to be in their sixties, seventies and eighties, and I wonder where the children and grandchildren are. Not one but two generations are missing from this village. The girls are treated like royalty, tempted into darkened sitting rooms only to emerge triumphantly clutching a *kikino*, a chocolate or a sweetie. Our eldest, Aria, seems to swallow the singsong Italian words that float around her, and immediately makes them hers. She chatters away, our little parrot, mimicking the sounds and accents she hears. It makes them smile, our neighbours, hearing this six-year-old Scot chattering away in dialect. Our neighbours are all born and raised in the area, and I ask about my grandparents, but so far I haven't found out anything useful. My nonna was from a nearby village, Sassi, and apparently there are no relations left. Nonno Giovanni was from Stazzana, of course, but being the only surviving son there were no other descendants. I ask if there might be cousins or second cousins still alive, but nothing is forthcoming. Everyone is polite, but I sense a reservation that I find hard to explain, even to Sam, who finds our neighbours charming. When I ask about the war and why my grandparents left people seem to become awkward, wary even. I realise how little I know about the history of the area, and resolve to do some research. Perhaps I will find in books what people here are loath to talk about.

Since the day we met in his field, Luciano has become a constant in our lives. A friend, a true friend. He has helped us all get to know the area in a way we could not have hoped to alone. He is our guide, our translator, teaching us new ways of seeing the land, understanding its secrets and its ways. Sam and he have become great buddies, despite the language barrier. I often come across them laughing together, great guffaws from Luciano, a departure from his usual quiet merriment, and Sam bent double with mirth, tears in his eyes. They try to explain, but neither can talk in any language at this point, and Maria and I just shrug, and return to what we were doing. Sam has taken to wearing a machete on his belt, à la Luciano, and can now name all the trees of the village in Italian. I hear him repeating to himself as we walk the land: *quercia, ontano, castagno.* Oak, alder, chestnut. As a carpenter Sam has always been fascinated with different types of wood and he has met a kindred spirit in Luciano. They've been spending the afternoons chopping logs, building up an impressive woodshed for winter. I remind him of Luciano's age, to take it easy with him, and he shrugs uneasily, admitting he forgets how old he is. I can see why: he practically springs around the land with an energy that belies his years. He can scale a slope in seconds, so sure of his footing is he. We struggle to keep up with him, a fact that amuses him greatly.

Aria and Luna have accepted him as one of them, a child trapped in an old man's body. There are always treats hidden in the depths of his pockets: a hazelnut, a dried fig, one of Maria's biscotti. He holds out his hands and they must guess which is the winning hand. He lifts Aria up high on his shoulders to pick the walnuts that grow around the edges of the fields at Stazzana, and then sits with her in the evening sun, showing her how to crack the shell open with a stone. Delighted, she shows me her treasure, and pops it into her open mouth. Luna takes his old hand in her tiny one, and knows he will follow wherever she leads, no questions asked. When they tire from their adventure they lay down on the grass in the shade, wherever they might be, and I find them fast asleep and gently snoring, while the bees buzz around them unawares, taking their siesta. In June the girls foraged for *fragoline*, the wild strawberries that grow on the ground, always making sure to prod the leaves first with a stick in case a snake is lurking in the grass. Luciano taught them how to do that, and made them each a 'poking stick', as they call it. Carved from walnut, strong and smooth, with their names engraved on the side.

For me, he has become like family. On the surface we have little in common, this elderly farmer from the mountains and I, a teacher from Scotland, but there is something that connects us. I know he understands how I feel about Stazzana, how my heart sings when we are out in the mountains. I know it grieves him not to be able to share this with his own children, and I think teaching us about the land has in some way reaffirmed his own love for it.

One morning I emerge onto the balcony with my morning coffee to find a huge bucket of *pomodori*, tomatoes, sitting there. Blinking in the morning sunlight I bend over the bucket, inhaling their sweet musty scent, instantly taking me back to my grandfather's greenhouse. On closer inspection there is a note written in Luciano's scrawling handwriting, and a recipe for passata. "For Emma," the note reads, "for your Italian education." There is also a basket full of glass jars and a strange metal machine, a sort of sieve with a handle. I smile and lug the tomatoes into the kitchen, where Aria and Luna fall upon them in delight. I let them take one juicy fat *San Marzano* tomato each – the first of Luciano's crop, I imagine – and they breakfast upon them, juice dribbling down their chins. Their excitement is contagious, and before we know it we are sterilising the glass jars and starting our first attempt at making passata, the rich tomato sauce I have bought so many times from supermarkets over the years, and never once thought of making myself. *Life's too short*, I might have said in the past, and with both of us working full time and two small children, it usually was. My mother was a great cook, and growing up there was always a freshly baked cake on the table, always a new recipe she was trying out. While my grandfather was alive he loved bringing her round produce from his garden. It was his way of showing his love, I always thought, like cooking was for her. The familiar sadness starts to prick behind my eyes, and I breathe deeply, determined not to let it overwhelm me.

"This is for you, Mama," I whisper, and tie my apron around my waist. Sam joins us and we set about washing and halving the tomatoes, scooping out the seeds and dropping them into the biggest saucepan I can find. The heat of the June day is already rising, and we are all flushed as the tomatoes start to bubble away on the stove, filling the kitchen with their memories of sunshine and earth, the scent clinging to our hands and clothes. Once cooked we allow the tomatoes to cool, and we turn our attention to the machine Luciano has lent us. In the recipe Maria calls it a *passatutto* and Sam soon has it fitted together and turning. It is a bowl-shaped sieve that the cooked tomatoes are poured into, and when the handle is turned blades force them through the holes, removing the skins and seeds. The girls take turns cranking the handle and when it suddenly spins sauce is splattered across our faces to shrieks of laughter. It's hard work, and we jokingly ask ourselves why we are putting ourselves through this in the heat of the Tuscan summer when we could be lying by a pool somewhere. There's more to these simple actions that we are going through though, and I feel it strongly. The magic of ritual and repetition connects me to my ancestors, to the generations who lived here, grew their tomatoes and made passata to last them through the winter months. I feel a link to the land that I was not previously aware was missing from my life, but that now seems obvious to me. Aria and Luna join in enthusiastically, sensing my own happiness and mirroring it back to me. They team up to make labels, Aria carefully inscribing 'Passata 2017' on the pieces of paper, and Luna sketching little tomatoes on the vine on each one. Once all the jars are filled, sealed and labelled, we proudly survey our morning's work. On Aria's suggestion we decide to take a jar to each of our neighbours as a thank-you for all the welcome gifts we received, finishing with a trip to Luciano's farm to offer him back some of the bounty from his farm.

"Your grandmother would have loved this," I tell the girls, smiling at their rosy faces. "She was a great cook, able to make a feast out of anything. She never used recipes, just listened to what the ingredients told her." They are watching me, drinking in my words, and I notice Sam looking at me too. I realise it's the first time I've talked about my mother since the accident, and that the process of making passata this morning has brought her closer to me. I resolve to try cooking some of her favourite dishes, and to learn more Italian recipes. She would have loved it here, cooking with fresh produce from the land. It was in her blood, and I so wish she could be here with us, discovering it together.

We make pasta for lunch, dousing it generously with our

newly made sauce, sprinkling on some basil from the balcony and grating *parmigiano* over the top. A simple lunch, no more than four ingredients, yet all bursting with flavour. This is Italian eating at its best, and we savour each mouthful. After lunch we retire to the bedroom where we siesta during the fierce heat of the afternoon, our shutters closed, the room dark and cool. Even Aria, who has not napped for a couple of years now, has quickly fallen into this new routine. We all wake in the late afternoon, re-energised for the rest of the day and the evening.

As the sun softens down towards *La Pania* the heat fades, and the mountains are bathed in a golden glow that coats every tree the colour of honey. The villagers start to emerge at this hour; their chores of the day complete, they are ready to relax and socialise. Most evenings they gather in the piazza to chat about the events of the day, the weather, occasionally politics. Our days here are governed by the weather and the mountains, as are the months and years. Our basket packed, we head down towards the piazza, where we greet several of the villagers. Often we join them in the evening, and the girls play in the falling darkness with the children if any are visiting their grandparents. Aria and Luna join in their games with that ability children have to communicate without words, the international language of childhood and imagination. Luciano and Maria never join these gatherings, their farm being a little outside the rest of the village. I suspect there is more to it than distance; I notice he rarely comes to our rental house. We either meet at his farm, or down at Stazzana. Another of the many mysteries that are so ingrained in this place.

This evening we carry on down the track towards Luciano's farm. It's nearly midsummer, and the crops around us are abundant. As we approach the farmhouse he and Maria are bent over weeding the zucchini patch, silhouetted against the flaxen bales of hay behind them. They straighten up as we arrive, calling, "*Buona sera!*", their arms outstretched in welcome. Aria and Luna run to them, and Luciano swings Luna up high, her giggles pealing through the evening air. The evening is too lovely to go inside and so we sit in the field looking over the valley towards Stazzana, where the house is hidden from view. Luciano ventures into the house to search for victuals, and I offer to help him. I hand over four jars of our passata, and he examines them, expressing his approval with a series of grunts. His silence encourages me to talk, our northern habit of filling the gaps, and I tell him how it made me think of my mother, how she loved to cook.

"My grandmother not so much," I joke, and he chuckles as he searches for a bottle of wine in the cellar.

"No," he agrees, "she always had too much living to do," and the affection in his voice catches my attention. It's dark in the cellar, lit by a single bulb, but I fancy I see the shine of tears in his eyes. His voice was thick with emotion, distant with nostalgia. I pause, confused, and I wonder what the nature of his affection for my grandmother was.

"Were you close?" I ask gently, hoping that he might finally answer some of my questions. He sighs in the darkness; he sounds suddenly tired.

"We were at school together for a while, up at Sassi," he tells me gruffly, wiping the dust from a bottle of wine with his sleeve. "She was older than me, of course, and married your grandfather not long after leaving school, just before the war. She stayed at Stazzana while Giovanni was away fighting in Africa."

"She lived at Stazzana?" I ask, incredulous. For some reason I'd never imagined my grandmother living at the house, although now it seems obvious, since they married before the war, and had my mother shortly afterwards. What could have happened there to make her so determined to put it behind her and never look back? I remember the emotion in his voice when he mentioned her, and wonder whether Luciano might have been in love with my grandmother. The age difference would have been too great, surely. Perhaps it was just an infatuation from afar? Does it explain why he is so fond of me, and the girls? Does he see her when he looks at us?

Luciano has said enough for one evening, and as we leave the cellar I see the sun has now set, throwing the mountains into relief, each black rock defined against the crimson sky. The mood is lightened by the others, and soon we are all laughing and toasting the summer. As darkness falls we see the first firefly of the evening, and the girls dash after it, convinced it is a fairy. The tiny light flashes and dances, and is soon joined by many others. The air is balmy on our skin and I breathe in the richness of the earth and the heady scent from the jasmine growing nearby. We drink wine made from grapes that grew here last year, and I feel part of it all, the whole cycle of life that has endured here in the mountains for so many centuries.

When we leave to walk home the moon slowly sails through the sky above us, casting silvery shadows as we walk up the lane. It's been an emotional day and more questions have been raised than answered, but I feel completely at peace. For the first night since the funeral I sleep through the night without nightmares, and wake up in Sam's arms to the scent of tomatoes lingering in the air.

10

Luciano

2017

A coward's choice even now, this holding back from telling her the truth. So many years have passed, and still the memories of that night haunt me. The nightmares have faded with time, disintegrating into the many horrors of the past, grown over with ivy like so much of our history. She came like an angel into my life, and perhaps she holds the power of redemption – but it could be beyond forgiveness. Can I risk telling her the truth? What is the truth, after so long? Will she understand?

We have grown close, like family, these past weeks. I have tried to teach them the ways of the land, the knowledge that has been passed down from generation to generation, the cadence of our lives here. How to coax crops from the fertile soil, how to collect the precious rainwater in anticipation of summer droughts. How to know when the blue sky will turn grey, when the wind whispers of a storm on the way. Where to hunt for *funghi, tartufi, fragoline*, in the passing seasons. They have learnt to recognise the wild herbs that grow in our fields; the little girls love to pick an *ortica falsa*, a false nettle, from the hedgerows and suck the nectar from the violet flowers. Emma is fond of chamomile tea at night to help her sleep, and I have shown her where the plants flower in June, near where the *grano*, grain, was planted the previous year. She has learnt how to dry the heads in the sun and store them in glass jars to use throughout the year.

Sam is slowly learning our language, speaking our old dialect like a native. In the beginning we had to rely on gestures and body language, but we got along just fine. As we say here, '*non si morebbe di fame*', we wouldn't die of hunger together. He is young and strong, and his energy reminds me of many I grew up with, before the war took them. Together we have chopped wood ready for the winter and I have taught him which woods burn fast, which slow, which make smoke that burns the eyes. Which are used to make furniture, which are fast growing and thus have weak root balls and are likely to fall in a storm. We have roamed the land together, united by our common love for it.

I can see Emma feels it, the connection to Stazzana. It is in her blood. She imagines her grandparents here and wonders how they could ever have left. She has asked me many times, and I have told her half-truths, looking away, using my age as an excuse. Back then, for being so young, and now, for being so old. Her bright eyes flick over me, searching for clues, and we return to safe ground, the ground under our feet. But I know the day will come when she will not be satisfied; she will grow tired of waiting. For the moment I will make the most of our days together, these happy times that I had not expected to know in my life. The fear is always with me, how she will look at me when she knows the truth. I have lived with the darkness for so long now I am accustomed. It keeps me awake at night; it reminds me that time is running out. I resolve to enjoy my time in the sun all the more, to take nothing for granted. This is how it is with old age. We might like the idea of giving in gracefully, ceding our place in the world when our time comes. But when it comes we find we are greedy for life. Another day, *Signore*, another week, another month.

Maria and I had become so stuck in our ways, halfway to the grave already. Our children gone, rarely to return. Unable to farm in the way we used to, we had sunk into a lesser existence, an apathy. Since Emma and her family arrived, I feel a new energy. My love for the land, now shared, has deepened. I have again become aware of the magic of this place, the value of the traditions passed on through generations. Threatened by the war, damaged by the occupation, reduced by the lost generation. But not destroyed: the fire still burns, low but constant. A thread, fine as spider silk, has held us all together, linking one to the other. Even across time and across space, across the ocean. Spider silk is the strongest material; it does not break. I think often of her now, far away, and I sense she is thinking of me. Occasionally, fondly, I imagine. It was always the way. I was the younger brother, the mild irritation, the chore.

I'd watched Giuliana and Matteo since we were children, yearned to be part of their exclusive club. I would beg her to take me with them on their adventures in the forest, but it was always the same story.

"You're too young, Luci, you'll get in the way, you'll get hurt, run along home." Even when we were all together, siblings, cousins, second cousins, even then they had a silent way of communicating. A look, a raised eyebrow; it seemed like magic to me then. How I longed to be part of their exploits, how much fun I imagined them having out in the wild, free like the wind, while I was trapped at home. Giuliana was older than me by four years, and was the most vibrant person I have ever known. People often commented that she should have been born a boy, and I think she herself wished that. She was frustrated with the feminine stereotypes she was supposed to conform to, and loved to rebel. Meeting her for the first time people were enchanted by her beauty, drawn to her charisma, and if they were honest, a little afraid by the spirit in her eyes. It wasn't what was expected of a young girl in those times, in a Catholic country under fascism. There was something of the wild in her green eyes, deep and dark as a ravine. They brought to mind the she-wolf howling at the moon, the Apuan buzzard swooping down from the sky, intent on its prey and nothing else in the world. Her movements were quick and fluid, and when caged at home helping our mother with domestic chores the latent energy within her would build until she burst out of the house and would make for the high mountain. She'd return hours later, worn out, scratched and sore, her soul at peace.

From a young age she could scale all the trees in the forest, scampering up them like a monkey, leaving the other children gaping and wondering where she had disappeared to. She learnt how to become invisible in the forest, how to silently track animals, how to use the wind and the sun to know where she was. Our parents knew it was no use looking for her in the mountains; she could never be found until she wanted to be. I never saw her afraid of any animal in the forest, even one time when she came face to face with the black viper, the most venomous snake in the mountains. She'd been crawling across the ground tracking a deer when she unwittingly came across a nest, and a defensive mama viper. I remember her describing how the dull black body, muscled and potent, froze, and the red eyes fixed upon hers. The tongue was the only part of the body that moved, flickering in and out. Giuliana also froze, her heart beating fast, every nerve in her body on edge. After what felt like an eternity the viper withdrew back to her nest, satisfied this human was not a threat. She said she felt like she'd passed a test; the viper's other-worldly eyes looked into her soul and judged her. Life and death both hovered before her, the two faces of the one reality. One bite, those fangs sinking into soft flesh would have meant certain death in those days. Now, if you make it to hospital in time by car, the anti-venom might work. If you are an adult, and the amount of venom is not too great. But back then nothing could have saved you.

Giuliana once told me that after Matteo left for the war she felt like half a person, that half of her soul was missing. I never saw her that way; to me she was always complete. She had the spirit of ten men, the courage of an army. In another time, another place, she could have been a warrior queen, leading her tribe to victory. She was brave, my sister, so brave.

I always knew, deep down, that I wasn't brave like she was. Even now I wonder if there was anything I could have done that night, the night our world as we knew it ended, thrusting us into the black hole that consumed everything. With time and adulthood I have tried to persuade myself it wasn't my fault. I was so young, and my motives were good. Well, if not good, they weren't bad. I was envious, curious, a young boy on the threshold of adulthood, aware of the action all around me but denied any part of it. Following Giuliana that night in the dark and the storm was perhaps the bravest thing I had ever done in my life up to that point. I told myself I might be able to help, that they might need me. I had my knife hanging from my belt, my face smeared with mud in an attempt at camouflage. They all thought they were so important, sneaking about the countryside with messages, hatching their plans. Really, they were just kids, kids playing at war. A few years before it had been *nascondino*, hide and seek in the fields of Stazzana, the air full of giggles and mirth. But somehow it had mutated into a deadly version of the game, and there were no winners, only losers.

I know that time is running out, that Emma will not wait forever, that she will demand answers sooner or later. That our friendship requires me to be truthful with her, even if that means the end. If it does, then it is no more than I deserve. I am a greedy old man, enjoying my time in the light when so many have lived and died in the dark. That I should have the gift of this time with Emma and her young family, when so many of her own family have been denied this joy, seems like a trick of fate. I have lived so long with guilt I can add a little more to my load and still carry on breathing. For a little while longer, at least. Until the day of reckoning comes, and then I will pray for a miracle.

11

Giuliana

1944

I close my eyes and in the darkness the years fall away, disappearing into the void. I see myself as I was, the sixteen-year-old who believed herself immortal. The winter of 1944 to 1945. A lifetime's excitement, fear, joy and despair – all in the course of one season. Autumn's reign was brief that year, and she quickly ceded her crown. The glow of the hills, every shade of gold and rust imaginable, gave way to the monochrome world of winter. The leaves fell, blown away by early storms, and with them went any hope we had of returning to our homes that year.

After fleeing the Nazi's invasion of our village, we quickly adjusted to life in the *metato*, the chestnut house, and the simple routine of our days. We made it our home as much as was possible, unpacking our few belongings, setting our *Madonnina*, our little figurine of Mother Mary, in a tabernacle in the wall. We were fortunate that the slopes and trees surrounding us hid the smoke from our small fire, and made us invisible to overhead bombers. We had a constant supply of clean drinking water from the river in which we could also wash, and initially a stash of apples and dried fruits that would supplement our diet of chestnut bread until they ran out. There was a *capanna*, a barn, up above Stazzana on the hillside that had a bread oven and the family who lived there made fresh bread every day. One of us, usually myself, would trek up every few days to buy some. I would avoid the main *mulattiera*, the mule track, and cut through the woods, alert for sounds of danger on the wind and evidence that anyone had passed that way. There was always the danger of bombs falling now, since the Germans had taken up the *Linea Gotica* here the Allies flew by regularly. We would hear the planes overhead and run for shelter in the *grotta* across the river from us, the cave that had been part of the mill in the past. Often we could guess from the ear-splitting explosions and gut-wrenching crashes where the bombs had fallen. Castelnuovo, a neighbouring town, was a popular target, and precious little remained after the war. Once a bomb fell just a little further up the valley, and we later learnt that a family we knew had all been killed, just like that. This was a war fought between armies, but the civilians paid the price. Little wonder that the civilians eventually decided it was time to fight back.

The first snow came in November, and we woke to a silent sylvan kingdom, each treetop painted white by an unseen hand. The sky had a pearly, luminescent quality, and our little *metato* wore a snowy hat that overhung its stone walls, decorated with icicles. I was the first one out that morning, the cold snapping at my cheeks, my sleepy eyes blinking against the dry air. The landscape that had become so familiar over the last few months had transformed overnight, wrapped in a white mantle. Pulling my woollen shawl tight around my shoulders I crunched down to the river, where our little bridge seemed to hover like a pale arc. The water was shockingly cold when I splashed it on my face for my morning wash, and I rapidly pushed my reddened fingers back into my gloves and clutched them to my body for warmth. I started to cross the bridge to a world as yet untouched by man, by worry, by the war. I noticed the prints my boots left in the snow, and on the other side soon became fascinated in seeing who else had been out in the early dawn. I saw the tracks of various birds, a wildcat and a fox. It occurred to me that the Germans would also be able to track footprints, and that we now had a new risk to be aware of. We were always careful when travelling around the woods. Going up to the farmhouse, hunting, going for bread, we knew to cover our tracks, to leave no sign of where we had been, but this would be harder now. Later would come more concerns: the difficulty of collecting chestnuts under the snow, the biting cold that was impossible to keep out even with the small fire that we permitted ourselves. But that morning I saw only the beauty. I was blissfully unaware of anything save the magic of the snowscape around me. It was a time of innocence, of wholeness, when I was one with the world around me. Strange to say, with so much wrong in the world at that time, but that morning I was *happy*. I was an innocent; I still believed that good would win out, that I could somehow mould the world around me to my wishes. That was when snow remained something pure, something sacred for me. Before it was soaked with salted tears, stained red with blood. There was more to my joy that morning than the pleasure of the snow, though I had no idea what it was to be. The day was marked, special, a day to remember.

I collected my basket and set off up the hill, for it was my day to fetch the bread from our neighbours. I took care to stay off the main track, skirting around the trees and the ravines, using the animal paths that thus far the soldiers had not found. There were now no leaves or bushes to use as cover, but I knew the land well and could use the steep terrain to my advantage, ducking and diving behind mounds and knolls. I was on my way home, making my way downhill, wary and watchful as always, when it happened. I spotted the lonely figure walking up the mule track he shadows lengthened. I thought of how ecstatic his mother would be at his return and knew that I could detain him no longer. I also warned him how close the Germans were, that they had set up a base in Montaltissimo, that if he was caught he would be rounded up and deported to Germany. *There is no more dangerous foe*, I thought, a shiver of fearful premonition running through me, *than a friend who has been crossed, and is now your enemy.*

Already I could see that home was not the safest place for Matteo to be, one hill away from the front line. For him to travel thousands of miles from the devastation of the Russian steppes, to come home only to be captured and shot if he tried to escape or sent away to one of the rumoured death camps, did not bear thinking about. As a deserter from the King's army, he would possibly be wanted by our own military. As a young man of fighting age, he would certainly be taken by the Germans, for work camps or worse.

"You must hide," I urged him, squeezing his bony hands in my own, in a reversal of the advice he had previously given me. "Retreat into these mountains we know so well, survive, and wait out the storm." He nodded, pale and suddenly exhausted. We agreed he would head up through the forest to the barn hidden higher up in the hills, that was used for storing and seasoning wood ready for the next winter. We called it the Lost Barn due to its hidden location, away from the main track and right in the thick of the forest. It had not yet been found by the Germans to my knowledge, whose numbers were still few at that point, and whose explorations of the terrain had been limited. I would go to the farmhouse and break the good news to his mother, and she would come up to him that night with food and blankets. I kissed him goodbye fiercely, trying to wrap him in a protective cloak of my love. I promised to come to the barn at dawn the following day and bring him what I could.

Benedetta had heard the dogs, of course, and came to the

from a good distance, and immediately dropped to the ground. My winter clothing no longer camouflaged with the forest floor now that the snow had arrived, and I stayed close to the trees, blending in with them where I could. I squinted at the figure approaching Stazzana. Who was this, friend or foe? Hunched and weak, with a slight limp, I could see even from a distance it was a male, and that he was painfully thin. No uniform, so not a German, and at that point the *fascisti* had not yet arrived in force. Still, no-one was to be trusted, and I kept guard as the figure got closer and closer. As he rounded the corner of the bend towards the farmhouse he suddenly stopped and lifted his head, as if he could feel my gaze. Knew he was being watched, perhaps hunted. As I saw his face, a shock bigger than any earthquake I have ever felt surged through me. How many times had I seen that face in my dreams, asked God and all the angels if he was still alive, begged for his return? It was Matteo, returned to us through some stroke of good fortune or the miraculous. In a daze I scrambled to my feet, slipping in the snow, and half ran half fell down the hillside, my bread and my caution forgotten. I flung myself into his arms and he staggered for a moment, before his arms gripped me so tight I could not breathe.

"*Giuliana,*" he whispered hoarsely into my shawl. "*È veramente te?*" I was laughing and crying at the same time; over a year of separation and anguish dissolving into the relief, the joy, that he was alive. I pulled back and looked into his face, taking it in my hands. It had lost all the roundness and naivety of youth; if he had left a boy then he had certainly returned a man. His face was strong, sculpted, more handsome than ever. He was filthy, his face and hands stained dark with dirt, his hair unruly under the hat he wore, and a dark beard now framed his lower face. His eyes spoke of sadness and loss, of disillusion, but they also burned with life, with love. I saw that he loved me still, had not forgotten me. I was suddenly shy, aware of the gaping gulf in our experiences. What he had gone through this last year? He had travelled, seen the world, perhaps killed men. What had I done? Moved down the track into his chestnut house? Becoming aware of our situation, I glanced up and down the track, realising how exposed we were. I took his hand and led him deep into the forest, retrieving my bag and the bread on the way. It was as if we were children again, playing out in the wild. We found a large oak tree and sat at its sheltered base, hidden by its thick branches overhead. I offered him the bread from my bag and he gratefully tore pieces off and wolfed it down; I wondered how many days it had been since he last ate. With the land beneath us and the sky above, as it had always been, we talked and talked. He spoke of his time in the army, in Russia. Of his initial pride at being part of Operation Barbarossa, the brainchild of Hitler and promoted by Mussolini as a vital show of solidarity. He spoke of the vastness of the Russian Steppes, the raw, savage beauty of the endless landscapes, nature on a different scale. Of initial victories against the retreating Red armies, of the celebrations, the camaraderie. But then winter had come and with it the cold, the worst weapon in their arsenal. He spoke of how the cold can hurt in places you cannot imagine, how it feels as though icicles are cutting you open from the inside, one organ at a time. He told me about watching friends die in the snow, the world reduced to a flag of blood red and frost blue. Last words drifting up to be frozen mid-air. How ill-prepared they were for the terrain, the climate, like lambs to the slaughter. Of how their hopes, dreams and patriotism had also died there in that godforsaken country. Of how he had been captured and was on the way to a gulag prisoner-of-war camp when the vehicle he was travelling in had broken down; how he had managed to escape and been hidden by a kindly Cossack family, at great risk to themselves. He had been with them a month, sick in bed for half that time, delirious with fever. They had nursed him, fed him nourishing stews, kept him warm by their fire: they had saved his life. Arranged to smuggle him to the coast, and on a ship back to Italy. I sent up

a silent prayer of thanks to whoever was listening
had broken down; had the angels intervened? I th
Russian family caring for Matteo, a stranger in th
enemy no less, and sent them my gratitude too. U₁
back in Italy he had very nearly been taken by the
but managed to slip away in time and stealthily m
across the mainland, up past Florence and Lucca
across the mountains. He spoke of his relief and j
back in the Garfagnana, and the kindness of varic
families who had offered him shelter and food alo
despite the danger they were in doing so. As far as
was the only soldier to return from Russia. Why h
saved, whether it was fate or chance, he did not know
had wondered many times.

"It was you, Giuliana," he told me, pulling me
kept me safe, my guardian angel. When I felt like
go on, when I wanted to die, your face would ap₁
mind, and I'd get the strength to carry on." He pau
smile crept across his face, some spirit returning t
"And I knew what a slap I would get if I dared to die.
remembering our last encounter, recalling the p₁
leaving. Overwhelmed by all he had told me, I nestle
to his body, listening to his heart beating. As the word
and the forest became quiet around us, we softened
other and the ground beneath us. I became aware of
around my waist, of his breath on my neck. He cuppe
in his hands and my vision swam as his lips touched
magical as the last time but filled with the passion that
up during the long months of separation. My body resp
his, unfamiliar sensations of desire shooting through ₁
body. We were in a shining bubble of first love, of p
The world had no dark corners, no sharp edges, nothin
We were oblivious to everything around us, to place
and time, to the war. Morning stretched into aftern

door to meet me, and tried to usher me into the warmth of the sitting room. She was surprised to see me of course; I rarely came to the farmhouse, and I knew she had plenty of work on her hands with the various family members who had fled their occupied villages to come to the relative safety of Stazzana. A pot of polenta bubbled enticingly on the fire and the warmth and comfort of the scene was tempting, but I knew I had to speak to her alone.

"Benedetta, I must talk to you; there is news," I said quietly to her, gesturing towards the hay barn. The fire cast a golden glow across her face that threw the deep ridges of worry across her brow into sharp relief, and her eyes flickered with questions. Nodding slightly, she closed the door behind her and followed me into the dark barn, which already had the first sparkles of frost settling on its roof. "It's Matteo," I whispered, clutching her hands. "He's here, he's come home!" She let out a small gasp and sank down onto a hay bale, overcome. The best possible answer to those ever-present questions.

"He's alive? Well?" she asked me, her voice husky with emotion. As quickly and quietly as I could I told her that Matteo was waiting up in the barn above the farm to see her, and for much-needed supplies. Benedetta was a formidable woman, and she immediately rose to her feet, brushing the hay strands off her apron. Finally, she could once again care for her youngest son, express her love, stagnant and aimless over the past year. I cautioned her about who she told the news to, for the moment, and to make sure she wasn't followed to the barn. She agreed to take no light, in case it was spotted across the valley, and fortunately the moon was already bright in the sky, an ivory coin glinting in the sooty skyscape. I bade her farewell and hurried home to the chestnut house, where I knew my own mother would be worrying. I barely remember my journey home; my feet made their own way and my heart was light. I felt as though I could stretch my wings and fly over the trees like the mountain eagle, silent and powerful in the dark. Everything looked different, lit by my happiness. The very trees seemed to me to hum their pleasure at Matteo's return. I was young, I was in love and my love had returned to me.

So many years have passed since that night, yet still a little shiver of that joy ripples through my wasted old body. My gnarled fingers try to clutch on to the images a little longer, willing myself back to the mountains, but with the dawn they are slipping away, back into the past, across the threshold to that shadowy world of memory. A door I have kept closed for so long, for to open it would mean releasing all the pain and devastation, as well as the joy. Many lives have been lived in darkness, and now the light must illuminate the lies. For so long I thought I was protecting her, being brave, being selfless, but perhaps it was only cowardice after all. Fear of rejection, fear that my decision was not the right one. All my protests, all my justifications, crumble to dust in the light of day. I feel the grave calling me, the voice growing stronger by the day. Night and day are blurring, and I long to give in, to sleep. But the truth will not let me, it must out, finally. My story must be heard.

12

Emma

2017

The summer flew by in a daze: endless days ruled by the sun, seeking out the coolness of the shade. Nights stretched out under our gauzy mosquito nets, cocooned away from the world. Our windows flung open, music and laughter from the village festivals floating across the valleys and into our dreams. Evenings sat on the balcony watching fireflies flash secret messages across the orchard, their merry dance a summer sister to winter fairy lights. Many nights we've sat in the piazza, chatting with our neighbours while the girls play, as I like to imagine my grandparents doing when they were children. Life in the village is wonderful, and I count many of our neighbours as friends, but our best times are always those spent down at Stazzana.

There was timeless quality to that summer, our first summer in the Garfagnana. Days flew by marked by the rising and setting of the sun, and we all relaxed into our new way of life. I put my quest for answers on hold, instinctively knowing that I needed this rest, and looking at the sun-splashed faces of my husband and children I realised they did too. Before we knew it *Ferragosto* had arrived, the mid-August national holiday initially created by the Emperor Augustus to give agricultural workers a well-deserved rest, and later becoming the Assumption of Mary: another *festa* appropriated by the Catholic Church. It felt like the whole of Italy was on holiday, and the pace of life, already slow with the summer holidays, came to a standstill as families celebrated together. We decided to spend it at Stazzana, and invited Luciano and Maria for a lunch cooked over our campfire. There is a lower meadow at Stazzana which leads to the woods by the stream, and there we have set up a little encampment in the shade of the hazel trees. Sam has dug out a fire pit and lined it with rocks from the river, and we bought a tripod and a Dutch oven to cook over it. The past few weeks he has been busy working on a new project at Stazzana, and when we arrive for *Ferragosto* there are cries of delight from the girls and myself as we spot the table and benches he has made for our al fresco dining. The table is huge, capable of seating at least ten people, and made entirely from a fallen chestnut, he tells me proudly. It is rustic and simple, and looks completely in keeping with the bucolic setting.

"I love it," I tell him, leaning in close for a kiss, and his face breaks into a proud smile. Together we set a white tablecloth upon the table, its edges dancing in the breeze. Aria and Luna set off with their baskets to search for wildflowers, and return with ox-eye daisies, old man's beard, pink sorrel and common mallow with its tiny purple flowers. Aria has also spotted some wild fennel, and I pick some to add to my mushroom risotto. We arrange the flowers in jam-jars to set on the table, and Aria and Luna dance around it, delighted with the effect.

Luciano and Maria arrive on foot, bringing home-made cheese, prosciutto and a couple of bottles of last year's vino. His farmer's jobs completed in the morning, Luciano is ready to play, and he heads off with the girls across the meadow ready

stion mark that hangs between us, a distance that we cannot
bridge. Whether Maria knows why I do not know, but her
fusion seems to imply she does not. Maria settles back into
chair, and the moment passes. I squeeze her hand and try
rround her with love, to let her know how sorry I am for
things are with Elena and Antonio. I can only imagine how
ld feel were that Aria and Luna. I would give anything to
my parents back; what a tragedy for them to have their
ts and yet be so estranged.

urn my attention back to the risotto which is at risk of
g, pouring in more white wine which rises as steam,
g a sweet smoky perfume. I toss in *nipetella*, the wild
hat goes so well with *funghi*, and the wild fennel that
und. I've also prepared a salad of *pomodori, mozzarella*
o, and I've brought an apple and cinnamon pie, made to
her's recipe. I send Sam off to fetch Luciano and the girls,
nutes later he returns with Aria on his shoulders, and
carrying Luna. The girls excitedly show us a porcupine
ey have found, and tell us how porcupines can climb
mething I didn't know myself until this day.

njoy our *Ferragosto* feast up at Sam's table, our laughter
in the stifling midday heat. Up above us sits the
se, a steady presence, watching over our festivities. I
lf gazing up at her as she glows in the afternoon sun,
g how my grandmother could have ever painted it so
h her talk of curses and danger. I feel only love and
. I notice Luciano watching me and smile at him,
how often he came to the house in wartime. How
ust be for him, to be back here after so many deca
d, nearly the span of his whole life.

nch we rest in the shade of the hazel and be
lower meadow and Luciano falls asleep
up in his arm. Maria dozes in a cam
rds with Aria, until she too succur

for whatever adventure awaits them. He pl
fashion which the girls adore, always compl
them. He teaches them about the wildlife
them in a way they love, never aware that
see them crouched over in the shade of th
sticks through the undergrowth, and I kn
for the last *fragoline*, wild strawberries, of tl
aperitivo for Sam, Maria and myself, and se
mushroom risotto. Sam has already lit th
into some dry leaves and building a trip
it. He coaxes life into the fire, gently blo
tending to it attentively. The smoke ris
stream, hanging in the sunlight that filt
I notice Maria watching Luciano playir
expression is difficult to read, her eyes
senses my confusion and gives a sigh.

"He loved it when Elena and Ant
to spend all day out in the field. It wa
he lost his way with them. They st
home, to socialise with friends, to sp
school rather than our old dialect. T
it was inevitable they would leave,
as rejection, of the old ways, of ev
all those who died in the war ha
speak, rarely return. Even the grar
now, and they barely know us. As
how we live." She wipes a tear fr
wine. "Since you've arrived, Em
would have believed it, but you'
mountains. His reason to get u
to continue and wonder what
this effect on Luciano. Do I re
the old days? Is it the children
missing, a piece of the jigsaw

que
yet
con
her
to s
how
I wo
have
parer
I
stickir
creatir
mint
Aria fo
e basili
my mo
and mi
Luciano
spine th
trees, so
We e
catching
farmhou
find mys
wonderir
darkly wi
peace her
wondering
strange it r
have passe
After l
that line th
Luna tucke
Sam plays c

from a good distance, and immediately dropped to the ground. My winter clothing no longer camouflaged with the forest floor now that the snow had arrived, and I stayed close to the trees, blending in with them where I could. I squinted at the figure approaching Stazzana. Who was this, friend or foe? Hunched and weak, with a slight limp, I could see even from a distance it was a male, and that he was painfully thin. No uniform, so not a German, and at that point the *fascisti* had not yet arrived in force. Still, no-one was to be trusted, and I kept guard as the figure got closer and closer. As he rounded the corner of the bend towards the farmhouse he suddenly stopped and lifted his head, as if he could feel my gaze. Knew he was being watched, perhaps hunted. As I saw his face, a shock bigger than any earthquake I have ever felt surged through me. How many times had I seen that face in my dreams, asked God and all the angels if he was still alive, begged for his return? It was Matteo, returned to us through some stroke of good fortune or the miraculous. In a daze I scrambled to my feet, slipping in the snow, and half ran half fell down the hillside, my bread and my caution forgotten. I flung myself into his arms and he staggered for a moment, before his arms gripped me so tight I could not breathe.

"*Giuliana,*" he whispered hoarsely into my shawl. "*È veramente te?*" I was laughing and crying at the same time; over a year of separation and anguish dissolving into the relief, the joy, that he was alive. I pulled back and looked into his face, taking it in my hands. It had lost all the roundness and naivety of youth; if he had left a boy then he had certainly returned a man. His face was strong, sculpted, more handsome than ever. He was filthy, his face and hands stained dark with dirt, his hair unruly under the hat he wore, and a dark beard now framed his lower face. His eyes spoke of sadness and loss, of disillusion, but they also burned with life, with love. I saw that he loved me still, had not forgotten me. I was suddenly shy, aware of the gaping gulf in our experiences. What he had gone through this last year? He had travelled, seen the world, perhaps killed men. What had I done? Moved down the track into his chestnut house? Becoming aware of our situation, I glanced up and down the track, realising how exposed we were. I took his hand and led him deep into the forest, retrieving my bag and the bread on the way. It was as if we were children again, playing out in the wild. We found a large oak tree and sat at its sheltered base, hidden by its thick branches overhead. I offered him the bread from my bag and he gratefully tore pieces off and wolfed it down; I wondered how many days it had been since he last ate. With the land beneath us and the sky above, as it had always been, we talked and talked. He spoke of his time in the army, in Russia. Of his initial pride at being part of Operation Barbarossa, the brainchild of Hitler and promoted by Mussolini as a vital show of solidarity. He spoke of the vastness of the Russian Steppes, the raw, savage beauty of the endless landscapes, nature on a different scale. Of initial victories against the retreating Red armies, of the celebrations, the camaraderie. But then winter had come and with it the cold, the worst weapon in their arsenal. He spoke of how the cold can hurt in places you cannot imagine, how it feels as though icicles are cutting you open from the inside, one organ at a time. He told me about watching friends die in the snow, the world reduced to a flag of blood red and frost blue. Last words drifting up to be frozen mid-air. How ill-prepared they were for the terrain, the climate, like lambs to the slaughter. Of how their hopes, dreams and patriotism had also died there in that godforsaken country. Of how he had been captured and was on the way to a gulag prisoner-of-war camp when the vehicle he was travelling in had broken down; how he had managed to escape and been hidden by a kindly Cossack family, at great risk to themselves. He had been with them a month, sick in bed for half that time, delirious with fever. They had nursed him, fed him nourishing stews, kept him warm by their fire: they had saved his life. Arranged to smuggle him to the coast, and on a ship back to Italy. I sent up a silent prayer of thanks to whoever was listening that the car had broken down; had the angels intervened? I thought of the Russian family caring for Matteo, a stranger in their land, the enemy no less, and sent them my gratitude too. Upon arriving back in Italy he had very nearly been taken by the authorities, but managed to slip away in time and stealthily made his way across the mainland, up past Florence and Lucca, and back across the mountains. He spoke of his relief and joy at being back in the Garfagnana, and the kindness of various farming families who had offered him shelter and food along the way, despite the danger they were in doing so. As far as he knew, he was the only soldier to return from Russia. Why he had been saved, whether it was fate or chance, he did not know, though he had wondered many times.

"It was you, Giuliana," he told me, pulling me close. "You kept me safe, my guardian angel. When I felt like I couldn't go on, when I wanted to die, your face would appear in my mind, and I'd get the strength to carry on." He paused and a smile crept across his face, some spirit returning to his eyes. "And I knew what a slap I would get if I dared to die." I flushed, remembering our last encounter, recalling the pain of his leaving. Overwhelmed by all he had told me, I nestled in close to his body, listening to his heart beating. As the words fell away and the forest became quiet around us, we softened into each other and the ground beneath us. I became aware of his hands around my waist, of his breath on my neck. He cupped my face in his hands and my vision swam as his lips touched mine, as magical as the last time but filled with the passion that had built up during the long months of separation. My body responded to his, unfamiliar sensations of desire shooting through my young body. We were in a shining bubble of first love, of perfection. The world had no dark corners, no sharp edges, nothing to fear. We were oblivious to everything around us, to our place in space and time, to the war. Morning stretched into afternoon, and the shadows lengthened. I thought of how ecstatic his mother would be at his return and knew that I could detain him no longer. I also warned him how close the Germans were, that they had set up a base in Montaltissimo, that if he was caught he would be rounded up and deported to Germany. *There is no more dangerous foe*, I thought, a shiver of fearful premonition running through me, *than a friend who has been crossed, and is now your enemy.*

Already I could see that home was not the safest place for Matteo to be, one hill away from the front line. For him to travel thousands of miles from the devastation of the Russian steppes, to come home only to be captured and shot if he tried to escape or sent away to one of the rumoured death camps, did not bear thinking about. As a deserter from the King's army, he would possibly be wanted by our own military. As a young man of fighting age, he would certainly be taken by the Germans, for work camps or worse.

"You must hide," I urged him, squeezing his bony hands in my own, in a reversal of the advice he had previously given me. "Retreat into these mountains we know so well, survive, and wait out the storm." He nodded, pale and suddenly exhausted. We agreed he would head up through the forest to the barn hidden higher up in the hills, that was used for storing and seasoning wood ready for the next winter. We called it the Lost Barn due to its hidden location, away from the main track and right in the thick of the forest. It had not yet been found by the Germans to my knowledge, whose numbers were still few at that point, and whose explorations of the terrain had been limited. I would go to the farmhouse and break the good news to his mother, and she would come up to him that night with food and blankets. I kissed him goodbye fiercely, trying to wrap him in a protective cloak of my love. I promised to come to the barn at dawn the following day and bring him what I could.

Benedetta had heard the dogs, of course, and came to the

door to meet me, and tried to usher me into the warmth of the sitting room. She was surprised to see me of course; I rarely came to the farmhouse, and I knew she had plenty of work on her hands with the various family members who had fled their occupied villages to come to the relative safety of Stazzana. A pot of polenta bubbled enticingly on the fire and the warmth and comfort of the scene was tempting, but I knew I had to speak to her alone.

"Benedetta, I must talk to you; there is news," I said quietly to her, gesturing towards the hay barn. The fire cast a golden glow across her face that threw the deep ridges of worry across her brow into sharp relief, and her eyes flickered with questions. Nodding slightly, she closed the door behind her and followed me into the dark barn, which already had the first sparkles of frost settling on its roof. "It's Matteo," I whispered, clutching her hands. "He's here, he's come home!" She let out a small gasp and sank down onto a hay bale, overcome. The best possible answer to those ever-present questions.

"He's alive? Well?" she asked me, her voice husky with emotion. As quickly and quietly as I could I told her that Matteo was waiting up in the barn above the farm to see her, and for much-needed supplies. Benedetta was a formidable woman, and she immediately rose to her feet, brushing the hay strands off her apron. Finally, she could once again care for her youngest son, express her love, stagnant and aimless over the past year. I cautioned her about who she told the news to, for the moment, and to make sure she wasn't followed to the barn. She agreed to take no light, in case it was spotted across the valley, and fortunately the moon was already bright in the sky, an ivory coin glinting in the sooty skyscape. I bade her farewell and hurried home to the chestnut house, where I knew my own mother would be worrying. I barely remember my journey home; my feet made their own way and my heart was light. I felt as though I could stretch my wings and fly over the trees like the mountain eagle, silent and powerful in the dark. Everything looked different, lit by my happiness. The very trees seemed to me to hum their pleasure at Matteo's return. I was young, I was in love and my love had returned to me.

So many years have passed since that night, yet still a little shiver of that joy ripples through my wasted old body. My gnarled fingers try to clutch on to the images a little longer, willing myself back to the mountains, but with the dawn they are slipping away, back into the past, across the threshold to that shadowy world of memory. A door I have kept closed for so long, for to open it would mean releasing all the pain and devastation, as well as the joy. Many lives have been lived in darkness, and now the light must illuminate the lies. For so long I thought I was protecting her, being brave, being selfless, but perhaps it was only cowardice after all. Fear of rejection, fear that my decision was not the right one. All my protests, all my justifications, crumble to dust in the light of day. I feel the grave calling me, the voice growing stronger by the day. Night and day are blurring, and I long to give in, to sleep. But the truth will not let me, it must out, finally. My story must be heard.

12

Emma

2017

The summer flew by in a daze: endless days ruled by the sun, seeking out the coolness of the shade. Nights stretched out under our gauzy mosquito nets, cocooned away from the world. Our windows flung open, music and laughter from the village festivals floating across the valleys and into our dreams. Evenings sat on the balcony watching fireflies flash secret messages across the orchard, their merry dance a summer sister to winter fairy lights. Many nights we've sat in the piazza, chatting with our neighbours while the girls play, as I like to imagine my grandparents doing when they were children. Life in the village is wonderful, and I count many of our neighbours as friends, but our best times are always those spent down at Stazzana.

There was timeless quality to that summer, our first summer in the Garfagnana. Days flew by marked by the rising and setting of the sun, and we all relaxed into our new way of life. I put my quest for answers on hold, instinctively knowing that I needed this rest, and looking at the sun-splashed faces of my husband and children I realised they did too. Before we knew it *Ferragosto* had arrived, the mid-August national holiday initially created by the Emperor Augustus to give agricultural workers a well-deserved rest, and later becoming the Assumption of Mary: another *festa* appropriated by the Catholic Church. It felt like the whole of Italy was on holiday, and the pace of life, already slow with the summer holidays, came to a standstill as families celebrated together. We decided to spend it at Stazzana, and invited Luciano and Maria for a lunch cooked over our campfire. There is a lower meadow at Stazzana which leads to the woods by the stream, and there we have set up a little encampment in the shade of the hazel trees. Sam has dug out a fire pit and lined it with rocks from the river, and we bought a tripod and a Dutch oven to cook over it. The past few weeks he has been busy working on a new project at Stazzana, and when we arrive for *Ferragosto* there are cries of delight from the girls and myself as we spot the table and benches he has made for our al fresco dining. The table is huge, capable of seating at least ten people, and made entirely from a fallen chestnut, he tells me proudly. It is rustic and simple, and looks completely in keeping with the bucolic setting.

"I love it," I tell him, leaning in close for a kiss, and his face breaks into a proud smile. Together we set a white tablecloth upon the table, its edges dancing in the breeze. Aria and Luna set off with their baskets to search for wildflowers, and return with ox-eye daisies, old man's beard, pink sorrel and common mallow with its tiny purple flowers. Aria has also spotted some wild fennel, and I pick some to add to my mushroom risotto. We arrange the flowers in jam-jars to set on the table, and Aria and Luna dance around it, delighted with the effect.

Luciano and Maria arrive on foot, bringing home-made cheese, prosciutto and a couple of bottles of last year's vino. His farmer's jobs completed in the morning, Luciano is ready to play, and he heads off with the girls across the meadow ready for whatever adventure awaits them. He plays in a timeless fashion which the girls adore, always completely present with them. He teaches them about the wildlife and fauna around them in a way they love, never aware that they are learning. I see them crouched over in the shade of the trees waving their sticks through the undergrowth, and I know they are looking for the last *fragoline*, wild strawberries, of the summer. I pour an aperitivo for Sam, Maria and myself, and set about preparing the mushroom risotto. Sam has already lit the fire, striking a spark into some dry leaves and building a tripod of kindling around it. He coaxes life into the fire, gently blowing air into its centre, tending to it attentively. The smoke rises and drifts across the stream, hanging in the sunlight that filters through the foliage. I notice Maria watching Luciano playing with the girls, and her expression is difficult to read, her eyes clouded with regret. She senses my confusion and gives a sigh.

"He loved it when Elena and Antonio were that age, happy to spend all day out in the field. It was when they got older that he lost his way with them. They started to travel away from home, to socialise with friends, to speak the Italian they learnt at school rather than our old dialect. They were so bright, so smart, it was inevitable they would leave, one day. But Luciano took it as rejection, of the old ways, of everything that his father and all those who died in the war had sacrificed. Now they hardly speak, rarely return. Even the grandchildren, they too are grown now, and they barely know us. Ashamed, I think, of who we are, how we live." She wipes a tear from her cheek and takes a sip of wine. "Since you've arrived, Emma, he's a changed man. I never would have believed it, but you've given him back his love of the mountains. His reason to get up in the mornings." I wait for her to continue and wonder what is special about us, to have had this effect on Luciano. Do I remind him of my grandmother, of the old days? Is it the children? I have a feeling that something is missing, a piece of the jigsaw I have not yet slotted into place. A question mark that hangs between us, a distance that we cannot yet bridge. Whether Maria knows why I do not know, but her confusion seems to imply she does not. Maria settles back into her chair, and the moment passes. I squeeze her hand and try to surround her with love, to let her know how sorry I am for how things are with Elena and Antonio. I can only imagine how I would feel were that Aria and Luna. I would give anything to have my parents back; what a tragedy for them to have their parents and yet be so estranged.

I turn my attention back to the risotto which is at risk of sticking, pouring in more white wine which rises as steam, creating a sweet smoky perfume. I toss in *nipetella*, the wild mint that goes so well with *funghi*, and the wild fennel that Aria found. I've also prepared a salad of *pomodori, mozzarella e basilico*, and I've brought an apple and cinnamon pie, made to my mother's recipe. I send Sam off to fetch Luciano and the girls, and minutes later he returns with Aria on his shoulders, and Luciano carrying Luna. The girls excitedly show us a porcupine spine they have found, and tell us how porcupines can climb trees, something I didn't know myself until this day.

We enjoy our *Ferragosto* feast up at Sam's table, our laughter catching in the stifling midday heat. Up above us sits the farmhouse, a steady presence, watching over our festivities. I find myself gazing up at her as she glows in the afternoon sun, wondering how my grandmother could have ever painted it so darkly with her talk of curses and danger. I feel only love and peace here. I notice Luciano watching me and smile at him, wondering how often he came to the house in wartime. How strange it must be for him, to be back here after so many decades have passed, nearly the span of his whole life.

After lunch we rest in the shade of the hazel and beech trees that line the lower meadow and Luciano falls asleep on the rug, Luna tucked up in his arm. Maria dozes in a camping chair and Sam plays cards with Aria, until she too succumbs to drowsiness, snuggles into his chest and falls asleep. The August heat is heavy, languid, and even the birds and insects seem to quieten down for siesta time. I close my eyes and enjoy the moment, noticing the part of myself that is one with the mountains, with the earth beneath my feet.

As the heat begins to drop we all stir, and come to in the rich golden light of early evening. Luciano and Maria bid us farewell and begin the trek back up to their farm before the light starts to fade, and I thank them for sharing the day with us.

"*Grazie a voi*," Luciano replies, gripping my hand, his face crinkling into a smile. I notice him glance up at the house as they cross the field, pausing a while. What memories lurk there; what ghosts call to him from the past? Is he imagining my grandmother there as a young woman, watching from the window? I wonder vaguely if I will ever know, if he will tell me the truth one day. Is he hiding something from me, or protecting me?

The girls' giggles draw me back to the present moment, and I see them skipping through the meadow, their fair heads bobbing about like sunflowers.

"I see one!" Aria shrieks. "A fairy!" And she and Luna are off again, following what I think is a dragonfly, but given the magic and mystery that seems to surround Stazzana perhaps it is a fairy after all. Sam and I sit in our camping chairs and watch them, and he passes me a chilled beer from the bucket of icy stream water. In the back of my mind I know there are things we should be talking about, concerns for the future, but in this moment I push them far away, aware only of the beauty all around us. He takes my hand and smiles over at me, that smile that still makes my heart beat a little faster. It was a perfect summer day at Stazzana, the pinnacle of the lovely dream that was our first summer in the mountains.

13

Emma

2017

All dreams must end eventually, and one day I woke up and realised it was autumn. The leaves were still green but they were darker, older, tired of summer and the drought. It hadn't rained for months, and the stream at Stazzana had all but dried up. The light was still golden, the earth warm with memories of the heat, but there was a breeze that spoke of change. Every drop of *la bella stagione*, the beautiful season, had been squeezed out, and it was time for the rains to return, for the wheel of the year to turn again. It led to a feeling of restlessness within me, questioning what we were doing here. My friend Cat is keen to know when we are coming home; I know she worries about me. She's asked whether we'll be putting the house in Italy up for sale, and I know that it would be the reasonable thing to do. It needs a huge amount of time and money spent on it, and our jobs and lives are in Scotland. Our friends, the girls' schools, Sam's family. But I'm not ready to make that decision, and I still haven't found any of the answers I came out here to find. The glamour of summer has blinded me to my goals, lulled me into forgetting my quest, but now the time has come to make some progress.

Sam and I finally managed to have a conversation about our plan for the next few months, and he agreed we can stay on until the end of the year. I know he worries about our financial situation out here, and being the only young man in the village he is luckily in great demand from our elderly neighbours for some of the heavier jobs on the land. Several ex-pats in the area have offered to pay him for strimming and chopping wood, and I know he feels relieved we are at least covering our expenses, if not earning what we were in Scotland. He's started building a treehouse for the girls down at Stazzana and he's built us a couple of bridges, ready for the winter rains when apparently the river will be too fast-flowing to cross on foot. He loves the freedom there, spending his days out in the sun, working with his hands. He grows stronger by the day; the physical labour involved in working such a steep terrain is much more demanding than his carpentry work back in Scotland. He returns home at the end of the day tired and happy, his hair thick with sawdust and bleached blonde by the sun. For the time being he is content, and I am relieved. So much lies unspoken between us these days, and I have no idea how he really feels about our life here. He's picked up the language much better than I thought he would, and can chat away with the villagers now without me being there to translate. I know he misses our friends and his parents, but he does seem to love the countryside. There is a distance between us that I don't know how to bridge; I fear it is growing despite all the time we have together. We never speak about the past or the accident, and I can't help but feel that he doesn't care how I am feeling. Many nights I fall asleep with tears coursing silently down my cheeks, and I long to reach out to him, to find comfort in his strength, but I don't. We are at an impasse, and I can't see a way forward. On the surface our marriage is as it ever was – we get on well, we joke with the girls – but it lacks the passion of the past, the ability to know what the other is thinking. For the time being I push these worries away, hoping against hope that if I can find what I am looking for here then perhaps I can find myself, and Sam will have his wife back.

I made our apologies to the girls' school back in Scotland and enquired at the local *Scuola dell'Infanzia* whether they might attend for a few days a week, which they happily agreed to. Fortunately, full-time school is not obligatory in Italy until the child is six going on seven, so we have no pressure there. No homework, no exams, just play-based learning while our girls learn a new language. They both settled in well, and are always happy to go in. Aria quickly made some friends and tells me all about her day in great detail. Luna seems content enough, watching the children playing and joining in when she wishes. She is one of the younger ones, of course, and the little ones tend to be cuddled and comforted by the teachers more, but our Luna is so independent. I laugh to see her polite refusal to be carried, her raised eyebrow when an adult addresses her in baby language. Once the school heard I was a teacher they invited me to start some English lessons for the children, a task which I happily agreed to, and two afternoons a week will easily give me enough time for my research too.

With the girls and Sam away from the house I find I have time to think clearly for the first time in months. For my initial research I have turned, as I have always done, to books. I spend much of my time studying at the local library in Molazzana, which is surprisingly well stocked. I'm learning about the history of the region and World War Two, when this area was occupied by the Nazis as they retreated up through Italy. The Gothic Line was a defensive line they drew across the mountains, initially passing through Borgo a Mozzano, further down the valley towards Lucca. When they abandoned this position to the advancing Allies the line was redrawn right through the heart of the village we live in, right through Stazzana. The little village of Montaltissimo was, I am surprised to learn, occupied by German forces. I think of Stazzana, so close by, and wonder how it was to live there in those times. I think of my grandmother and my great-grandmother living there, a house full of women. Were they scared? Were they raided? I read that at the height of the occupation there were up to fifteen hundred Allied flights a day, all dropping bombs on the mountains. I can only imagine how terrifying it must have been. I find a tattered old book in the library about the Resistance in the Garfagnana, and I'm gripped by the stories of bravery that emerge from within its pages. It seems that a few locals formed themselves into groups of freedom fighters and resisted the Germans by whatever means they could, at enormous personal risk to themselves and their families. By this stage they were not only fighting the Nazis but also the Italians still loyal to Mussolini and fascism, the blackshirts fighting alongside the Germans. A civil war, friends and brothers fighting one another. I start to understand some of the horrors that afflicted this area during the war, and why people even nowadays are reluctant to talk about it. My little book paints the members of the resistance as heroes but describes how unpopular they were with many people at the time because of the risk they posed. The *rappresaglie*, the reprisals, left a scar on this land that will never heal. Innocent civilians, rounded up and killed, punishment for partisan coups. Ten villagers for every German.

I remember one Monday I was reading my book in the library, dictionary to hand, translating it as I went. The girls were at school, Sam was working down at Stazzana, and I was enjoying the peace and quiet. My chapter was recounting a partisan success whereby a landslide crashed down upon a convoy which included some senior Nazi officials, and killed ten men. Furious, the local commander ordered the deaths of one hundred villagers, and civilians were rounded up the very next day. Half were released following interventions from local priests, but that evening the remaining fifty were shot. I'm reading this as a history book, gripping but removed from me personally; these are, after all, events that happened three quarters of a century ago. I'm glancing through the list of names of the victims, and a shiver runs through me despite the heat of the day as I read the name *Luca Bonini*. In Italy married women keep their maiden name, and my grandmother's surname was Bonini. My mind rationalises that it might have been a common name, but I somehow know it was someone close to her. My heart beats faster as I wonder if this is why she left, why she never wanted to look back. Was the pain of losing this relation too great for her to bear? I decide to ask Luciano if he knew this man, since he seems to know more about my grandmother than I initially suspected.

I realise it's four o'clock and time to collect the girls from school, so I borrow the book from the friendly lady in charge of the library and head back home to Montaltissimo. The late September sun illuminates the vines and the olive trees as I enter the village, and the scene is so perfect it's hard to reconcile with what I've been reading about the horrors of war. I force myself to leave the past behind and focus on the present as I walk up to the school gates, where Aria and Luna are waiting for me.

14

Giuliana

1944

I can still feel the cold of that winter we spent in the chestnut house; it has never really left my bones. I was young and strong, but so many did not survive. Young children, the elderly, the infirm. It was a mixed blessing, the mountain winter. It certainly hindered the Germans' progress, and must have caused them to doubt the wisdom of choosing this terrain for their famous *Linea Gotica*. The autumn storms brought weeks of heavy rain, flooding their trenches, ruining much of their equipment. Landslides, always a peril here, occurred unexpectedly, blocking their routes and crushing their fortifications. Sometimes the hand of nature, sometimes the work of the hidden enemy, the secret army defending the land that was rightfully theirs. The storms were followed by long stretches of blue-cold, deep snow and icy conditions. A lack of food and warm clothing affected nearly everyone in the mountains, no matter whether they were Germans, locals or *sfollati*. Anything was used as firewood, even family furniture, and many barns were pulled down to pillage their wood. We were lucky indeed, in the chestnut house, to have food and firewood, and fortunate to be sheltered in the base of the valley, hidden by the trees around us and not bombed by the allies. Neighbouring Castelnuovo di Garfagnana was razed to the ground and we heard it all, the crashing destruction echoing around the valley, that moment of silence before worlds ended. It was a strange paradox: despite our hidden location we were so close to the front line, just a hill away, and the Allies were just another hill away again. We were protected in our own bubble, and yet just a stone's throw from the epicentre of the fighting, a microcosm of the war. It was an odd feeling, to be so close to home and unable to return there. I wondered who was living in our house, what we would find on our return. *If you ever return,* an inner voice reminded me.

By this point we were completely cut off from the wider world. The newspapers and letters had long since stopped getting through, and although a few people managed to be smuggled out across the line each month, taking little-known and dangerous mountain passes, no-one was crazy enough to want to come in. We had no idea who was winning the war; we kept our heads down and concentrated on survival – never an easy task in a mountain winter, even less so in an ancient barn never intended to be lived in.

Hunger was our daily companion. My youngest brother Luciano suffered the most, I believe, as a growing boy. Already a pale child, he grew ever thinner, and his frustration at being kept home with the 'womenfolk' grew by the day. My sisters Margherita and Rosa pined for our father, their friends, their old lives. They lived in fear of the Germans and never ventured out much further than the confines of the chestnut house. They tended the fire and helped our mother where they could, spending their days reading the Bible and darning our clothes, making do with what we possessed, for there was nothing new to be had. Luciano and I had patched up the chestnut house against the cold as best we could, and every morning I would collect more firewood to be dried out by the fire before burning.

By November the last of the chestnuts were hidden under a thick mantle of snow, and I had to seek them out with frozen fingers. I had amassed several sacks, but I was still concerned whether it would see us through the whole winter. I worried about them being taken, for we had no weapons to defend ourselves with. German patrols regularly passed along the track that lead up to Stazzana and then on up to Sassi, and in all probability they now knew of our presence. I did not think that our chestnuts would be enough to tempt them, but I worried for Renata, our cow. Many farms in the area had been raided for supplies and taken at gunpoint. Benedetta had already had such a visit, and one of her three cows had been led away. We all lived with our animals in those days, cared for them from the day they were born. My heart wept when I heard the news, and I can imagine Benedetta watching the cow being led away: the anger and sorrow she must have felt.

That autumn had also seen the arrival of the *San Marco* and the *Monterosa*, Mussolini's army of Italian soldiers fighting for the Italian Social Republic. Allied with the Germans, with Mussolini a puppet figure, his strings pulled by Hitler. They were from all over Italy, some even from the Garfagnana. These young boys, most of them having been too young to fight when the war began, were dealt a cruel hand. All soldiers suffer, that is a soldier's lot, and has ever been. But most know that if they die for their cause, their families will be proud of them, their country will honour them. These *alpini*, these *fascisti*, were from a country divided, a state ripped apart by politics and war. A nation that changed allegiance, turned against their former friend and suffered the horrific consequences. Some were spat upon by their own loved ones; some were disowned, told never to return home. *Vergogna*, shame, was worse than death for an Italian soldier.

Matteo's return to the mountains changed everything for me. The hardships of daily life and the danger of our situation all disappeared into the shadows when I thought of Matteo and the next time I would see him. I was lit from within with a radiance that I could not have hoped to hide from my family. They noticed the change in me when I returned to the chestnut house after my reunion with Matteo and pressed me for the cause of my elation. I told them, my heart relieved to share how I was feeling. If Matteo had returned, there was hope for our father. I missed out much of what he had told me, of the defeats and slaughter, of how our country was humiliated, divided. I swore them to secrecy and omitted telling them where Matteo was hiding. My mother urged me to be cautious, not to seek him out again, but I think she knew that was an impossible thing to ask of me. As we crouched around the fire warming our hands against the gelid night I was already elsewhere, looking for Matteo in the flames, asking the fates to show him to me. I knew that where he led, I would follow, that I would risk everything for him. Never again would we be separated, I vowed, war or no war. I thought of him alone in the dark of the old barn, listening to the lonely owl's hoot, the frost settling on the snow outside. I knew Benedetta would have brought him blankets and food, and that he would be better off than he'd been all those previous nights crossing the mountains. *He is home*, I thought, and deep inside me something relaxed. I was sixteen, so young and naïve, but even I knew that hard times lay ahead. But with Matteo by my side I believed we could do anything, that we were invincible. I was wrong.

The next morning dawned as bright as my mood, the sun cutting like glass through the bare branches, reflecting off the snow and blinding me as I emerged from the dark of the chestnut house. The snow was glimmering with frost, and ice glinted from the shallower pools of the stream. Carefully I set off through the forest, on my usual route to the farm that made bread. The guns were quiet, the sky blue as the ocean over my head, empty of whirring planes, and I could almost believe myself back in peacetime. As I neared the farm I was careful to track around its boundary, and set off in a northerly direction. The terrain was steep and I climbed nimbly from one tree to the next, clutching at branches and roots to steady me as I went. The barn was well hidden and would have been very hard to find had I not gone this way so many times. There was no track to the barn and the only access was on foot. The way was overgrown, and it was only the familiar contours of the land that led me to the barn. *The only way to the Lost Barn is to follow your heart.* Our childhood words floated back to me as I climbed, making me smile, thinking how true they still were. As I drew closer I was gripped with the fear that I had imagined it all, that the barn would be bare, and I a foolish girl alone in the woods. *Coraggio*, I told myself, and felt a glow of warmth on my hands where they had held Matteo's just the day before. I knocked gently and pushed open the heavy wooden door. There he was, asleep on a sack, wrapped in woollen blankets and propped up defensively against a stack of logs. He heard the creak of the door and jumped, immediately on guard, reaching for his knife.

"*Sono io*," I said, pushing back my hood, "Giuliana." He exhaled with relief, and I crossed the barn and tucked myself under the blankets with him.

"I was dreaming," he told me, his eyes half-closed, "dreaming I was an old man by the fire at Stazzana. You were sitting beside me, and all around us were our children and our grandchildren. They were so perfect, so full of life." He groped for my hand under the blankets and looked into my eyes, his own full of sadness and regret. "I should never have left you, Giu, I'm sorry." I pulled him close and felt the flame ignite between us. I willed some of his sorrow and his pain to leave him and come to me, I wanted to share this burden. I summoned images of our childhood, of our merriest times in the woods, of the feeling of a never-ending summer day. The magic of the evening we lay in wait for the wolves; the night of the *vendemmia*, when we finally saw the pack up close. His breathing deepened, and I felt some of the tension leave him. We stayed that way, savouring the seconds together, for as long as we dared. Matteo told me that his mother had advised him to head higher into the mountains, up to a village about an hour's walk from Stazzana. He had family there who would take him in and hide him for the time being.

"When will I see you again?" I asked urgently, searching his face.

He smiled at me then and took my face in his hands. "Nothing can keep me from you now," he assured me with a kiss. I pressed my forehead to his and stayed that way, feeling the bond between us strengthen. I watched him head off uphill, following the paths of our youth. Back then we told tales of monsters in the dark, werewolves and dragons, but what was out there now was much scarier. I whispered a prayer of protection and forced my feet homeward. Every inch of me yearned to stay with him, to follow wherever he might go, but I knew he was safer alone.

Two whole weeks passed, and it felt like a lifetime. The sun rose and set, and I went about my chores, but I was constantly checking upriver for visitors, and a couple of times I risked the journey to the farmhouse to see if Benedetta had heard anything.

"Don't fret, child," she would tell me, kindly. "He'll have reached his *zio* and *zia* just fine, and they're safe up there. The soldiers haven't bothered them up there yet." The *yet* hung in the air between us, filling my head with images of Matteo being captured, killed, sent to Germany. I was restless, bad-tempered with my sisters and Luciano, and rude to my mother. The selfish ways of young lovers, who always believe themselves the first to have ever felt that way. It was evening time in late November, perhaps around nine o'clock, when I heard the birdcall. No-one else reacted – the woods were full of animals – but I would have recognised that sound anywhere. It was our secret signal as children to let the other know we had arrived and were waiting, ready to head off on an adventure. My body thrilled at the noise, and I could feel my heart beating fast against my ribcage. I made an excuse about fetching some water, and luckily no-one queried me. He was there, waiting at our meeting spot by the stream, like no time had passed at all. I threw myself into his arms, covering his face with kisses, restraining myself from crying out with happiness. We retreated to a quieter spot in the woods, out of sight of passers-by or curious members of my family. Matteo looked well, already much more like the young man who had left to go to war. He was clean, and his face had lost its pallor. His dark curls bounced again, and I wrapped my finger around one, marvelling at his beauty. He told me he was safe with his aunt and uncle, and that his cousin Raffaello had also returned from the war and was staying there. So far the village was safe, but there were reports of the Germans and *fascisti* ranging further up the mountain, and there was a cave they had prepared with supplies in case they needed to leave the village and hide out. The shepherd Dino, the man who had given Matteo the Maremma puppies, had passed through the village just a few days previously. He roamed all over the mountain range with his flock and his dogs, and was a valuable source of information. He told Matteo and Raffaello how the Germans were fortifying the new front line through the mountains, but the weather had been against them and the allies had gained ground and were now down in the valley at Gallicano and Barga. Matteo told me of a man whose name was kept secret smuggling people out of the occupied area across a little-known mountain pass. Jews, young men, residents of Florence, Lucca and other cities who had fled to the mountains for safety, only to be caught behind enemy lines.

"Will you go?" I asked him, wondering if I would join him, and knowing with a sinking feeling that I would not be able to abandon my family. Matteo shook his head, looking down at the snow, searching for the right words.

"Giu," he leaned closer, his voice dropping to a whisper, "we were fools, led blind into the wrong war by Mussolini, believing all the Fascist rhetoric. Hitler pulling our strings, using our country for what he wanted. He's still doing it, although he's lost half the country now. America has joined the war, and Hitler can't beat Russia, they're too strong. The King has sided with the allies, and the people are waking up. *I* am waking up, *amore*. We need to take action, to fight for our country. To rid ourselves of the *tedeschi* and the *fascisti* and take our country back." The passion burned fierce in his eyes, and I was confused, my head muddled. Memories of another speech on this spot crept back to me, and he saw it in my face.

"It isn't like before," he promised me. "We were so stupid, so naïve. This time we fight for the right cause, for ourselves." We had never been political, in the Garfagnana. News from Rome filtered through eventually, pre-war, and some of us were more learned than others, but mostly we didn't really believe it concerned us. When the war took our men, our houses, our freedom, our *lives*, we were all forced to become political. What Matteo was saying fanned the flame that had been lit within me that first night at the chestnut house, lying listening to the gunfire in my village. He was right, I realised. We were warriors, hunters, he and I. We'd had too much taken from us already, and it was time to fight back. "*Sì*," I whispered, meeting his gaze.

"I knew you'd understand." He clutched me tight, and I felt the heat between our bodies crackle through the cold night air. He then explained how a small group of men, some from the area and a couple from the coast who had ended up there by chance, were organising themselves into a resistance group. There had been calls from the Allies on leaflets dropped into the area for local people to resist the enemy, to keep the spirit of free Italy alive despite the occupation. It was early days, but through the shepherd Dino they had already been in contact with a couple of other groups in the area who'd been carrying out acts of sabotage for several months now. *Partigiani*, they were known as, partisans. Freedom fighters, acting beyond the guidance of the state, the only law their own moral compass. I knew now that Matteo would not leave these hills, that he was already committed to this cause.

"I want to help," I told him, and he knew better than to argue with me.

"You need to know this is dangerous work," he told me, frowning with concern. "If you get caught, there is torture and death. And the danger is not only for you, but your family, the village. The reprisals can be against innocent villagers, the old and the young, women and children."

"My family must not know," I replied, after some thought. "Mother would worry, and my sisters talk too much. Luciano would want to help, but I won't put him in danger. He's too young, and Mother couldn't face losing him." Matteo nodded, and kissed me. As usual thoughts of the war disappeared, and we two were all that existed, drawn together like magnets. I could have stayed there all night, but I heard my mother's voice calling my name, and reluctantly I bade him good night.

"I'll return in a week," he told me, blowing a kiss. I watched as he faded into the woods, my dashing ghost.

That was the night I first heard about the partisans, the movement that would become famous after the war, capture the hearts and the spirit of a nation. Back then they were young lads, naïve and inexperienced, taking on an enemy that outmatched them in nearly every way. The one advantage the partisans had was what allowed them to operate for so long, so successfully, and eventually to contribute to winning the war. They knew the mountains. The enemy had entered their playground.

15

Emma

2017

I got my chance to ask Luciano about Luca Bonini a few days later, when he announced the conditions were perfect for mushroom hunting. It was October by this point, and about a week before we had had the first of the autumn storms, days of heavy grey rain and thick mists that hid us away from the rest of the world. All the views we'd grown so used to disappeared, and even the trees in the orchard loomed blearily out of the fog, coming and going as the wind pushed the clouds along. We were up in the clouds, quite literally.

"You must feel at home!" our neighbours joked to us, but in truth this was like nothing we'd ever experienced in Scotland. That rain had apparently woken the mushrooms up, and now they'd had a few days to grow and the weather had improved, the time was right for one of the most sacred of Tuscan traditions. Luciano informed us we should meet him at six in the morning by the gate to his farm, and that he would bring breakfast. I dreaded to think what time Maria would have been up in order to make the bread that I knew would be part of the breakfast victuals. The day dawned clear, the pink glow slowly spreading along the horizon, illuminating the rocky tips of the mountains. Further down, where the tree line began, the beeches had all turned red, and once the sun's rays hit them it looked as though the mountain was on fire. Lower down still the chestnut woods began, covering vast swathes of the mountains. The chestnuts were a kaleidoscope of colours, ranging from yellows that popped like cider to bright pumpkin oranges and browns dark as allspice. I had always thought spring was my favourite season, but this year autumn was giving it a good run for its money. We pulled two drowsy children from their warm beds with whispered promises of *cornetti* and hopefully lots of *funghi*, and strapped them onto our backs, where they nestled sleepily in for another snooze.

Luciano was waiting at his gate, armed with two large baskets. He'd woven them himself, he told us proudly, from willow. They were gifts for us, for our mushroom-collecting adventures. It's important to use a basket, he told us, so the spores from the mushrooms may drop through and spread as you walk, ensuring the future is provided for. With a small laugh he told us it was even the law in Tuscany these days; potentially you could be fined for using a plastic bag. The baskets were beautiful, rounded and deep with a plaited handle, and I thanked him, tears springing to my eyes. The hours he must have spent making them. He brushed my thanks off with a grunt, but I could see that he was pleased.

Once we reached Stazzana we entered the woods by the river, and started to follow an animal track running parallel to it. The girls had woken up by this point and were running about the woods in the morning sunlight, searching for mushrooms. Luciano just kept walking, explaining that here the forest was a mixture of alders, beeches, poplars and birches, and that the mushrooms we were looking for preferred chestnuts and oaks to grow under. Most of the mushrooms the girls were pointing out were either *tossico*, toxic, or merely *non commestibile*, inedible. We pressed on, further along the river than Sam and I had been before. We were soon surrounded by chestnuts and oaks, and the ground was dotted with spiky green chestnut cases, some of them split open to reveal shiny bronze nuts within. The girls were desperate to collect some, and so Luciano showed us how to check the nut for the tell-tale worm hole, and if there was one to throw it back on the ground. If the nut was a decent size and worm-free, it could go in the basket. Collecting chestnuts was a perilous occupation, prising the jewels from their prickly shells, and the woods was soon filled with cries of, "Mummy! Daddy! 'Ciano! Over here, there's a big one!"

Once our baskets were weighty with chestnuts Luciano drew our attention to a mushroom that we would have missed, camouflaged as it was with the forest floor and the patchwork of leaves that covered it. The king of the mushrooms, he proudly declared, the delicious *porcino*. It was about three inches across, and with a stalk nearly as wide as its head. I had only ever seen them in restaurants, usually served on top of pizza, and I wondered at its stocky proportions and pungent aroma. Luciano cut it with his knife, near the bottom of the stalk. It amused me that the Italian for stalk was *gamba*, leg.

"You don't pull it from the ground," he explained solemnly to the girls, their fair heads bent over the mushroom. "You leave the roots in the earth to let another mushroom grow. Give it a little shake, like this, to release the spores back into the ground, like sowing seeds for more baby *porcini* to come." The girls practised the motion and promised that they would remember to obey the 'Code of the Mushroom' all their lives.

Engrossed in our *funghi* hunting, I was surprised to look up and see a tumbledown barn in front of us, where two streams met. It was nestled into the woods and had a magical quality that made me think of fairy tales like *Hansel and Gretel*. I felt rather than saw Luciano's reaction, and I sensed his aversion as much as I was aware of the building drawing me closer. Ignoring him, I approached the little barn, jumping over the stream to the other side. Ivy coated the remains of the walls, and great rocks and roof tiles lay scattered around. The clearing was quiet, peaceful, only the gurgling of the river to disturb my enchantment. Sam and the girls were following me now, hop skipping over the stream and climbing around the building, imagining what it had been in the past. I wondered if we were still in Stazzana territory, or if we had passed the boundary. Luciano waited for us on the other side of the stream, resting on a large rock. Eventually we returned to him and I saw he looked tired, deflated. Older, somehow.

"What is this place?" I asked him. "Are we still at Stazzana?" He nodded wearily, and explained that this was a *metato*, a chestnut-drying barn. That the chestnuts were laid out on the raised floor and a fire lit underneath, which smoked them dry over the course of several days. There were many in these mountains, although now there was only one working *metato*, up in the higher mountain village of Sant'Antonio sulle Alpe.

"It is yours now," he told me, so quietly I had to strain to hear him. "Part of the Stazzana estate. It has not been used since before the war." He hesitated, as if trying to summon up the strength to continue. "It was lived in, during the winter of the occupation. The winter of 1944." As I let this sink in my mind raced, trying to imagine people living in this tiny ramshackle building in the middle of the woods. I waited, sensing he was on the point of crossing some line, telling me some of the information I had so desperately been seeking. I didn't need to ask, *"Who lived here?"* The question hung unspoken in the air. He lifted his head and met my eyes. A resignation, a sadness, filled them, which I could not fathom. His voice thick with reluctance he told me, "I lived here that winter, with my mother, and my three sisters. When the Germans took our house in Montaltissimo we fled down here, where we were safe. We stayed here from the autumn of '44 to the spring of '45, when the liberation came." I knew I was staring at him, searching my mind for a response and finding nothing. I had so many more questions, but I couldn't quite voice any of them, and we stayed like that, mute. Luckily Sam and the girls saved the day, reaching us and diffusing the tension.

"I'm starving!" Aria announced loudly. "Can we eat now, Luci?" He smiled, as if a weight has been lifted. His face broke into a thousand wrinkles and I tried to see him living here as a boy. How old would he have been? A young teenager, at the most? Too young to fight, fortunately, though I imagine his father would have been enlisted.

We spread the picnic blanket on the damp forest floor, and ate a fine breakfast of fresh *pane*, *cornetti* filled with apricot jam, and sugared coffee hot from the flask. The aroma of coffee and sweet jam mixed with the earthy smells of fungi and rotting leaves, and our silence was interrupted with the occasional soft thud of a chestnut falling from a tree. After breakfast we headed back the way we came, our baskets full of chestnuts and *porcini*, and a couple of *galletti* – or chanterelles, as I know them – wrinkled yellow mushrooms. As we left the *metato*, I glanced back, and I noticed Luna looking back as well.

"Did you like the little chestnut house?" I asked her, squeezing her chubby hand. She nodded, thoughtfully. Before I could ask anything else, she dropped my hand and rushed off to join Sam and Aria, who were bent over examining some pawprints in the mud.

"It might be wolves!" I heard Aria yell out, and they all started following the tracks. I fell in line with Luciano, as we followed them.

"Go on then," he announced, a smile playing around his lips, "ask me. I'm an old man, you know, you might not have much time." I laughed at his Tuscan directness, always getting straight to the point. I also wondered at what had changed; he had been so evasive in the past. The words spilled out from him now, and he told me of the day they had to flee their home when the Nazis invaded, and how they had to adjust to life in a barn. How autumn turned to winter, how ill equipped they were to cope with the weather, the cold. How hungry he was every day, how he tried to hide it from his mother who already had so much to worry about. I asked about his sisters, and he told me that thankfully they all survived the war. Two married and moved to neighbouring villages; the other left shortly after the war and made a life for herself abroad. He tells me his sisters who stayed in Italy both died in their eighties, having lived good long lives. His father never returned from the war, and his mother lived out her days as a widow in Montaltissimo, taking pleasure from seeing her grandchildren grow. None of them ever returned to the chestnut house after that winter; they all tried to look to the future, not the past.

I remembered how I wanted to ask Luciano about Luca Bonini and I seized the moment while he was in a talkative mood.

"Who was Luca Bonini?" I asked him. "Was he related to my grandmother?" He stumbled, uncharacteristically, and as I tried to help him and check if he was OK, he batted me off crossly, muttering under his breath. He took a moment to recover, so I continued: "I found his name in a book I'm reading about the Resistance, and I wondered if he was a relation, and whether this was why my grandmother left?" I realised I was rambling, and when I glanced over at Luciano I was worried to see him bent over coughing, looking worse than ever. He looked exhausted, and a flicker of fear flitted through me. *Is he ill? Has this morning been too much for him? Have I gone too far with all my questions?* "I'm sorry," I murmured, taking his arm. "Are you alright?" He nodded, composing himself, and there was a pause while he seemed to think about what to say.

Eventually he nodded, and said, "You're right, Emma, Luca

was Assunta's brother. He was in Castelnuovo the day after a partisan attack, and was rounded up as part of the reprisals. He was shot in cold blood, like so many." He sighed, and seemed to sag under the weight of memory. "Assunta was devastated. She didn't talk to anyone at Stazzana for a month, so deep was her grief." He looked across at me, and his expression was so conflicted, that I wondered again what he felt for my grandmother, why speaking about her is so difficult for him. I'm fond of Luciano, he's been such a friend to us, and yet I always have an uneasy feeling that he is hiding something. We walked on to join the others in silence, and when we reached Luciano's farm the sun was high in the sky. We thanked him and urged him to take some of the *porcini* home to Maria for lunch. As I embraced him to say goodbye he told me, "Soon, Emma, soon," and I nodded. I had come so far already; I could wait a little longer.

16

Luciano

2017

The countdown has begun, and I can feel time slipping through my fingers, gathering pace. I wake most nights in a panic that I have left it too late, that I have no time to make amends. Perhaps my life is coming full circle, at the end I must confront what happened at the very beginning. Emma's question about Luca Bonini startles me; for up until now I have kept her in the present, despite her endless questions about the war. Afraid of losing her, of releasing the pain that lurks in the shadows of the past. My time with Emma and her family has been a blessing I never expected, and never deserved. To have this time with her while so many have been deprived of it seems grossly unfair, but there it is: I am all she has left. I believe she needs me as much as I need her; for some reason our fates are intertwined. I saw today her determination, her need to know the truth. She sensed, goodness knows how, that Luca was dear to Assunta. She is desperately seeking the truth about why her grandparents left, but the truth is not mine to tell.

I remember the day we heard about the shooting: innocent civilians rounded up and shot, vengeance for the partisans' latest war games. We heard the screams from the farmhouse all the way from the *metato*, and later heard from Benedetta how Assunta's only brother was one of the victims. I vaguely remember Luca from school days, though he was ten years older than me. A hard-working boy, a quiet soul, his life should have followed the usual lot of a *garfagnino*. He should have worked his land, married a local girl, attended Mass at the village church. Instead it all ended one winter's day, leaving a grieving sister who had already lost her parents, and did not know if her husband would ever return. The *rappresaglie*. The scars on this land which will last a thousand lifetimes. The price paid in innocent blood for the partisan's war games. Taunting the Germans with their home-made bombs and their landslides, enraging the blackshirts, the *fascisti*, with their ambushes. The bitter war between countrymen, between Italians, between friends. Ten villagers for every German killed. Free rein for the *fascisti* to do what they like, to whoever they happened upon. God help them if they had been drinking.

Seeing the chestnut house after so many years opened a door in my mind that has long been sealed shut. Plastered over, hidden from sight. But now the plaster is cracking, and the cracks are spreading. Nature has reclaimed the chestnut house, ivy spreading over its ruins. It is barely standing now. *A little like you*, the voice taunts me. I returned home to the farm the day of the mushroom hunt pale and shaking, and gave Maria quite a fright.

"You've overdone it, you old fool," she scolded me. "Trying to keep up with the young ones. And at your age! You think you're still a lad, not an old man of eighty-six!" She sent me off to bed for a siesta, and I acquiesced. I could not sleep though; there was something urgent I needed to do. Something I should have done the day Emma fell in my field, the day I saw those green eyes. I found a pen and paper and started writing in my stilted, uneducated handwriting. A farmer's hand, more used to digging than to writing letters. It was a brief letter; I've never been very good at expressing myself. We have exchanged letters, over the years. Usually a postcard on her behalf, from some place in the world, different each time. I sent news of my marriage, our children, grandchildren. Spoke of the farm, the village, never in any great detail. Safe subjects, for both of us. I had an address in America where I knew she was based in later years, when she was able to travel less. In this letter I wrote, as kindly as I could, about the sudden deaths of Giovanna and her husband, and about the arrival of Emma, Sam and the children in the village. She needs answers, I wrote. Answers it is not my place to give. As I wrote Maria's words came back to me: *An old man of eighty-six.* Was I really that old? That would make Giuliana ninety. Could she still be alive? Surely, I would have heard if she had passed. I would have known, in myself. Felt the difference in the world, a world in which she no longer breathed. A lack, an absence, a fading of colours. The letter finished, I collapsed into my bed, exhausted. I felt every one of my eighty-six years.

When sleep came it was fitful, interrupted with dreams of the past. Sensations and memories that I'd thought gone forever drift back to me, transporting me back to those war years. An intense, strange period for us all – long stretches of boredom and mundane daily tasks interspersed with terrifying moments. The ever-present ache of hunger, the longing for something fresh, something that wasn't made with chestnuts. Even now their sickly, earthy taste brings back memories of the war and the post-war era, and I avoid them as much as I can. I see chestnut flour in the supermarket these days, priced higher than any of the other flours on offer. *Artisanal product of the Garfagnana,* I read, smiling wryly. There is chestnut-flavoured pasta, even chestnut liquor. Now it is a gimmick, something to sell at inflated prices to tourists. Back then it was our survival. I avoid eating them, but I will always be grateful. Without them, we would have all starved that winter.

I remember our evening meals around the fire in the chestnut house, the smoke dispersing among the leaves above the patchy roof. I remember Mother reading from the Bible, and my sisters and I listening, calmed by her soothing voice. I remember the games we played on those long winter evenings to alleviate the boredom, and to distract us from the hunger pains. Mostly what I loved about our time in the chestnut house was having my sister close by, my best friend. Once Matteo returned to the mountains she was brilliant, alive, full of fire and passion. She was my hero; so brave, so funny, so strong. I soaked up every bit of attention she paid me, and my greatest joy was when she would hug me and squeeze my cheeks and exclaim, "Luci! Isn't it a beautiful world?" Despite our circumstances, she was happy there. Her cheeks glowed with it; her eyes danced. She was at home in her mountains, and she was in love. She had time for me, by day, and we would collect chestnuts together, trap rabbits for dinner, care for Renata and gather firewood. These were my happiest times, just being with her. But then that whistle started coming in the evenings and she would sneak out under some pretence, and I knew she was with him. I didn't begrudge her that; I liked Matteo and I was glad he had returned. I could see how happy he made her and hoped that one day he would be my brother-in-law. But then came the longer absences, the lies to our mother and a distracted furrow appeared in her brow. She was no longer fully present during our times together, she no longer marvelled freely at the world around her and she started to overlook me, again. I had been cut out of their games, as I always had been. I begged her to tell me what she was doing, where she was going. I would threaten to tell Mother and she would take me by the shoulders, finally noticing me.

"Luci," she would say, fixing me with those intense green eyes. "It's for your own good. Please don't ask me, I can't tell you, it's not safe. I don't want you and the family caught up in this. Do you understand?" I would nod reluctantly and, satisfied, she would let me go. She never told me what she did, where she went, but I learnt a little of what she was involved in afterwards.

I can hear the voice growing louder, stronger, its presence starting to emerge from the shadows and draw closer. To drag me screaming to some hell of my own making. I am still running, refusing to look at it, terrified of what I will see. Is it him; is he the voice I have feared so long? The ghost of what should have been? A strange life I have lived, with all the drama at the beginning and the end. A story that has all the action at the extremities, and a peaceable blur in the middle. Years of nothing in particular. Now I must wait for a reply and pray that I am not too late.

17

Giuliana

1944

From that night on I lived a double life, the mundane domesticity of life in the chestnut house contrasting with the excitement and danger of my life as a partisan. By day I would help my mother with the chores, keep my sisters and brother company, and try to keep morale up. Winter dragged on, our food supplies dwindled and the cold tightened its grip on the mountains. There was little to eat, and even our cow Renata gave only a cup of milk a day, thin as she was. Each morning I would check the traps and prepare any meat I had caught for cooking on the fire. Once a week I would trek up to our neighbours who were still managing to make bread and bring home a precious loaf, which would be rationed out into meagre portions.

By day we were all regular country folk, farming, tending to our animals, surviving. But at night, farmers, shepherds and priests alike slipped off their pre-war selves like a cloak, and became freedom fighters, saboteurs, assassins. A small network of resistance slowly spread across the mountains, fragile veins reaching out to one another, fed by hope and faith alone. A tiny band of mutineers, hidden in the forests, taking on the might of the Nazi army which had razed its way across most of Europe. An inexperienced, juvenile group of idealists, with no weapons and no support, entering into guerrilla warfare with a vastly superior enemy. Ridiculous, many would have said, and indeed that was the attitude that most people took. Beaten down by loss, hunger and terror, most of the residents of the Garfagnana now cowered in fear, focused only on surviving the war. I couldn't blame them, really. At least in the beginning. Later, when they chose living peaceably with the enemy over standing up for their own, then I came to despise them for their narrow-mindedness. For their blindness, preferring to live in oppression and safety rather than fighting for something better. After the war suddenly everyone was a partisan, cheering on their valiant efforts in contributing to the Allies' victory. Singing 'Bella Ciao', the now-famous song of the partisans, and burning Mussolini's picture. But the reality was very different.

The night Matteo took me up the mountain to meet the rest of the group I was shaking with nerves. He had already told me that several members of the group were opposed to the idea of a girl enlisting, and I could well imagine that was true. He laughed when he saw how tense I was and cupped my face in his warm hands.

"They haven't met you yet," he told me, encouragingly. "Believe me, they'll soon realise you're worth more than any man!" Matteo's cousin Raffaello was the leader of the group. At twenty-one he was one of the older members and had experienced fighting with the Germans in the Balkans. A recent arrival in the group was Canzio, a young man from the valley who had enlisted with *fascisti* under duress and trained in Germany. He had heard about the partisans and followed his heart, at great risk, deserting to join their ranks. Initially the group had been wary, for it was not unheard of for the *fascisti* to send a spy in to join the partisans, only to betray them. But after several weeks of menial duties tending the fire and cooking for the group Canzio had eventually convinced them of his worth. A surprise encounter on a mule track with two *tedeschi* had led to him saving Raffaello's life with his quick reactions, and since that day he had been a trusted member of the band. There were also two university students from Pisa, Ottavio and Silvano, studious young men who had left the comforts of unoccupied Pisa and their family homes to live a life of danger in pursuit of their ideals in the mountains. I already knew the shepherd Dino, a quiet man who had taken the flock over from his father a few years before. He knew the mountains better than anyone from his many years of moving the sheep from the higher pastures in summer down to the lower more protected *pianura* in the winter. This year nowhere in the valley was safe, and he moved his flock from barn to barn, ostensibly looking for grazing but in reality monitoring the Germans' positions and reporting to the various resistance groups he was in touch with. A gentle man, he gave the impression of being a simple soul and passed unsuspected by villagers and soldiers alike. But behind the unassuming exterior he was a treasure trove of information, his mind a detailed map of the Gothic Line and its fortifications. A valuable asset to the partisans, and eventually the Americans at the Office of Strategic Services.

The last member of the *banda* was the parish priest, Don Franco Fratelli, a miraculous combination of holy man and warrior. Completely fearless, and with little regard for his personal safety, he spent the war helping threatened minorities escape the occupied zone and negotiating the release of prisoners the Nazis had taken as part of the *rastrellamenti*, the round-up operations. By 1944, however, he was a wanted man with a price on his head of thousands of *lire*, and was in hiding like all the men that were left in the mountains. Already fluent in Latin and Greek from his ecclesiastical studies in Florence, he had also learned German in order to better negotiate with the enemy. Before they became suspicious of him he managed several very successful operations leading to the release of a number of prisoners. With his quick mind, ability to converse in their tongue and aided by the excellent wine he always brought along, the padre was a welcome visitor for those German soldiers who were far from home and clearly hated by most of the civilians they came into contact with. Don Franco had a talent, perhaps a gift from his service to God, for sensing which man was essentially good, and which was not. I remember the fear in his eyes the night he told me about his meeting with one SS Oberführer based in the Garfagnana: Walter von Steinbrinck. He recalled how his skin had crawled with primal fear, that he just knew, on the most basic level, he was in the presence of evil. He made his excuses and left the room, vomiting violently in the bushes outside. We all saw the war from a different point of view, but for Don Franco there was no doubt that this was a holy war; a war between good and evil. He would not be there the night I met the partisans as his visits were only when strictly necessary, and then usually done at the Church at Sant'Antonio, under the guise of confession.

Matteo and I headed up the mountain together in the dark of night, a few stars blinking through the bare branches above our heads. We were soon warm from the uphill climb, and despite my nerves I was thrilled to be out at night with Matteo. To be part of something, to be by his side. We took the steepest, most dangerous route, keen to avoid German or Fascist troops that might also be passing in the night. Since the Allies had been bombing all the main routes the enemy had been taking the mule tracks more and more. They had been here several months now and knew the area much better than in the beginning. After an hour we reached the little village and approached a barn on the outskirts. Matteo gave the call of an owl, haunting and low, and from the bushes on the other side of the barn came an answering call.

"The guard," he whispered. "I think it's Silvano tonight." We quietly crossed the few metres to the barn, where Matteo knocked four times on the door and was ushered inside. A small group of men was crouched around a fire at one end of the barn, and they jumped to their feet as we entered. They looked incredibly young, their faces lit by the dull glow of the fire, dirty and patched clothes hanging off thin bodies. Knives and machetes were strapped to their waists, their only weapons at this point. Recognising Matteo they relaxed and sat back down, although those who did not yet know me continued to eye me with a mixture of interest and wariness. Matteo's cousin Raffaello embraced me warmly with a kiss on each cheek. It had been several years since I last saw him, and he'd grown from a gangly youth into a formidable young man. He grinned at me, welcoming me to the barn, and I could immediately sense the natural leadership within him. Dino was there by the fire, warming his hands, and he gave me a nod of acknowledgment. Raffaello led me over to meet the others, and to introduce me.

"This is Giuliana," he told them. "Matteo vouches for her, and I have also known her all my life. Her spirit is as strong as any man's. She can track and shoot, and she could be valuable to us as a messenger. As a woman she may be able to go unsuspected into places that we cannot. I ask you to welcome her to the group and accord her respect." There was a pause, as the men considered. Canzio shifted uncomfortably from one leg to the other, and I sensed an objection coming.

"We must all be in agreement," Raffaello added. "There must be complete trust within the group." He looked at Canzio, who was encouraged to speak.

"We are brothers, family, here. Pledged to die for each other and the cause, if need be. I know you didn't trust me to begin with, I had no right to expect that and I didn't. I earnt that trust by living and working with you. How can you now ask us to trust our lives to this young girl, who has never fought before?

Probably never even left her village?" This remark cut me to the quick, precisely because it was so true. What could I possibly bring to this group? I knew what he meant about trusting their lives to me, simply by being brought to the barn that night I now knew their identities and their whereabouts, prized information that the Germans and the fascists alike would be desperate to get their hands on. Under interrogation, even torture, would I be able to resist? The whole group looked to me to respond, to make my case. I knew then that I wanted to join them more than I had ever wanted anything in my life. My heart went out to this brave group of young men, including my Matteo, my world, who were willing to risk their lives to rid their homeland of the enemy. To fight for a brighter future, perhaps not for themselves but for future generations. To restore some ounce of pride to a defeated and fallen nation that had once been great.

"Don't trust me," I told them quietly, raising my eyes to meet theirs. "Let me earn your trust. Give me a mission, let me prove myself to you. I swear I will give everything I have to succeed, or I will die trying." As I spoke the men listened, and a calm seemed to settle over them. One by one they nodded and came over to shake my hand. Matteo smiled and squeezed my hand, his face full of pride and light. The meeting began in earnest then, and I sat by the fire and listened, flushed with excitement. These men were few and barely armed, but their ambitions were grand. Inspired by other active partisan groups with whom they had been in contact, they had great plans to disrupt the enemy. Their location was unique, being just above the Gothic Line itself, the centre of the action. The Germans' Todt Organisation was using forced labour to build fortifications, and the group planned to attack and destroy their efforts. The most pressing problem for the group was their lack of weapons. There were reports of the Allies being willing to airdrop supplies in, but communications were difficult, with the Germans able to intercept any radio communications.

"We need someone to cross the Front Line," Raffaello told me, gravely. "To go in person to the Americans and arrange for supplies to be air dropped to us. To give the exact coordinates for the ravine where we can light fires which will not be visible except from the air." He paused and looked over at me. "It's a lot to ask, Giuliana. It would be incredibly dangerous. You could be intercepted and interrogated by either the Germans or the Fascists, or both. There's also the risk of getting caught in the crossfire of the fighting, or the bombings. We'd recommend you take the mule track down the mountain, which is both steep and perilous, and we would only be able to accompany you part of the way. From there you will need to cross over No Man's Land at the *pianura*, cross the river, and reach the OSS in Barga on the other side of the valley. Were you to fall into enemy hands, we would be unable to help you: you would be at their mercy. At this point you have limited knowledge of our operation, but we would have to assume that under torture you would give that information, which is why we would need to move to a new location until your return."

"No," Matteo said, standing up and shaking his head. "It's too dangerous. Too much, too soon. There must be another way."

"There isn't," Raffaello replied gently, but firmly, and I saw a flash of the unwavering courage of his convictions that would make him such a great leader. Personal sacrifice was demanded of all; death was expected, sooner or later. At the centre of everything was this fight, this way of life.

"I can do it," I heard my voice saying, and my eyes met Raffaello's. He nodded, pleased, and went on to discuss the details. It was approaching midnight when we left, and Matteo insisted on accompanying me back down the mountain.

"I don't need guarding," I protested weakly, keen not to be given any special treatment because of my sex.

"I know," he smiled, "I just want more time with you." Grateful for his company, and by now exhausted with the evening's events, we made our way quietly back down the mountainside, dimly lit by a sliver of moon. The crescent moon, I realised, life and death, the ebb and tide of life. My new life as a partisan, perhaps. As we approached Stazzana I knew my mother would be worried at my late return, and I would have to think of a reason to absent myself for several days for this mission. There were so many things to think about, but with the moonlight reflecting off the silvery snow, alone in the mountains with Matteo once again, they all slipped from my mind. I felt only a deep peace, a sense of the earth beneath my feet, and of being part of something greater than myself. Something that would prove to be greater than any of us individually, greater even than our love story.

18

Emma

2017

Autumn gave way to winter, and we were still in Montaltissimo. No-one here ever questions our plans; we just live life day to day, in a sort of lovely protective bubble. Scotland and our life there seem a distant memory, a distance I am happy to have, with all the painful reminders that await me there. Christmas loomed suddenly on the horizon like a black star, and the very thought filled me with dread. Memories from childhood, happy times with my grandparents and my parents at the house in Ayrshire. Flashbacks of us all wearing Christmas cracker hats, playing charades, laughing ourselves silly. My father pouring the wine and toasting to us all, my mother red-faced and merry in the kitchen, wearing her festive apron. Last Christmas both my parents and Sam's had joined us in our little house on Murray Place, and we had all crammed around our dining table, Aria and Luna presiding over the festivities with great delight. How happy we were, I muse, naively assuming the year would bring us good things, that we would all still be together the following year.

I force myself out of downward spiral, to think of my children. I remind myself that life is precious, and we must not waste one moment of it. They deserve a joyful holiday. Their childhood Christmases are numbered, and not one must be tainted with loss. The magic of a child's Christmas is a sacred thing, to be protected. I'm just not sure I can do it this year; I'm not sure I can hide the sorrow inside me. The thought worried away at me for a few days, and so when Sam approached me with an offer to stay at his parents I knew at once it was the right thing to do. Sam's parents, Archie and Daisy, are a kind couple I've always got on well with. They live on the shores of Loch Leven in an old Victorian hunting lodge, a romantic remnant of the past. I realise with a flash of guilt that we haven't seen them in months, and that they will be missing the girls awfully. I wonder again if I'm being selfish keeping Sam and the girls out here, far from family and friends while I follow a wild goose chase, a vain attempt to find the family I have lost. Before I could sink any further under the weight of my guilt I told Sam to accept the invitation, and set about looking for flights and planning what presents to take back with us.

December shot by in a grey blur of sleet and mist, and I somehow managed to get by from day to day. The grief of losing my parents and facing Christmas without them seems to intensify, and I feel like a failure, that I'm going backwards instead of forwards. Isn't time supposed to heal? It's like winter has brought reality home, and the bleakness is setting in to stay. Perhaps the light of the summer and the novelty of being in Italy postponed the grieving process; perhaps when I thought I was doing so well I had merely put it on hold. I fear I'm submerging a little more each day, and that one morning I won't be able to lift myself from my bed. Sam tries to help, but I can't find the words to talk to him. He comes up with extra energy to deal with the girls, to play and laugh with them, as well as helping around the house. I realise he is counting the days until our return to

Scotland, and the thought strikes me that perhaps he will not want to come back after Christmas. We have few possessions here, no ties that could not be severed. I have booked return flights, but was Sam hoping they would be singles? The distance between us seems to grow by the day, and I realise we are hiding behind the children, unwilling to discuss the spreading cracks in our relationship. We haven't slept next to each other in months, haven't touched each other, even to hold hands. I am unwilling to share my misery, to colour another life with my grief. I'm lost in the darkness, and I struggle to see a way forward. The way back to myself, to be the girl that he married.

In a strange parallel to me, Luciano has also sunk into a dark depression as winter has progressed. He is withdrawn, distant. We rarely see him and I worry that he is ill and not telling Maria how he is really feeling. He refuses to see a doctor, of course, stubborn old man. Even the children fail to lift his mood, try as they might. He looks at me with such sadness in his eyes, as if there is much he wants to tell me, but something is stopping him. I've given up asking now; I was foolish to imagine I could unravel whatever mystery has lain here for so many decades. These people are too stubborn, their secrets too well buried. Stazzana is also suffering with the cold weather, and I fear a few more winters will be the end of her. The rot from the water ingress is worsening, and some of the beams look on the point of collapse.

The night before our flight it starts to snow, and we all watch from the window as snowflakes drift down, settling softly on the ground. A peace descends on the village and I am reminded of our first evening here, of the colours and the heat. How we sat outside on the balcony and watched the fireflies dance, sipping our chilled white wine and admiring the beauty of the mountains. Now from the balcony I see countryside that is familiar to me, stripped bare of its summer finery. As I watch it is again transformed into something new, dressed in a coat of white. Sam brings me a mug of mulled wine; I wrap my hands around it gratefully and manage a small smile.

"The first snow," he whispers, pressing his body behind me, attempting a *rapprochement*. I feel the warmth emanating from his chest, a contrast to the icy bite in the air. We stay like that, watching the snow envelop the land, kissing the trees it lands on. I sip my wine and its heat spreads through me, comforting and spicy. Despite my sadness I feel a strange reluctance to leave Montaltissimo, this little world we have become a part of.

Christmas at Loch Leven is just what we need. I find I am relieved, comforted, to be back in Scotland, the country of my birth. I can see that Sam is also happy to be able to communicate easily, not struggling to make himself understood all the time. Snow has already fallen, and the hills around the loch are buried deep in crisp, perfect snow. The lodge dates from Victorian times and is full of character. Built of dark grey stone and with huge bay windows looking out over the loch, the house appears to be watching for our arrival.

Archie has been busy decorating and the front of the house sparkles with thousands of fairy lights. A huge wreath of holly and ivy hangs on the front door, replete with a jolly red ribbon. As soon as we arrive it feels like we are home. We enter the warmth of the lodge, fires roaring in the hearths, and Archie and Daisy shriek with delight and usher us in out of the cold. Archie enfolds me in a bear hug, reminding me where Sam inherited his strength from. Daisy dusts the flour from her hands briefly on her apron, and as she embraces me I smell mince pies and spice. Her blue eyes are full of kindness, and I feel relief flooding through me that we are here. The children are spun around ever higher by Archie, then fussed over by Daisy as she removes their coats and shoes, and within moments we are settled by the fire, a cup of tea and a slab of fruit cake in our hands. Inside in the lounge they have put up an enormous Christmas tree, and I find myself wondering how they got the tree in place, and how much swearing was involved. They've waited for the girls to decorate the tree, to their great joy.

Sam was brought up here at the lodge, and as much as his parents moan about the heating bills, the damp, the constant repairs, I know they love it as much as he does. The thick velvet curtains that hang in the bay windows are a little faded by the sun, and the rugs that adorn the flagstone floors are threadbare in places, but it feels like a real home. I can relax here with the girls, not worried that they will stain or ruin anything. The family dog, a deerhound named Macbeth, lurks near the girls, waiting for crumbs to be dropped. Aria chatters away while she eats, using her hands to gesticulate in what I realise is a very Italian way. She is telling Archie and Daisy all about the kitten she has rescued, and her friends at school. Luna listens and eats her cake, cosying up to her grandmother beside her. Her big blue eyes catch mine, and she smiles, a secret smile just for me.

The days pass in a merry blur of festivities, and I let myself unwind and be in the moment. In the mornings we spend time outside tramping through the snow, making snowmen and sledging down the hill leading to the loch. The girls shriek with joy as they whizz along, rosy-cheeked and bright-eyed. At lunchtime we return to the house, the tantalising aromas of roasted meat and vegetables greet us, and we all enjoy a large and delicious lunch. It feels so wonderfully indulgent to be cooked for, to be cared for. In the afternoons we are all sated and content, and we settle by the fire in the living room, the girls happy to play with their toys on the rug, and the adults to doze and chatter. Later we muster the energy to play some games, and the girl's favourite is hide and seek, the old house being full of nooks and crannies to hide in. It's the traditional family Christmas we all need, and I am so grateful to Sam's parents for all they've done for us. When I thank Daisy she tells me it is a pleasure, that they are thrilled to have us there.

"It would be so sad were it just us two old folks pottering

around at Christmas," she tells me, bustling about the kitchen. "It's a joy to have you, and those little angels." We watch through the kitchen window as the girls and Sam engage in a snowball fight, Sam falling to the ground and lifting his arms in defeat as the girls run and jump on him. Archie creeps up on them with an armful of snow, and there are more shrieks as he throws it over them, a mischievous look in his eyes. "You've had quite a year," Daisy turns to face me, worry in her eyes. "It will get easier, my dear. Time is a great healer. You must miss them so much, especially at Christmas." I nod, unable to say anything, struggling against the rising lump in my throat. "We're always here for you," she reminds me, and I manage a, "Thank you," mumbled into her thick jumper as she pulls me in for a hug.

Daisy doesn't say anything to me directly, but I suspect her sharp blue eyes have noted the change in our marriage. The distance, the politeness that now marks our exchanges. With great subtlety she and Archie start to offer to take the girls out for a morning walk and to read bedtime stories with them in the evening, so that Sam and I can have some time alone. One evening Sam tells me he has booked a table at the local pub, the Old Forge, and asks me if I would like to accompany him. He catches my eye, and his own have a twinkle in them I haven't noticed in months. I blush, suddenly shy, which I tell myself is ridiculous. This is Sam, I remind myself, my husband whom I've been through so much with. Born two children with. I've not only lost sight of myself and who I am, but I've forgotten who my husband is. I accept with a smile, and when Daisy leads the children upstairs for their bath I get dressed in our room, choosing my outfit and make-up with care for the first time in months if not years. It feels novel, exciting even, to have a date to go on. I settle on a dark green velvet dress that I bought for Christmas years ago, and have never worn until now.

Sam is waiting for me in the lounge, and I note the smart blue shirt he is wearing, a present I got him for his birthday one year.

The blue sets off his eyes, and his honey-blonde hair is combed back, still damp from the shower. He kisses my cheek in an old-fashioned move, and it feels like we are off on our first date. We borrow Archie's Land Rover and drive through the snow to the local village. The pub is lit with tiny fairy lights, an enticing glow from the low windows beckoning us in.

Sam is greeted warmly by neighbours he grew up with, and spends a few minutes catching up while I take a seat. The fire is crackling away merrily, the hum of chatter and laughter filling the place. The sense of history is everywhere, from the ornaments hanging over the fireplace to the centuries-old wooden bar. So much of our life in Italy takes place outside, which I love, but it's cosy being in a proper Scottish pub after so long. It's a real treat being out without the girls to watch, and I start to relax as I see Sam heading towards me with a pint of cider and a glass of red wine. We chat about the holidays and Christmas, and stay on safe ground while we order our meals. It's the most we've talked for such a long time. It feels fun, flirtatious even, and I'm reminded of our early dating life, the days when our biggest concern was where to go for dinner. Flushed with the warmth from the fire and the red wine, I broach the subject that's been playing on my mind the whole trip.

"Do you hate it in Italy? Do you want us to come home?" I study him for a reaction, and his eyebrows knit, confusion flitting across his face.

"No, babe, I love it. It's been hard with the, er, situation, but the rest of it, I love it. I've always wanted land, the freedom to farm it, to work with wood of my own. The time with the kids too, that's been so special. I feel like I've got to know them, who they really are, and they know their father too. I was so busy before, too busy to really appreciate them as I should. I don't want to go back to that." He shakes his head, and looks down at his cider, twisting it on the mat. "I know I've not been what you needed. I haven't known what to say, how to help. I hate how helpless I feel, how stupid I've been. If there was anything I could do, I'd do it in a flash. If I could bring them back… but I hate seeing you that way, and I'm scared, so scared that I'll lose you." He glances up at me, and I see the love and the hurt deep in his eyes, and understand how difficult this has been for him too. I take his hand and breathe deeply, trying to take it all in. I have felt alone, in my darkest moments I've thought he didn't care. Many nights I've laid in the same room, tears silently coursing down my cheeks, soaking the pillow, wondering how he could possibly not guess how I was feeling. I see now that he does care, and has been as lost as I have been, dealing with this terrible year.

"It was always going to be an awful time," I say eventually, attempting a small smile. "But I know you're with me, that you care. You won't lose me. I do feel lost, a lot of the time, but you and the girls, you're my anchor. You keep me grounded; you keep me with the living." We lean across the table to kiss, and the kiss is so familiar, so *right*, that I do feel I am home. The same heady desire that connects me to the past, our dating, our wedding night, arises and I am giddy with relief. I can see a way forward, and I know Sam feels the same as I see his grin widening.

"We could renovate the house, you know," he suggests. "Sell the house, your parents' house, or ours if you're not ready to part with your childhood home. With the money we could do Stazzana up, make it a home again?" I'm shocked he has thought about this, that it's something he would consider. His blue eyes shine with excitement and love, and I'm amazed at his bravery. I know he is saying what he thinks I want to hear, but I feel a curious reluctance.

"Not yet," I reply, trying to think how to explain it. "I still don't know why my grandparents left, I'm still not sure where we fit in…" I trail off, aware that it's a weak response to such a suggestion. It isn't that I haven't thought of it, of course. The longing to be there, to wake up to the view of those hills, to breathe love once more into those crumbling walls, it gets stronger every time we go there. The reluctance to leave, the anticipation of our next visit, how she will look in autumn, winter, spring. I wasn't aware until now that Sam feels it too, that the magic is rubbing off on him as well. There's more to it though; as well as the practical concerns there is the warning from my grandmother lurking in the shadows, making me fear for our safety, for the girls. How she said the place was cursed, how she hinted at the dangers that lay there. The fear she instilled in my mother, so much so that she never returned to the place of her birth. Sam doesn't push me to explain, and we agree we will give it another few months in Italy, to give me time to try and find some answers. He holds my hand over the table and I feel the delicious thrill that always used to accompany his touch. Feeling closer than we have since the accident, we leave the pub hugging each other tight as we emerge into the starlit snow scene outside.

19

Emma

2017

One morning, sometime after Christmas, I wake from a vivid dream and though the details of the dream quickly start to slip away I see an image of my parents' house in Ayrshire, clear as day. I am reminded of the letters from William, my solicitor, confirming that the house is now mine, and realise that while we are back in Scotland I really ought to visit it. I haven't been since just after the funeral, and I imagine we should check the house over while we are here. I know I need to think about putting it on the market, but I've been avoiding making that decision. Reluctant perhaps to cut my last link to my parents, the house I grew up in, where so many memories lie.

Archie and Daisy agree to look after the girls, and Sam and I set off the next day, early in the morning. It's two days until Hogmanay, and the roads are quiet in the lull between Christmas and New Year. Scotland sparkles with frost and snow, and I'm reminded how beautiful this ancient northern land is. I've been in touch with Sally, a long-time friend and neighbour of my parents, who has been checking on the house every now and again and forwarding me the post. She knows we are coming, and as we pull up onto the drive she hurries over to greet us. She hugs and kisses us and enquires after the girls. She wants to know how life in Italy is, and is full of questions and interest.

"I've turned the lights and the heating on for you, Emma dear," she tells me. "I didnae want you arriving to a cold, dark house. It's hard enough anyway." I glance at the front door, and can almost see my mother opening it, standing in the entrance smiling and waving us in. I'm grateful to Sally for her help, and for trying to make it easier for me.

"We'll come and say goodbye when we leave," I reassure her. "And we can have that cup of tea." I think she senses my desire to get into the house, as she presses a packet of biscuits into my hand and scurries back across the road to her house.

We enter the house, and despite the light and the warmth, the silence is overwhelming. I look about me, noting objects that are familiar to me, yet the stillness renders them alien, strange. *Where are you?* I wonder, and my question seems to be absorbed into the house somehow. I wander from room to room, looking for them. In the kitchen Sam busies himself making a cup of tea with the supplies Sally has left, and I wander into my parent's room, running my palm over the wooden wardrobe, noting the reading glasses on the bedside table. I take the book my mother was reading in my hands, and hold it close, running my fingertips over its smooth cover and raised letters with the author's name. I flick through its pages, trying to conjure an image of my mother reading them. A bookmark slides from the pages near the end, one I gave her a few years ago, with photo booth-style photos of Aria printed down the middle. *How frustrating*, I think, *she never found out how it ended*. I realise this is minor, in the scheme of things, but I know it would have bothered her. My mother was a voracious reader, and always had a book with her.

"I'll read you the rest," I promise her, and slip the book into my bag. Since the accident my memories of my parents have been distorted with grief, each happy image tinged with pain. Here in their room I am surrounded by everyday reminders of their lives, and it is comforting. Not yet, perhaps not for months or years, but I glimpse a time in the future when I will remember them and smile, holding on to the good times. Maybe it is a self-preservation technique but part of me has blocked them out, these past few months. I've not allowed myself to dwell, to remember, scared the pain would swallow me up. Safe in my childhood home I allow myself to think of them.

As a small child I saw my mother as an angel, my best friend. For many years there were no boundaries, I couldn't tell where I began and she ended. Her dancing eyes, her magic smile that could banish nightmares; she was always there for me. As I grew more independent my love for her only grew stronger, and I appreciated her gentle warmth, her kindness, the love she bore for us. She and my father met while they were studying, and discovered a mutual love of hiking in the mountains. When I was a baby they would carry me in a rucksack, and when I was four they bought me my first pair of hiking boots along with little red socks to go with them. I can still remember them to this day. There's a photo of my first hike hanging on the wall here in their bedroom, and I run my finger over it gently. My mother is holding my hand, the sun glinting off her shiny black hair, and my father is grinning, one arm slung around her shoulders. His sun-streaked hair is standing up in the wind, his blue eyes full of joy. I am standing between them looking proud of myself for climbing my first mountain, my red socks pulled up above my trusty new boots.

They were our favourite times, out in the mountains, just the three of us. We didn't need a mad social life; the wind and the sky were company enough. Interesting, I ponder, that my mother loved the mountains so. Did she ever wonder about the place her family originated from, the mountains of the Garfagnana?

She never spoke to me about it, but looking back it must have been hard for her. She would have stood out at school, with her Italian parents and her dark looks. She wasn't Scottish, and yet she knew nothing about her roots. My grandmother insisted they embrace their new culture, but that must have left my mother in No Man's Land: not quite Scottish, but not really Italian either. She married my father young, in her early twenties, and I know that theirs was a happy marriage. Perhaps it was this that saved her, where she found her place in the world. My father was so strong, so bright; he always made us feel safe, like we could do anything. He adored my mother; it was clear from the way he gazed at her, loved to surprise her, caught her in his arms and danced around the kitchen with her when he returned from work. This last memory is so vivid it catches me off guard, and I gasp with the force of it. The images fade away, back into the silent room around me, and I reluctantly get up and leave the room, aware that I have taken a big step.

Sam and I have our cup of tea in the kitchen, and it starts to feel more normal being there. Ever the practical one, Sam is keen to check the water and electrics are all sound while we are here, and he heads out to the garage to check the meters. After a while I follow him, and wander aimlessly around, looking at all my dad's tools and the neatly labelled boxes that cover one shelved wall. 'Christmas decorations', I notice, sadly left in their box this year. 'Emma's University Folders', and I wonder what I would think of my essays now. Then one catches my eye, one I have never noticed before. It is simply labelled '*Mamma e Papa*', in my mother's handwriting. I manage to pull it down, blow away its layer of dust and carry it through to the warmth of the kitchen. I can't remember much of the time following my grandmother's death. I know my mother sorted out their house for sale and gave most of their clothes and possessions away to charity. This box seems to hold the few sentimental things that she decided to keep. As I open the box up a musty, sweet scent rises from it, the fading essence of their memories. I pull out a photo of them, a young dark-haired couple, with my mother as a toddler on their lap. The family Bible, which I knew my mother had saved. A couple of religious icons, and things from my mother's childhood: her first ballet certificate, a few old school reports. At the bottom of the box there is a folder, full of old letters and postcards, mixed in with photos and other keepsakes. As I flick through them, I notice an envelope, marked simply with the letter 'G'. It is sealed and for a moment I hesitate, feeling I should ask permission before opening it. *This is your family,* I remind myself, *and besides, there's no-one to ask.* Taking a deep breath I open the envelope, and I see it is full of postcards, dating from 1947 up to 2001, the year my grandmother died. I note they are all written in Italian, in a bold, forward-slanting hand, and a spark of excitement flickers inside me. Who are they from, and why did they save them? It must have been someone from the past, from Montaltissimo, surely?

I carry the postcards over to the sofa, wondering if my mother read them, guessing from the seal on the envelope that she probably didn't. I tuck my legs under me and sink into the comforting space of my parents' worn blue sofa. I take the first postcard, sent from Barcelona in December 1947. It is black and white, wrinkled with age around the edges, and entitled '*Llano de la Boqueria y Rambla de las Flores*'. Smaller than postcards today, I have to squint to read the tiny print and what is written on the back.

Cari Giovanni & Assunta,
Christmas greetings from Barcelona! How are you? How is Giovanna? I hope you have settled well into your life in Scotland. Are the people friendly? Is it very cold? Are you learning English well? It is so different to our native tongue. I am in Barcelona and have found work

as a waitress. Spanish is very similar to Italian, so I am
getting by. I have a nice little apartment in the city centre,
and the sea is close by, which I love. I enclose my address,
below.

With warm wishes,

G

Intrigued, I stare at the writing, and wonder who 'G' is. Clearly, a
friend or relation who also left Italy after the war, but one of the
few who stayed in touch with my grandparents. I wonder if they
replied. I turn to the next postcard to find my answer, and see
an image of the infamous New York skyline, a bit less crowded
than it is today.

Cari Giovanni & Assunta,

Thank you so much for your card, and the photo of
Giovanna. She is so beautiful, and I am pleased to hear
she is starting to speak both Italian and English, what an
advantage for her in this world. I am now working here in
New York in a restaurant. The city is very large and noisy,
but an exciting place to be. All best wishes for Christmas
and the New Year,

G

I try to imagine New York in 1948, just a few years after the
end of the war, and think what a huge contrast it would be
to the little villages of the Garfagnana. I know many Italians
emigrated to America after the war, so I imagine he or she
would have found fellow Italians to socialise with, perhaps even
work with. I look back to the first postcard, and notice the word
for waitress, *cameriera*, is used in the feminine form, so 'G'
must be female. Pleased with my detective work, I feel a rush
of emotion at finally getting closer to finding out more about
my grandparents, and their lives before I was born. The tone of

the postcards confuses me a little. It is both friendly and warm, and yet somehow distant, as if the writer was holding something back. *Why postcards,* I wonder, *instead of a letter in which one might write more?*

I continue to read the postcards for another hour, as Sam fixes some fault he has found in the garage. It seems that 'G' spent some years in New York, qualifying as a nurse at night school, before then volunteering out in Africa. The postcards are rarely from the same place; it seems that almost every two years to the dot she moved to a different country, working in many of the African countries and some far-flung places in Asia. She kept an address in New York, however, and seemed to return there every few years for a period of several months, eventually buying a small apartment there. The postcards always followed the same format, I notice, arriving once per year, in December. They always enquired after my grandparent's health, and after my mother, and provided some update about G's working and living situation. Friends or partners were never mentioned, and I deduced that G was something of a nomad, always on the move. It was a bit like I was reading a history book, interesting but not personal to me, until I read the 1982 postcard with a start.

> *Cari Giovanni & Assunta,*
>
> *Thank you for your card, which eventually caught up with me here in the Sudan. I am working at a refugee camp for those fleeing the war in Ethiopia, and life is hard here. So, it was wonderful to receive your card and the joyous news about baby Emma's arrival. What a sweet baby she is! So fair, she must take after her Scottish father. How is Giovanna adapting to life as a mother? I send you all my best greetings for Christmas and the New Year,*
>
> *G*

I stare at the postcard and run my finger gently over the words, the faded black ink blending in with the yellowing card it is written on. To think that this little postcard had flown from a camp in Africa the year I was born, to Scotland, to my grandparents' house. I wonder why they never mentioned 'G' to me, and as far as I knew my mother had never known about her. What a fascinating character, to have left the mountains of Tuscany and gone on to see so much of the world, and to help so many people in need.

When Sam finishes and comes to find me, I am buzzing with a new energy, with pride and excitement at having made such a discovery. My head is full of questions, and I have a feeling that 'G', whoever she is, holds some of the answers. I carefully pack the tiny postcards back into their envelope and tuck them into my bag, intending to study them further back at the lodge.

I remember my promise to pop over to Sally's before we go, and we cross over the road to her bungalow as the streetlights start to flicker on. She ushers us into the warm and busies herself in the kitchen, making us tea and cutting pieces of cake for us. She is so pleased to see us, and I feel guilty that I haven't given her a thought over the past few months. She was always close to my mother, popping in and out of each other's houses for cups of tea and glasses of wine over the years. She was a rock on the day of the funeral, so supportive, though her eyes were red-rimmed from crying. She's keen to hear news of the girls, and how life in Italy is treating us. She's never been herself, never ventured further than the border.

"It sounds lovely though," she says, peering over her glasses. "I know your mother thought about going, over the years. But she wasn't one for breaking promises." Confused I stare at her, waiting for her to elaborate. She seems surprised I don't know to what she is referring and stirs her tea thoughtfully, wondering I imagine if she should tell me or not. Sally is a good lady, a regular church-goer. A faithful friend, even in death. "Aye, perhaps she had her reasons. Perhaps part of her wanted you to be free, not to be bound like she was." I'm intrigued now and ask her what promise she meant.

"Your grandmother was always strict, as you know, a strong influence in your mother's life. Aye, she loved her, but she laid down the law alright. On her deathbed she became delirious, with the morphine and all. She ranted on about betrayals and danger, and she made your mother promise never to go to Italy. She was distressed, in pain, and your mother wanted to ease her suffering. All her life she'd never dared disobey her, and in this last request she couldn't deny her. She was drawn, of course, to this place she'd inherited, where her father was born, but she never could bring herself to go against her mother's dying wish." Sally looks at me, concerned, and I can see she is already doubting whether she should have told me this.

"Thank you, Sally." I reach out to squeeze her hand, wanting to express my gratitude. "It explains a lot. I need answers, after what happened, and this solves part of the mystery why my mother never went there. I still don't know why she never talked to me about it, though. We were so close, we told each other everything."

"I think she intended to, one day," Sally replies, "but life went on, and she thought she had time. We all did." Tears swell in her eyes, and she hastily wipes them away with her pinny. "She loved you, so much, you know that. They both did. You were their world, you and those two little angels." I nod, smiling at her through my own tears, and I promise we will bring them to visit her the next time.

We need to start our journey back to Loch Leven, but it has been a good day, despite the pain associated with coming back here. The light is starting to fade outside, the sky growing darker than the snow-cloaked land. It's a sort of reversal of a regular winter's day, when the earth is dark and barren, and the sky pale and bleak overhead. I glance across at the house one last time before I get in the car and I whisper, "Bye, Mum. Bye, Dad."

My words drift up into the night sky, and I know that they are not here at this house, but with me, wherever I go. The thought comforts me, and I turn my back on the house, and the old year, and head with hope towards the new one.

20

Giuliana

1944

In the end I could tell my mother neither the truth nor a lie. I simply told her I would be gone for a few days, and that this was something I needed to do. We were sitting by the fire in the chestnut house, the small space that had become our home. She took my hands in hers and looked at me, searching my eyes for clues. She seemed older, frailer, thinner.

"*Figlia mia*," she said, finally. "My little girl, you have always been different. So strong, so full of spirit. You were ever that way, even as a tiny baby. Many told me you should have been a boy, that life would be hard for you. But perhaps you are just what's needed now; perhaps your strength can save us. I won't ask where you are going, or what you are doing. It's better that I don't know. But please, stay safe. For my sake, for your father, for your sisters and brother. May the angels be with you." She gave me her blessing, with a kiss on my forehead. I knew how hard that had been for her, and I started to understand how there are different types of strength in this world. Perhaps my mother, in her quiet way, was the strongest of all.

"Thank you," I mumbled, taken aback. We agreed that the official line would be I had travelled to see family in San Pietro in Campo, as I had an aunt and uncle there. It was a weak pretext, I knew, but we hadn't been able to come up with a better one. If stopped I would feign ignorance about the dangers of such a visit and play the part of a simple country girl. Snow still lay on the ground in a thick white mantle, and I dressed in my warmest woollen clothes. My boots had thankfully lasted the war thus far. Many by that stage were without any footwear, and managed by cobbling together bits of leather and straps as best they could. The only weapon I took was my hunting knife, and I packed a small bundle of food and my water bottle.

The night before setting off I declined Matteo's offer to accompany me down the mountain; I didn't want to put him in any danger that wasn't absolutely necessary. We met by the little glade of trees outside the chestnut house, and I was reminded of another meeting, another goodbye, when it had been Matteo who was leaving. This time the roles were reversed, and part of me, I'm ashamed to admit, was pleased that it was I who was off to have the adventure this time. Matteo tried to protest again, and up close I noticed his eyes were smudged with fatigue, his jaw tense. He told me I didn't need to do this, that they would find another way.

"I won't be able to help you, Giuliana," he said, pacing up and down by the stream, smacking his fist into his palm. "If they take you I won't be able to save you, and I can't bear the thought of it. Of what they might do to you. It's torture, just thinking about it. I haven't slept since this ridiculous idea was conceived." I stopped him in his tracks, put my arms around his neck and pulled him close. His mouth found mine in the darkness and we pressed closer, drinking each other in while we could. He held me tight and I whispered how he had to trust me, that it would be alright. I didn't know that, of course, but I wanted to comfort him. I needed him to let me do this, to prove myself.

"This is bigger than us," I reminded him. "Have faith in me. I will come back to you, I promise." I closed my eyes, willing some of my peace and conviction to surround him, to cloak him in my love. I was aware for the first time of my own power, my strength. I felt Matteo respond and relax in my arms. He covered my face in soft kisses and I felt the familiar heat rising between us, his body under its winter clothes seeking mine out. I gasped as his kisses moved down onto my neck, and I felt the urgency of our connection growing stronger. My head swam, crimson waves of desire swirling around us, the energy rising from the earth beneath us. Once again we were all that existed, he and I and the forest floor below us. We started to sink down onto the bed of snow together, our passion rising in a crescendo that only we could hear, a call we had to follow. Out of the darkness came the scream of a fox, shattering the moment, wrenching us apart. Matteo pulled back abruptly, cursing as he strode away and punched an oak tree, cursing again as the blood poured from his knuckles. I hurried over and pressed my handkerchief onto the injury, watched the blood slowly soaking through the fabric, terribly dark against the white fabric and the pale snow beneath. He sat, hunched over on the forest floor beside me, tears in his eyes, the image of a broken man.

"It's more than I can bear," he murmured. "To be near you, to kiss you, and not to... to do what a man does with his wife. It gets harder every time." I blushed furiously, hearing Matteo say this. I was so innocent at sixteen, completely uneducated and unexperienced in matters of love. I had heard my sisters' hushed whispers and giggles, but they were as innocent as I was back in those days. I didn't know much, but what I did know was how I felt about Matteo, and I knew with complete certainty that he was the only man in the world for me. With a boldness that surprised me, I climbed astride Matteo and pushed him firmly down onto the bed of snow beneath us.

"So do it," I whispered in his ear, brazenly, and I felt the shudder of desire ripple through his body, setting my own on fire. "Do it and make me your wife." He searched my eyes and saw his own passion and love mirrored back, a circle that would last through eternity. He kissed me fiercely, and I felt his need to possess me, to make me his before I left the next day. When we were together it felt like something took hold of us, something stronger than we were. Love, destiny, passion, I'm not sure. All I knew is we were made for each other, and I yearned for our union more than anything. That night we were interrupted by my mother coming out of the chestnut house and calling my name, perhaps her own maternal senses warning her something was going on. For that night at least, my virtue remained intact.

The next morning I left at first light, in the pale glow of dawn. I aimed to have reached my goal by the six o'clock curfew that the Nazis had imposed on the valley. Anyone found out after six in the evening would be automatically imprisoned. The mountains were silent, the snow absorbing what little noise there was. I began the steep and rocky descent down the wolf track that lead from Stazzana along the river and down through the woods, passing the village of Cascio down to the *fondovalle*, the valley bottom. Lost in concentration I tried not to think about the dangers that lay ahead of me, how I was planning to cross the front line from occupied Nazi-Fascist territory over to the Allies. I had no idea how I would achieve this and tried only to think of the next immediate hurdle on my journey. I was well-rested and physically fit, and the first part of my journey went smoothly. I met no patrols and there were no Allied bombings that morning, no familiar whirring of engines headed across the sky to wreak devastation on our villages. A few times I heard the cracking shots of machine-gun fire ricocheting around the valley, but the fighting was mostly light that day. I didn't know it, but the Allies were waiting the winter out at that point, distracted by the fighting in France.

Once I reached the edge of the woods on the valley floor there stretched out ahead of me the flat fertile plains of the *pianura*. There were a few small hamlets, all abandoned by this point, and some copses of trees and bushes, but it was still incredibly exposed. The valley spanned the two mountain ranges: the Apuan Alps on my side, the Apennines on the other side, where Barga lay. The cathedral, unscathed by the war, rose up out of the low-lying mist that floated through the valley, the weak sunlight illuminating the bell tower. It had been some months since the church bells of the Garfagnana had fallen silent. The Germans had become suspicious that the partisans were using the bells to communicate with each other, and the death penalty had been issued for all members of the clergy and the local mayor of any village whose bells were to ring. The fear of this among the local population was so great that many steps to bell towers had been bricked up entirely, to remain thus until the end of the war. In some churches the entrance was not blocked but the ropes were cut, muting the church bells that had rung for centuries.

My eye was drawn to a series of ditches that ran through the flat fields of the *pianura*, a drainage system to avoid the valley flooding when the torrential rains came in autumn and spring. It occurred to me that thanks to the mist I could perhaps cross the valley by staying in the ditches. With my dark clothes I would be reasonably well camouflaged. I would have to hope that a sniper did not spot me, and that no fighting broke out across No Man's Land, but it seemed to be my best chance. There was still the question of the river to be crossed, and I shivered involuntarily as I spotted the brown body of water snaking its way through the valley. Swollen and fast-flowing following the autumn rains, it was a different beast entirely to the shallow blue waters of the summer.

I began the slow and arduous task of slogging through the ditches, up to my waist in thick muddy water. I gasped as I entered the freezing water and soon my legs and feet were numb with cold. I could feel my muscles screaming as I struggled to keep moving. It was like some nightmare where you want to run but can only move in painfully slow motion. There I was at the epicentre of the war, crossing the front line, and all I could do was press forward inch by inch, in an agonisingly slow fashion. I was obliged to follow the ditches as they meandered around fields, staying low and keeping in motion, lest the muddy bog start to pull me under.

Eventually I reached the river and struggled gratefully out of the ditch, lying on the riverbank as I caught my breath. I was somewhere in between the two bridges that crossed the river, at Campia and at Gallicano. The first was heavily guarded by the Germans at this point, having been attacked several times by other partisan groups already. The bridge at Gallicano, I was told by Dino, was often the subject of enemy fire, being the Allies' main way across. The river, dangerous as it was, remained my only way. In the summer we often swam in the rivers and lakes, and I was a strong swimmer. But I had never swum in a current like this, or in the depths of winter with all my clothes on. The river rushed past me, angry and intent on reaching the sea, and my heart quaked at the thought of entering it. I said a quick prayer and thought of Matteo to give me courage. There was no turning back at this stage. At the last minute I picked up a fallen log, some driftwood that had washed up on the shore of the river. At least I would have something buoyant to hold on to, while I fought my way across the river. The shock of the cold water took my breath away, as did the speed with which I was swept along. Kicking my legs as hard as I could and using one arm to plough across the river, I was nevertheless pounded by the force of the water like a piece of flotsam, and I knew I would end up washed out to sea, where no-one would ever even find my body.

Perhaps the angels really did help, perhaps the current was just kind to me, but somehow I managed to cross the river and cling on to a low-hanging tree on the other side. I managed to crawl onto the bank by the river, my clothes heavy and sodden, and lay coughing up river water. I was staring up at the pearly sky overhead, realising to my surprise that I was still alive, when I heard voices approaching. Too weak to move, adrenalin now flooding my veins and making me shake uncontrollably, I looked up and found myself staring into a face that was as black as the night sky. My head span and my eyes closed, and when I opened them again, curiosity winning out over my fear, the face was still there, attached to a body in green uniform crouched down beside me. The face was kindly and concerned. It belonged to a young man with a twinkle in his coffee-coloured eyes, and although I could not understand the words he was speaking, I knew from his tone he meant me no harm. He was part of a patrol of ten men who were respectfully keeping their distance, all with the emblem of a buffalo sown onto their shoulders. *Americans*, I realised, relief flowing through me. *"Americani,"* I murmured, attempting a smile. The young man flashed brilliant white teeth in a bigger smile than I had ever seen, and nodded. He offered me his hand in a polite and formal gesture, and I struggled to get up from the mud. My waterlogged clothes dragged me down, and in the end to my embarrassment it took two soldiers to help me up and onto my shaking legs. I could only mutter, "OSS," under my breath to my rescuer, before my shaking became more violent, and he realised he needed to get me to a place of warmth and safety before hypothermia set in. I later discovered I had in fact been washed a kilometre downstream, fortunately further into Allied territory. It was incredibly lucky that this patrol, returning to Barga after duties further up the valley, happened to come across me beside the river. I vaguely remember being helped into a vehicle, the first I had ever ridden in in my short life; it's a shame I have so little memory of it. From there I was taken to a house in Barga, given warm clothes, food and drink, and I slept for a few hours. A friendly lady called Maira checked on me several times, taking my temperature and treating a small head wound I had sustained in my struggle with the river. When I surfaced from my exhausted sleep my head was foggy, but I knew I could waste no more time. My clothes were dry and folded by the fire that burnt in my room, and I struggled to get dressed, aware that having got this far I now needed to reach the OSS. Maira contacted the soldiers and my rescuer from the riverbank returned to escort me. I imagine that during my sleep my belongings had been searched and some research been done into who I was and what I was doing there. I wished I knew some English to converse with this soldier who had helped me so much already, but all I could do was smile and accept his offer of chewing gum. It was the first time I had ever had chewing gum, and I saw the alarm on his face when I chewed it politely and then swallowed it. His concern was swiftly followed by booming laughter, and his whole face creased with mirth.

"No swallow," he said loudly, miming the act to me, and showing me what he was doing himself. "Just chew!" I nodded and gave it another go, succeeding this time in keeping on chewing. *How strange*, I thought to myself. *Are their supplies so low they must chew their food but never swallow?*

Barga, an ancient hilltop town, had been bombed heavily both by the Allies when it was held by the Fascists, and by the Germans and the Fascists once it was taken by the Allies. Many of its once-beautiful buildings now lay in piles of rubble, but the medieval stone walls defending the town remained strong. As we set off in the American Jeep my escort apologised and brought out a black scarf, and I understood he needed to blindfold me to protect the security of the location of the OSS. I nodded my assent, and he gently secured the scarf over my eyes. This was wartime, after all, and there were spies and double agents everywhere. No-one was to be trusted without good reason.

After a short journey we arrived and I was guided by Benjamin, as I now knew his name to be, into a building, and then into a small room where my blindfold was removed.

I waited, alone, for a period of about ten minutes, before two older white men, who I also believed to be Americans, came into the room. They had with them a younger man, who I soon discovered was American but of Italian descent, and he was to be the translator. Initially reserved and wary, they asked me many questions, and I replied as best I could. The truth was that I was a teenager straight out of a mountain village, ignorant to a great deal of what was going on with the war, and I think to begin with they couldn't decide if I was being evasive or if I was genuinely that under-informed. I answered their questions truthfully and waited patiently while my every word was translated and discussed, until I decided to take charge of the situation.

"Look," I said, leaning forward in my chair, summoning up every ounce of courage I had. "I've climbed down a mountain, waded through boggy ditches and nearly died crossing a river to get to you with an important message. My mother is waiting for me back home, worrying herself silly, and I've still got to make that same journey back. My colleagues want to help you win this war, they're in a strong position, and they're ready to act. But they need weapons, which we were led to believe you can help us with." Once my words had been translated there was a silence, and the two older men surveyed me with an expression of bemused admiration.

Finally, the more senior one said something to the translator, with a barking laugh, and the atmosphere in the room seemed to relax. The young man smiled at me bashfully and told me, "He's asking if all Italian girls are so bossy!" From that point on we got down to business, and maps emerged of the mountains. It was strange seeing the mountains, so familiar to me, mapped out on paper, and it took me a while to get my bearings. I soon located the ravine we had agreed upon for the drop-off, and I also showed the officers the area we were based in. As predicted, they were very interested in our proximity to the Todt operations, and the Nazi base at Montaltissimo. Dino had told me some limited information about the TODT fortifications, and the men eagerly listened to this and marked it all down on the maps. They asked if I would be prepared to continue to act as a messenger and gave me the details for a safe house over my side of the valley, in enemy territory, along with the code words that would identify me as a member of the Resistance. There I could arrange safe passage at an allotted time across the bridge in Allied territory, and they would arrange transport up to the OSS for me. I agreed readily, flushed with pride at the success of my first mission, and the respect that now showed in the eyes of the Allied officers.

As I left the office we shook hands, and the officer I now knew was Officer Mark Anderson shook my hand.

"A pleasure meeting you, Miss…" He paused for a moment and conferred with his colleague. "You must no longer use your real name," he told me, thinking. "Miss Rivers," he said, a small smile playing at the edge of his mouth. That was the day that Miss Rivers was born, and my life as a *staffetta*, a messenger between the partisans and the Allies, began.

21

Giuliana

1944

My long journey home began that evening, following my meeting with the OSS commanders at Barga and my initiation into the ranks of the informers across Italy. Benjamin, the American soldier who had saved my life on the banks of the River Serchio, accompanied me across the bridge and over No Man's Land under the cover of darkness. I already felt the warm stirrings of friendship for Benjamin, with his kindly eyes and his calm, solid presence. Without a common language we could only smile and gesticulate, and I resolved to learn what English I could in order to be able to communicate with him in the future. He left me at one of the safe houses I'd been told about, pressing a chocolate bar into my hand as we parted. These safe houses belonged to a network of people trusted by the Resistance and the Allies. Simple people, taking enormous risks every day. With time I came to know many of these places and people well, although we never spoke more than was strictly necessary. No-one could afford to take any more risks than were essential.

I left the safe house at first light and immediately veered off the main track, heading straight up into the mountains. I was further south than I'd ever been before, but the summit of La Pania guided me, visible as it is from virtually every hill in our region. As far back as I can remember, La Pania had always been a presence in my life, the highest point in the whole mountain range. I had scaled her heights many times as a child and marvelled at the view from the top which stretches all the way to the coast, to the gleaming blue sea. Not knowing which were in enemy hands I decided to avoid all the villages and hamlets on my route home, skirting the edges and sticking to the animal tracks that criss-crossed the hillsides. The going was hard, and I knew I had to keep up a good pace in order to reach home by nightfall. I was young and fit, and buoyed up by an incredible elation at having succeeded in my first mission. My heart swelled when I imagined how proud Matteo would be; I had proved myself worthy! No longer was I a schoolgirl from nowhere – I was now 'Miss Rivers', partisan spy returning from a mission with the OSS! I was already imagining the drop-off, our band of students and misfits transformed into proper freedom fighters, with real weapons and supplies. I could start to see a future where the Allies chased the Nazis out of Italy, where some ounce of national pride could be restored thanks to the work of brave heroes such as my comrades. And yes, I must admit that my joyful visions of the future were not only about national pride and politics, but also the idea of Matteo and I living together as man and wife at Stazzana, lying wrapped up in each other night after night, never again to be separated.

Pride comes before a fall, as they say, and what a fall was waiting for me on that mountainside. With the success of the previous day pumping through my veins, and these lofty and lusty thoughts preoccupying my mind, I forgot my hunter's instincts. I started to relax into the mountains I knew as home, and I virtually walked straight into a patrol of Germans. I believe they were also taken by surprise, for they scattered at the sight of me, some dropping to the ground and raising their weapons, some throwing themselves into the undergrowth. I later learnt that many partisan ambushes took place on tracks such as these, and this must have been what they feared was happening. I was lucky not to have been shot on sight. What a fool I was! I who had been careful for so many months, who knew how to read the signals, how to make myself invisible in these hills I had grown up in. A moment of success went to my head and I forgot it all. I fell to my knees, cursing myself, my hands raised in surrender. I heard shouting in German, and felt real terror shooting like black ice through my veins as I waited. I was approached cautiously by a man I assumed was the commander, and my hands tied. They shouted the same question at me several times, the only word I could distinguish was '*allein?*', and I guessed they were asking if I was on my own. I nodded dumbly and focused on trying to control my breathing, which was coming in sharp, ragged gasps, fear coursing through my body in waves of red panic. After some discussion I was made to stand, and my legs shook so badly they scarcely held me. I was searched for weapons, and my little knife taken from me. Back in formation the patrol set off down the mountain, back the way I'd just come from, and I realised we were heading in the direction of Gallicano. I risked a nervous glance at the men who were my captors – these t*edeschi* I'd heard about but never seen. Under their severe grey overcoats they seemed as thin and gaunt as my countrymen, and they were paler than any men I had ever seen before. The commander appeared to be young, with watery blue eyes, and I was surprised by the humanity I saw in them. I found myself wondering if he had a wife or a sweetheart back in Germany, waiting for him. This was the enemy, assuredly; I had heard the horrific stories of massacres and retributions. And yet, aside from the strange, spiky language, this seemed like just another group of boys, caught up in a war they no longer wanted any part of. We walked for the rest of the afternoon, finally arriving at a grey building on the edge of Gallicano. There were bullet holes on the walls, and the confines were guarded by soldiers who eyed me with a mixture of suspicion and interest as we approached.

I was led to a makeshift prison, a room that was bare except for a chair and a table, and had several locks on the door. I was brought water and left for about an hour. A bleak time for me to imagine my mother and my family waiting and watching upriver for my return, fretting and imagining the worst. And the worst had truly happened – I was in the hands of the enemy, completely vulnerable and unable to escape. Would I be tortured? Killed? Would I be raped? Sent to one of the work camps in Germany? I had always thought of myself as strong, but now I felt that strength ebbing away with the fading light. I frantically tried to think what to say, how to convince them I was no threat. Could they possibly know about my visit across the valley to the Allies? Surely not, and yet there were traitors everywhere, perhaps even at the so-called safe house. I felt my spirits dropping lower and lower as I realised that I had failed the partisans at the first hurdle, that I was even now putting them in danger with my presence here. Visions of Matteo and our last evening together filled my mind, and I longed for his embrace, yearned for his warm body against mine. I tortured myself with images of him pacing the woods, waiting anxiously for news of my return.

Eventually the door opened and two Germans entered the room, one older, one younger. They brought two more chairs and sat down facing me. The elder was clearly superior in rank, and when I risked a glance at his face his glacial blue eyes froze me to the spot. What I saw there I shall never forget: a being without soul, a man missing a conscience. I was reminded of Don Franco telling me about his experience with evil, and I felt instinctively that this man would show no mercy. The shadow of death was all around him, yet his eyes burned with a zeal that told me he justified every death with a higher cause; his self-belief was absolute. No guilt dogged him, his power was enough to hold the shades at bay, and in that split second my entire belief in the world I had been raised in wavered. It may have been the moment my belief in religion faltered. The fact that this man could exist in the world and remain unpunished went against everything I had ever been taught. Where was the retribution, the justice?

The younger German was the translator and had a gentler demeanour. He seemed to be in fear of his superior and permitted himself no show of friendliness, but I sensed in him an empathy lacking in his colleague. The officer barked out questions, and the private translated for me, in stilted, broken Italian. He wanted to know where I had been, and where I was returning to. I told them I had been visiting family in the village of Calomini, near to where I was captured, and was returning home to Stazzana, near Montaltissimo. It was a weak story, but I had nothing better to offer. I tried to come across as a simple country girl, which wasn't too far from the truth. They then demanded to know whether I had come across any partisans in my area, and whether I was carrying messages for them. I dared not meet the stare of the officer, which I could still feel upon me: cold suspicion probing me, trying to strip me bare, to reveal the truth that I carried within. I kept my eyes low to the ground, feigning modesty. I called upon all my wit and denied any knowledge. I lived quietly at home, I told them, with my mother and my sisters. It was harder than I would have ever imagined, bringing the lie to my lips. As determined as I was to defend my comrades and Matteo, I knew with sickening dread that the officer's will was stronger than mine, that with time he would hunt down the truth, spin it out of me. I was aware of his presence expanding, icy tentacles tightening all around me. Was this the power of the devil he commanded, to search a soul in such a way?

My salvation came in the form of a knock on the door, and he was summoned outside. I felt the pressure around me ease and I slumped into my chair, the air flooding back into my lungs and I was able to breathe again. I looked up, cautiously, and saw that I was left alone with the younger German. I summoned up the courage to ask him what they would do with me, and he shifted uneasily in his chair and replied that he didn't know. It was possible that I would be released, but more probable that I was would be transferred to the prison at Castelnuovo for a time and interrogated further.

"It's not so good for women, in prison," he told me, his mouth forming the words with difficulty. "Many bad men. If you know something, is better to talk now. If you will be released, you can go to Germany, to work, until war finish." My heart sank at these prospects, and I realised that at this stage of the war the Germans were suspicious of everyone: man, woman or child. The partisans had been hitting them hard for over a year now, and they were taking every precaution. Perhaps earlier in the war I would have been released, but at this late and desperate stage all bets were off. I felt tears prick my eyes as I realised I would never see my family again, or Matteo.

Just then the door re-opened, and as I looked up I realised with a shock that it was not the officer who had entered, but a figure who, even through my misty vision and the dim light, I recognised. He was wearing the Fascist uniform of the San Marco division: dark green jacket and trousers, and a hat with a feather typical of the *alpini* soldiers. Taller, thinner, older, it was still unmistakably Matteo's cousin Fiorlindo, whom I had not seen in several years. The sight of a familiar face and a ray of hope in my blackest hour lead me to fling myself at him, sobbing, and he held me and stroked my hair. He made a gesture of dismissal to the younger German and closed the door, leaving us alone together. He sat me down and offered me water and bread, which I gratefully took. His thin, handsome face scrutinised me while I ate, and I felt his gaze travel down my body, cool and calculating. I blushed a little, remembering how I had thrown myself at him just moments earlier.

"I couldn't believe it was you," he finally said, leaning closer to me. "Little Giuliana, grown to be a woman." He smiled appreciatively at me, stroking my face with one finger. I froze at his touch, feeling a shadow of premonition. I hid it as best I could, aware that he was my only way out at this point. Brusquely he sat up straight, the moment past, reminded of his duty. In a harder tone, he questioned me. "Giuliana, what were you doing out alone so far from home?" I repeated the same story I had told the Germans, and he nodded. I'm not sure he believed me any more than they had, but he gave no sign of this. "Do you know how much danger you are in?" he asked me, becoming frustrated with my apparent stupidity now. "If I hadn't arrived today, you would be in prison tonight – do you know what they do to young girls in prison? What desperate German guards do after a few bottles of wine?" He sighed and gave a gesture of desperation. "Even what the *alpini* will do, for that matter. Men are men and there are few pleasures to be found in wartime."

He looked much older than his twenty-odd years, and I found myself wondering what sort of man he had become in these war years. How long he had spent in Germany, whether he had killed any partisans, his own countrymen.

He stood up then, his decision made. "I will use what influence I have to get you out. I will vouch for you, explain that I have known you since childhood, that you are a good Fascist girl who doesn't understand the dangers of war. That you will promise to stay at home in the future. You will stay home in the future, Giuliana?" I nodded dumbly, grateful for any way out.

"*Si, Fiorlindo,*" I told him, "*Grazie.*"

A short time later I was released from custody, ushered into an army vehicle, and Fiorlindo and two soldiers drove me back up the mountainside to where the track to Stazzana began. He signalled for the other two to stay in the vehicle, and he led me off the side of the track. The hour was now late, and we were cloaked in inky darkness.

"Thank you," I mumbled awkwardly. "Thank you for saving my life." I knew he must have risen the ranks of the Fascists to have enough power to have me released, and for that I was grateful, even though I knew him to be on the side of the enemy. He was still staring at me, trying to figure me out, I think. I sensed a potent blend of mistrust and desire emanating from him, and I was confused and exhausted, desperate to get away.

"You can make your way on foot?" he asked me, holding my shoulders and forcing me to look up into his face.

"Yes, I think so," I replied. "*Buona notte, Fiorlindo.*" His grip tightened and he leant in to kiss me goodnight, murmuring his goodbye in my ear.

"I'll come and see you, Giuliana, bring you and the family some food when I come to visit my mother. She is at the farmhouse now with *Zia* Benedetta."

"*Grazie,*" I murmured again, and slipping from his grip I disappeared off down the mule track, aware of his gaze following me as I went. The chestnut house had never seemed so welcoming as it did that night, our little haven in the woods, and my family all cried tears of joy to see me home again. I could not speak of my adventures, nor my escape, and with great relief I collapsed onto the bed by the fire and fell into a deep and dreamless sleep.

22

Fiorlindo

1944

They have no idea, these partisans, what loyalty means. Duty, patriotism, honour. They switch sides with such ease, allying themselves with our enemies: the *Americani*, the *Inglesi*. After all Il Duce has done for our country they cast him aside for what they perceive as the winning team. Taunting the Germans with their home-made bombs, hiding in the woods like cowards. Raining destruction down upon the innocents: our mothers, fathers, grandparents. They are weak, badly organised, they will not endure against the might of the Reich and the Italian republic.

I've wondered for a while whether Matteo might have found a way home, whether he could have joined the ranks of the traitors. I knew he would have headed for Stazzana, unable to resist the pull of home. Of seeing his mother, and *her*, of course. They always were inseparable. Running off to the forest together, sneaking away from the rest of us when they thought no-one was looking. But I was always watching, aware even then of the power Giuliana exuded, the beauty she would grow into. Not a suitable wife, in many ways, but the only one I have ever wanted. Not just wanted but longed for, for years now. The thought of Matteo taking her before I have a chance, before the war is won, maddens me with a red rage that I cannot see past.

I regularly make the trip to Stazzana to visit my mother who is staying there with her sister, my Aunt Benedetta. My mother knows nothing of his return, certain her sister would have told her, but I remain suspicious. Assunta is also living there now, my cousin Giovanni's wife, and she may be my best hope. She is sharp, observant, a devout Fascist girl. I always admired her at school; in many ways she would have been the perfect choice for me. She knows where her loyalties lie, and she has always disliked Giuliana. Envied her, I think, for her restless beauty and her quick wit, her easy popularity. If Matteo is back and if Giuliana is, as I fear, involved with the partisans, Assunta may be my way to them.

I bring much-needed food to Stazzana, and they have my assurance that their remaining livestock are safe. She is easy to charm, Assunta. She is alone, an orphan, her husband far from home. She is a plain girl, not blessed with Giuliana's beauty. She blushes easily under my gaze, is soft and pliable in my arms when I embrace her on arrival. I bring her small treats, when I can. She has a sweet tooth and eats them while I watch. Good girl, I tell her. Il Duce would be proud of you. She is so starved of affection. I drip sweet words into her ear, and ask her to be my eyes and my ears in the valley. To watch out for people coming and going in the night, for gossip she might hear from other women in the house. My smart uniform, my authority, my gifts; they all turn her head. I will keep you safe, I tell her, you are all my family here at Stazzana. My mother, my aunt, my cousin's wife. They have my protection, and my relations with the tedeschi remain strong. I learnt some of their language when I was there for my training, in that low, grey country where it did nothing but rain. I can see why they long for *lebensraum*, space for their race to grow and expand. As a rule they are dismissive of us, scathing of our failures in Africa and Greece. Of how our King submitted to the Allies, how half our country is lost. But they respond to strength, and I have earned their respect these past few months. I have proved myself loyal, a true ally. Since the partisans started their war games many of our *alpini* have been divided, unable to see where their duty lies. When it comes to the capture and execution of traitors, whatever nationality they may be, I have no qualms. As Il Duce himself commanded, traitors are to be shot in the back. Some of my colleagues have not the stomach for it; they still see them as fellow Italians, countrymen, *garfagnini*. To them they remain brothers, friends, schoolmates. To me they are the enemy, and I do not hesitate. My love, once declared, is eternal. For my country, Il Duce, the Italian republic. For Giuliana. She will come to see this, to appreciate the life I can offer her. A respectable role as a wife and mother. She will set aside her wild ways and embrace the life of a good Fascist wife. Obedient to her husband. I believe in our future as I believe we will win this war. My faith is absolute.

If she has been led astray by these fools, it will be Matteo's fault. She is young, and of the weaker sex. She needs a strong hand to guide her, to mould her. To discipline her. A task for her husband, and she would come to respect and then to love me. I would be her saviour, rescuing her from a life of sin, the life of a traitor. She could be shot, if she is involved. I will have to be careful; she would need protecting, and as a capitano I would be able to do that.

I have visited her regularly since the day I rescued her, bringing food to her family at the chestnut house. She is grateful, polite, but as slippery as water when I try to express my intentions. Several times she has been absent and her mother tells me she is checking traps, collecting chestnuts, buying bread from Abetone, the farm above Stazzana. Her absence is suspicious; I have warned her of the dangers of venturing far from the house. The mountains are crawling with soldiers, deserters, escaped POWs. Desperate men, more than a match for an unarmed woman on her own. She is disturbingly careless about her own safety; she shrugs off my warnings with a toss of that black mane, and I am left frustrated, driven to distraction by her. I know she thinks me a cold fish, a figure of authority. I see how she stiffens when I embrace her. I have not the charming words of a poet, the romantic touch of young lover. Can she not see the love in my eyes, the growing need within me to make her mine? I could offer her so much. Security, a home, a place in society. Travel, perhaps, with my career in the Italian army. Il Duce will reward us richly, the *alpini* who stayed loyal to him. When the war is won, when our German allies have secured their hold over Europe, when the Italian empire is re-established, we will be victorious. And she could be by my side, partake in all the glory. I will forgive her misdemeanours, show her the way to redemption. She has been left to run wild for too long, but now she is a woman and she needs a firm hand. I must admit the thought of being the one to tame her keeps me awake at night, pleasure and pain combining in delicious dreams. The perfect contrast of strong and weak, soft and hard, male and female. I wonder if she enchanted me with those green witches' eyes, since the day I set her free my nights are full of her, I cannot escape, and I wake every morning with the taste of her on my lips, salty and wild and sweet.

For now I must do my duty; I have precious little time. I will continue to use my authority to visit Stazzana, both to bring food to my family and my intended, and to gather information. I know the partisans are operating around there; I can sense it. I will sniff them out and eradicate them like the rats they are, hiding in the ditches. Traitors to our country, trouble-makers, rebels. If my cousin Matteo is among their number, I will show no mercy. Any blood ties we share would be void. We will liberate our people, show them the way, allow them to live in peace again. And then I will claim my reward – my Giuliana. I will save her from this war, and from herself. I will lead the way, back to God, back to her country, back to her true nature and into the arms of her loving husband.

23

Giuliana

1944

I remember the months following my escape from the Nazis as the happiest of my whole life. That seems strange to say, considering the danger we were all living in, but it's true. Despite the bitter cold and the never-ending gnaw of hunger I woke each day with a passion for life that I have never again experienced. I had a purpose, a mission; I was part of something wonderful. A brave band of heroes fighting for a better world. We were so idealistic, dreaming of a free Italy, a democracy, a society of equals. After twenty years of repression under the Fascist regime, more than my lifetime, it felt like anything might be possible. Women were finally granted the right to vote in the February of 1945, and after years of misogyny under Il Duce, we started to see the glimmer of a brighter future ahead.

I became ever busier with my work as a *staffetta*, a courier between the OSS and the local partisans, as the war continued on into 1945. Our valley remained the epicentre of the fighting. Germans, Fascists, partisans and Allies were all trapped in a deadlock, while the civilians just tried to survive the winter and escape reprisals.

The night of the airdrop remains as clear and sharp in my memory as if it were just the other day, instead of over seven decades ago. Raffaello and his *banda* were overjoyed with my success at the OSS and my safe return, and I saw a new respect in their eyes that thrilled me. But as the date for the drop-off drew nearer we all grew jumpy, quick to find fault with each other as we doubted ourselves and the Allies. Would they show up for us? Would the night be quiet, or would there be unexpected Nazi or Fascist patrols in the area? Would our signal fires be spotted? We knew that in the dark and with the hazardous mountain conditions the drop-off would not be exact even if it happened, and there was the risk of our supplies being lost, destroyed or falling into enemy hands.

In the end the spirits of the mountains were smiling upon us, and the night of the drop-off was clear and starlit, a half-moon high in the sky. The conditions were perfect, both for lighting our signal fires and for the plane to spot them. Once the pale winter sun slipped over La Pania the temperature started to plummet, and being a clear night we knew it would be well below freezing. The partisans had provided me with men's clothes, including my first pair of trousers. I can still remember those trousers to this day: how strange they felt on my legs, how my movement felt different immediately, more masculine somehow. One simple pair of trousers, but a monumental shift for the culture of our time. A fork in the road, a step towards the modern world, towards equality.

My mother and sisters were greatly distressed by my new attire, which struck me as amusing given the changes that had already taken place in our lives.

"Giuliana!" my sister Margherita lamented, wringing her hands, the first time she saw me in my slacks. "Who will ever want to marry you now?" There was a pause as my mother, Rosa and I all considered this question, and moments later a great burst of laughter escaped first from my mother and then my sisters and I, until we were all collapsed on the bed, laughing until our stomachs ached. The question took us back to pre-war teasing of this sort, and it seemed such an absurd comment given our current predicament. It made me realise how quickly life had changed in all sorts of ways, and how even once the war ended, we would find ourselves in a different world. I for one would not be giving up my trousers after the war, even if it did put off a potential husband! Besides, there was only one man in the world I would consider for that position, and I do not think he objected. There was a lot of hardship and worry that winter, and I remember those precious moments of laughter with my mother and sisters fondly. A moment of lightness in an existence that weighed heavy with danger and risk.

Dressed in my warmest clothes, tightly belted in and with a scarf wrapped around my head, I was ready. Before the snow I would have blackened my face with soot from the fire to blend into the night, but since the snow had fallen camouflage was harder. I headed up the mountain to our hide-out, where I found Dino on guard. Together we headed uphill before descending into the ravine that had been chosen for the drop-off. I had identified its location for the Allies using the maps they provided, and now I fervently hoped I'd been correct. Raffaello had calculated and tested the theory that the fires would not be seen from the German-occupied surrounding villages, but on such a clear night we feared the smoke might carry further than usual.

Three large fires were lit by the time Dino and I arrived. They formed a triangle around the ravine, and the plan was for our supplies to be dropped in the centre at midnight. We all retreated to our defensive positions and crouched down on the ground, pressing our bodies into the snow. We could only watch and wait. There was no gunfire echoing around the mountains that night and I fancied I could hear the frost settling on the surface of the snow, tiny crystals forming all around us. My breath formed a cloud of mist as I exhaled, floating up to the stars. My body became numb, frozen in place. Dislocated from my body I felt my soul wander, become one with the mountain beneath me and the sky above. It was like a beautiful dream, and I wondered whether this was how death felt, just freedom and open space, liberated from the restrictions of our human shells.

Just after midnight there was the distant whir of an engine, and I was back in my body, aware of a sharp pain in my fingers and toes, and I struggled to raise myself up, to re-awaken my sleeping limbs. With a flurry of activity we all sprang into action, and the fires were fed with the driest wood, reaching their tongues of flame upwards to the stars. The plane grew closer and came into view – a metal bird gliding down from the heavens. As she passed overhead we saw several bundles tumble out and softly parachute down into the ravine, like mushrooms blooming in the night sky. Then the plane was off, fading from view into the distance. Instead of dropping the bombs that decimated vast parts of our homeland this time she left gifts, vital supplies that would transform our band of misfits into warriors.

The hardest task remained ahead of us: finding the packages under the darkness of night, on rocky and treacherous terrain. The fires were rapidly doused and we began our search plan, as previously organised by Raffaello. Dino and I were to start at the southern end of the ravine, while the others had been assigned their own areas. I was glad of the shepherd beside me, as agile and sure-footed on the rocky slopes as his herd. We had no lights to aid us, but our eyes adjusted and the moonlight aided our travails. We found one bundle caught up in a tree, and together we managed to carefully free it from the tree's embrace. It was heavy and we lugged it back to the barn together, excited to discover what we had found. We found Canzio and Ottaviano back at base, with a bundle of their own. Canzio was limping, having sprained his ankle slipping on a rock, and I quickly set about packing it with camomile and calendula from the little bag of dried herbs I always carried.

Raffaello and Matteo joined us shortly after with a bundle of their own, and later Dino and Don Franco, with two more parcels. One more would be found in the light of day the next morning, and in total we retrieved six. It was like the *Befana* had come, the good witch who in my childhood brought us presents for Epiphany each year. We were as excited as schoolchildren opening our presents, greedy for what lay within. Ottaviano and Dino took up their positions outside as guards, while the rest of us opened the packages, one by one. We found weapons – machine guns, pistols, ammunition, explosives, hand grenades and knives. These were well wrapped with warm woollen clothes and thick jackets, and to our great joy there were stout boots for those men who had none. There was food, precious jam and dried fruit, bread and cheese, *salame* and even some bars of chocolate. These supplies would not only feed our men but would be distributed to the most needy in our surrounding villages, where some families and children were already on the brink of starvation. We also discovered, wrapped up in several pairs of thick socks, a radio set, which would allow us to communicate with the other partisan groups and the Allies.

We worked all night by the light of our small fire, sharing out the clothing, allotting weapons, and dividing up the supplies between our members and those we had already identified to receive some of our bounty. The weapons and what was left we hid carefully in the cave; we couldn't risk them falling into enemy hands. It was dawn when we finished, and I knew I had to get home. Matteo accompanied me down the mountain and we walked together in easy, exhausted silence. We were still incredulous that it had actually happened: the Allies had taken us seriously and followed through on their promise. I knew Raffaello would already have a plan made for our next meeting, and that the life of our little of band of freedom fighters was about to really begin.

Matteo had a spring in his step despite the late hour, and I think we were both fuelled by excitement at what we could now achieve. The dawn was spreading across the Apennines; the clouds that clung to the Passo Delle Radici were glowing crimson, gently furrowed like a newly ploughed field.

"This land," Matteo murmured softly beside me, "this Garfagnana. This is why we fight." I looked across at him, and saw his eyes were fixed on the horizon, his long eyelashes strung with tears. His eyes were misty with feeling, his mouth curved in a small smile and my heart swelled with love for him. His focus moved to my face, his smile widened and he leaned in to kiss me. His embrace sent little sparks of pleasure travelling through my body, and I pressed myself closer, seeking to tie myself to him for all eternity. Our need for each other grew stronger with the dawn, until it felt like we'd been waiting our entire lives for this moment. We were near the Lost Barn, and we somehow made it the last few metres before falling down upon the pile of hay, our makeshift bed. I felt his weight upon me, the shape of his body, the delicious contrast of soft skin and hard muscle, the sensation of being willingly trapped beneath him. I ran my hands through his dark curls, pulling them tight, and he sighed a little in my ear, saying my name over and over. I slipped my hands inside his shirt, feeling the warm skin underneath under my icy fingertips. I sensed the force of his passion and it thrilled me, making me aware of my own power, the possibilities of my body to enchant, tease, delight. He kissed me harder and I responded, instinctively speaking the language of love, and his hands worked away, deftly removing my men's clothes. The chill of the dawn air only heightened the sensations, the silver chill in the air contrasting with the heat we were creating. My head span as his kisses covered my body, as sacred as an act of worship, and when we finally became one I remember crying out with bliss and not caring whether the Germans heard. I remember that first, perfect time so clearly, though it should make an old lady blush to remember. We made love as equals, friends, partisans, soulmates. We were made for each other: the perfect match. The physical sensations of desire sated in each other were more than matched by the love we felt, a love that was both fierce and gentle.

Afterwards we lay nestled under our coats in the silence of the winter dawn, marvelling at what we had done. We gazed up at the chestnut rafters of the barn above us, listening to the winter woods waking up. We were hidden away in the Lost Barn; it was our sanctuary, our escape from the war. It has always been this way, this sacred trio. Myself, Matteo and the mountains. Were we a part of them, or were they a part of us? I can no longer remember. What I remember is the happiness, the feeling of being complete. One with the natural world, the beating heart of the earth beneath us. A place beyond words, beyond time and space, beyond the impermanent.

"Now you are my wife," Matteo whispered in my ear, dropping a warm kiss on my frozen cheek, where it melted like snow. "And I will love you through all eternity."

24

Giuliana

1945

I continued my work as a *staffetta*, a courier between the partisans and the Allies, and I crossed the front line countless times, carrying messages that were too sensitive to transmit via radio. I was never again re-captured for I had learnt my lesson and was always on high alert. On many occasions I had an uncanny sense that the mountains colluded to hide me. There were near misses, but by some stroke of luck I remained out of sight, hidden by a sudden mist or a handy thicket of bushes. I was grateful for my knowledge of the terrain, and my love for the mountains deepened every day.

I spent many hours with Don Franco learning English so I could better communicate with the Allies, and some German in case I should ever need it. Don Franco was still in hiding, concealed by the good people of the mountains who loved him so dearly. He worked tirelessly throughout the whole occupation to get food to those in need, provide medical assistance to the injured and sick, and to smuggle many hundreds of people across the front line to the liberated zone. He was a warrior priest, a holy freedom fighter and one of the best men I have ever known.

After the airdrop our little *banda* of rebels went from strength to strength. Various bridges that the Germans relied on were blown up under the cover of night, the soldiers guarding them taken out by shadows that appeared out of the mist with no warning. Landslides occurred while convoys of Nazi vehicles were travelling up the valley, thundering fists of rock crashing their fury down upon helpless travellers. The sleeping giants of the mountains were awakening, scared young soldiers whispered amongst themselves. The witches and sprites of ancient times were there, watching them from the darkness that cloaked the valley, night after night. This was a terrible and cursed place, a valley of death and danger. The rumours grew, and the reputation of the hidden army of partisans spread. The Todt fortifications were attacked again and again, attacks that came from nowhere, from men cleverly hidden in the rock formations they knew so well. The Germans, up against local knowledge and the harsh winter conditions, stood no chance. Within weeks the half-built fortifications were raided, stripped, abandoned.

Our last and greatest victory came in early March, when the snows had started to thaw and the river by the *metato* ran fast with meltwater. I saw the first snowdrops pushing their brave little heads up through the slushy snow and there was a sense of optimism in the air, both for the coming of spring and the end of the war. I was well-informed from my work with the OSS, and I knew the Allies would make their move in the spring when the conditions were better. Some key German officials were already negotiating their surrender by this point, and the Fascist deserters continued to flock across the front line. We never let ourselves relax, for we realised how crucial it was to keep the momentum up.

By this point I was used to the procedure for crossing over

the front line to the OSS, and I was well known at the safe house near the river. On this occasion as on many before it, Benjamin arrived to pick me up, his ready grin flashing white in the darkness.

"Ciao!" he greeted me with his American drawl, and I jumped in the Jeep, familiar by now with its strange workings. Thanks to Don Franco I could communicate fairly easily with Benjamin and his colleagues, and even differentiate between the American and the British accent.

"How's your family?" I asked Benjamin, as I always did, and he'd tell me about his mama back home, and his brothers and sisters. It intrigued me even then, this America he spoke of. We chewed gum as we crossed the bridge, and I marvelled at how accustomed I had grown to events that would have been unthinkable to me just a few months ago. Travelling in a motor vehicle across the front line with a black American soldier, chewing gum and chatting away in English! Already I barely recognised the naive teenager I had been at the start of the war. With my work as a *staffetta* and my relationship with Matteo, I admit I felt quite grown up. Benjamin dropped me off at the premises where I would meet with Officer Anderson, who was still my main point of contact at the OSS.

"Miss Rivers," he greeted me dryly, getting straight to the point. "I hope your journey went smoothly today." Always polite, he ushered me into my chair at the desk, and I detected an animation in him today, a schoolboy enthusiasm that told me he had received good news. He whizzed through the usual security checks and updates, his blue eyes sparkling with excitement. "I have news," he said, "news that might be extremely valuable to us, if we can use it to our advantage." Although the room we were in was completely secure, he lowered his voice and leant towards me. "We have the date and time of a convoy that is to include SS Oberführer Walter von Steinbrinck, among other senior German officials." He sat back and waited for my reaction, and

I think he was not disappointed. I gasped, remembering Don Franco's description of the man the night he had met him. *Pure evil*, he had told me. *A soul that has long lost sight of God and is working wholeheartedly for the other side.* My heart began to beat faster as I realised what Officer Peterson was asking of me, of our group of *partigiani*.

"You want us to set off a landslide," I murmured. "Take them all out in one go." He nodded, pleased I had understood, and pulled out a map. He indicated the route they were due to take, and I asked how he had come about the information.

"A double agent," he replied, "who must remain unnamed, of course."

"Can you trust them?" I asked, worried it might be a trap.

He paused, and frowned slightly. "I believe so, Miss Rivers, though in these times it is hard to be completely certain of anyone." Together we examined the place on the map where the landslide would have to occur, and I knew from the terrain it would not be easy. Setting off a landslide is never an exact science, and relies as much on luck and good timing as skill.

"Perhaps we should set up an ambush as well," I suggested, "have some of our party hidden near the roadside further down the valley. If the landslide fails they have a second chance to take him out."

"Good thinking, Rivers," Officer Peterson praised, "and good luck." He shook my hand and I made my way back outside to where Benjamin was waiting. He raised his eyebrows when he saw my expression and touched my arm in concern.

"You alright, Ma'am? You look like you seen a ghost." I was far away, my mind whirring with ideas for how we could accomplish this task. I had heard other stories about Walter von Steinbrinck, stories of torture and killing, of terrible, unnatural acts that will always haunt me. The part he played in several reprisals, executing helpless old people, women, children, even babies. I felt passionately that if we could achieve this, if we could remove such a person as he from the war and from the world, then it would all have been worthwhile. I forced a smile for Benjamin and jumped back into the Jeep.

"Yes, thank you, I'm fine. Just a little tired."

"Here." He pushed me a bar of chocolate which I gratefully took.

"You are too kind, Benjamin. A real friend. *Grazie.*" To bring me back to the present I chatted with Benjamin on the way back across the front line, asking him to tell me more tales from his homeland. I loved to hear his deep voice talking with his rolling American accent, and the way he moved his large hands to gesticulate. His homeland sounded so different to Italy, and yet the same values of family, friendship and working the land connected us.

"Maybe I'll visit you one day, after the war," I mused, and he laughed, the sound booming around the vehicle.

"You'd be most welcome, Miss Rivers," he told me. "You'd always have a place with me and my mama." The war hung heavily around us all in those days; it permeated everything, every experience, every waking moment. To allow ourselves, however briefly, to imagine a time and a place free of the war was always to lift the curtain for an instant, to remind ourselves of how sweet life once was, and could again be, if only we could believe it.

I made my way home carefully with no incidents, and the very next evening I was up at the partisans' barn, telling them the news. Raffaello immediately began pacing the barn, his mind racing to come up with a plan. There were only three days until the date Peterson had given me, and preparations would need to begin straight away. The rest of us waited by the fire, Matteo holding my hand tightly.

Raffaello's plan, as usual, was simple but brilliant. Using what explosives we had left, half of our number would set off the landslide when the convoy was in sight, hopefully taking them all out in one go. Should it be delayed and some or all of them continue on up the valley, then the rest of us would be waiting ready to ambush them, armed with hand grenades and machine guns. Dino, Ottaviano and Silvano were chosen to carry out the first part of the mission, while Raffaello, Canzio, Matteo and myself would take care of the second part. The convoy was due to pass at dusk, which made it safer for us to remain hidden but harder to aim accurately.

The day dawned cloudy but dry, which we took as a blessing since the explosives would not get wet and we would be more agile without our clothes getting sodden with rain. The morning dragged on, and it was with relief that after lunch I set off up the mountain to our meeting point, able to release some of my nervous energy during the uphill climb.

I met up with the others in the forest near the barn at Sant'Antonio, and I took a bag to carry so we could share the load. We split into small groups to travel, so that even if some of us were apprehended hopefully the others would be able to escape. The snow had nearly all gone and once again we camouflaged ourselves as best we could to blend in with the mountains. We smeared mud on our faces and wore dark clothes, and with the cover of the trees we were adept at disappearing into the landscape. Our progress was slow and careful, always aware of the explosives we were carrying. We reached the summit within an hour, the place identified to set off the landslide. Dino had become an expert with explosives, his patient, careful nature making him the ideal candidate. He would keep watch up the valley until he saw the convoy, and then it was up to him to get the timing right.

The summit towered over the mountain road below, and looking down I saw it winding along the valley bottom next to the river. I shivered to think of the huge chunks of rock crashing down the hillside, gaining deadly momentum as they went. We had chosen a spot that had no houses or barns nearby, and within occupied territory as there was little chance of anyone other than the enemy passing by.

Raffaello, Canzio, Matteo and I still had a long walk to reach our location for the ambush, so we wished our friends good luck and set off. I carried a bag full of hand grenades and my machine gun, and Raffaello chose me to lead our group, trusting my highly developed instincts to detect any danger up ahead. The approach to the rocky outcrop where we would lie in wait was bare, and I was painfully aware of how exposed we were as we crept towards our hiding place. If an enemy sniper had been watching we could easily have been picked off, but fortunately we made it there safely.

The light was starting to fade, but we still had a clear view of the road, and we settled into our positions, preparing our weapons. I prayed that Raffaello's calculations were correct, and that the landslide would not spread along the ridge and take us out as well. The part of the road that the landslide was supposed to take out was around the corner and out of sight, but when the explosives went off they were as loud as thunder, like a great angry roar from the heavens. We cowered behind our rock, deafened by the noise, the vibrations passing through the earth under our feet. Unseen rocks crashed down the hill, an ocean of stormy waves, and it seemed to go on forever. A cloud of debris came towards us from the road, and I smiled grimly to myself. Dino had certainly got the explosion right, but had the rocks hit their mark?

I felt Matteo tense by my side as a vehicle emerged from the dust, and then another. Two *panzerwagons*, armoured cars, were travelling towards us; they must have just escaped in time. We had been informed the convoy would consist of five vehicles, so I guessed that three of them had been hit by the landslide.

"Steady," Raffaello said as they drew nearer. "*Ora!*" And we launched our hand grenades down onto the road, exploding with flashes as they hit their targets. The vehicles drew to a stop, and we started to shoot with our machine guns, several soldiers jumping out and returning fire. To my horror they continued to emerge from the vehicles, at least ten soldiers, and whilst I saw at least a couple fall to the ground I knew we were outnumbered and would quickly be overwhelmed.

"Retreat!" Raffaello shouted over the gunfire, and the four of us started to back up the mountain, crossing the exposed rocky expanse that would lead us back to the forest. The Germans continued to shoot after us, but they were just out of range. I could hear from their shouting they were coming after us, a tricky climb up the rocks, but they were fuelled with fury after our attack, and I knew they would not give up easily.

When we reached the woods we split into two groups as planned: Raffaello and Canzio heading straight up the mountain, while Matteo and I took a northerly direction, heading deeper into the forest in an attempt to lose the enemy. Dark was falling around us by the minute, and with no stars or moon I knew the black night would be impenetrable. We had no torches back then, and although I suspected the Germans would I knew they would be reluctant to use them in case they attracted the attention of a passing Allied aeroplane.

Matteo and I fled into the woods, making as little noise as we could. As the undergrowth thickened around us we slowed to a walk, listening out for signs that an enemy soldier was close. My heart beat loudly in the silent forest; I felt the terror of the prey animal with the hunter close at its heels. I grasped Matteo's hand, trying to slow my breathing and find my centre. For some reason an image of the night of the v*endemmia* appeared in my mind, that last happy festa before the war. I saw myself and Matteo crouched up in the old oak tree at Stazzana, watching the wolves below us. In the darkness my eyes made out a thick trunk, and feeling the bark under my fingertips I realised it was an oak tree.

"*Matteo*," I whispered, squeezing his hand, "up here!"

Quickly and quietly we scaled the oak tree, feeling the way with our hands until we reached a point in the tree where several branches met and I hoped we would be hidden from sight. We cuddled together, taking care that our faces and hands were not visible from below, and stilled ourselves, becoming part of the forest around us. A few minutes must have passed before we heard voices, and we froze in place, praying to the Madonna to protect us, to keep us hidden. I heard orders barked out in German, and at one point I believe they were right under us. It was a strange echo of the night of the *vendemmia*, but this time the hunters were our fellow humans, stalking their own kind. I remember the beauty of the wolf's golden eyes, the wisdom of the alpha male that had been aware of our presence and accepted us. This time we prayed we would remain unseen, for we knew what capture would have meant.

We stayed that way until dawn, grateful for the cover of night and the cloud cover that kept the frost away. Our bodies pressed together for warmth, we were saved by the mountains that had always looked after us. When we finally descended the tree that had been our salvation we could barely move, so stiff and cold we were, but as we started the trek home the blood started to flow again, and the movement warmed our joints. We were exhausted and hungry but exhilarated from our success and our near escape.

We returned to the barn at Sant'Antonio, desperate to know if Raffaello and Canzio had escaped as well. To our great joy they were there waiting for us, and we all hugged, hardly able to believe we had made it.

"I've had radio contact," Raffaello told us, his face glowing with pride. "Von Steinbrinck was in one of the vehicles that was crushed by the landslide! We got the bastard!" Canzio had cracked open a bottle of wine, and we all toasted the news by the fire.

I can still see the faces of my comrades, the glow of the fire softening their faces into something beautiful. Weary and war-worn we were fuelled by our spirit, our idealism, our dreams of a free Italy. I recall it so keenly, that lost happiness. What I would give now to sit by the crackling fire, to listen to the earnest chatter of those brave boys. With my friends around me and Matteo by my side I was complete; I wished for no more. We hoped we had contributed to the beginning of the end of the war, and I believe we did. Little did we know it was the last time we would all be together, the high point from which the descent into the abyss would be steep and unforgiving.

*

25

Assunta

1945

This place has become my prison, this house that I hoped would be my home. I was so happy when I arrived; life was sweet. I had my Giovanni, my love, my husband, and our future was bright. We looked forward to starting a family, seeing them grow at Stazzana, taking over the farm from his parents.

Giovanni is the first-born son and will inherit the farm, as per tradition. He is well cut out for the role: responsible, righteous, hard-working. He has always known the time will come when he will be in charge, and although he attended the village school to gain a rudimentary education, work on the farm has always come first. We have known each other since we were children, and I always liked and respected him. As we crossed the threshold to adulthood we began to court; it was a gentle courtship. Shy words exchanged after Mass, a dance at the midsummer festa. Sitting next to one another at the *vendemmia*, our parents nearby chaperoning us. They were never concerned with more than appearances; they knew we weren't the sort to do anything improper. Giovanni knew I would make an excellent farmer's wife, hard-working and tolerant of the long hours a farmer must work, especially at certain times of the year.

Our love for one another was true, but ours was also a practical arrangement. We knew that we would work well together, our families approved of the match and everything went according to plan. Giovanni proposed, I accepted and we were married in the little church at Montaltissimo. I moved into the farmhouse at Stazzana with him, where his parents and his two brothers still resided. His brother Francesco is the middle son, a friendly boy whom I get on well with. His youngest brother Matteo, however, is the troublemaker of the family. Spoilt by his mother, he always was a cheeky child who knew how to get his own way. The youngest son, free to run wild in the hills, without the responsibilities which shape a man. He was a good-looking child, I'll admit. Curly black hair, large eyes framed with long lashes, altogether too pretty for a boy. His smile when it came was wide and brilliant, and I saw the effect it had on women of all ages. He was a charmer, and I worried for his soul. I am not beautiful, and I thank God for that. In my experience it does not go hand in hand with godliness, for the body is weak. Vanity leads us astray, leads us to temptation. To ruination, to the hell we read about in Dante's *Inferno*. I tried to help Matteo upon my arrival in the house by setting a good example for him. I read my Bible aloud to the family every evening; I made sure we never missed a Mass.

Perhaps on his own, he might have listened to me. But he is rarely on his own; he is always with *her*. As children they shared a special bond, to the exclusion of the rest of us. They were wild children; they cared for little else save each other and running amok in the forest. It's a wonder neither of them were ever savaged by the beasts that live there. I myself never venture there alone for fear of the boar, the snakes, the wolves. They were always a thorn in my side, but for the most part I rose above their childish ways. I was a grown woman, married to a good man, with a household to help run. Soon there would be children of my own to care for, and I was too preoccupied with my own life to care too much what those two were up to.

The arrival of war, and the departure of my father-in-law, Francesco, and my dear Giovanni, changed everything. The life we had planned disappeared overnight, and I prayed constantly that Giovanni would be returned to me. The only male left was Matteo, who was too young to enlist initially. Responsibility was good for him: he started to become a man, managing all the farm work in the absence of his father and brothers. He spent much less time with Giuliana, which as far as I could see only had a positive effect on him. Matteo left to fight once he came of age, to the distress of his mother, and our workload increased again.

We coped fairly well, those first few years, our household of women. I had faith in Il Duce, our army and our brave soldiers. We worked hard, we shared our meals, we prayed for the safe return of our menfolk. But it felt like our prayers went unheeded, for our situation continued to worsen throughout the course of the war. We certainly never imagined, tucked away in the mountains, far from all the world, that we would end up being at the centre of the action. First came the armistice, and the King betraying our great leader with his surrender. The so-called fall of fascism, the ideology that had made us great once more. Slowly, some of our menfolk started to trickle home, tattered remnants of the men they once were. I waited and prayed for Giovanni; I hadn't had a letter from him in months by that point.

Then our mountains saw the arrival of the Germans, as they drew their line of defence across our mountains. *The Gothic Line*, they called it, recalling the dispelling of the Goths in ancient Roman times. We were a household of women on our own, vulnerable and weak, and we soon lost a cow to the hunger of the exhausted German soldiers. They based themselves in

Montaltissimo, and the villagers all fled their homes. Giuliana and her family came to live in the *metato* by the river, though to my relief we rarely saw her or her family. We were all busy just trying to survive by that point in the war. Food was scarce, and we knew the winter of 1944 to 1945 would be the hardest yet, living with the Germans stationed all around us. For them we had become the enemy, the traitors.

In 1944 my parents were killed by an Allied bomb, their house in Sassi blown up as they slept. I wept for my loss, but I was just one of many at the time. No-one came through the war unscathed; loss and grief became part of our everyday life. The only family member I had left was now my brother Luca, who had been conscripted to work for the Todt fortifications. He was young, just fifteen at the time, and I prayed he would keep his head down and work hard.

Fiorlindo came back into our lives at just the right time. We were losing hope, fearing the last of our supplies would be taken, scared that we would be rounded up ourselves. Raped, killed, deported to Germany. The Allies were dropping bombs every day, we trembled to hear the approaching engines and spent hours hidden in the *cijere*, the cellar under the house. They were dark days, any faith I had left was but a glimmer, a spark that was nearly extinguished. When Fiorlindo came to Stazzana to see his mother, Giulia, it gave us all something to believe in. Smart in his *alpino* uniform, fresh from his training in Germany, he had quickly proved himself to our German allies and been made a capitano. He always was a sharp child, quick to learn. He had grown into a man, strong and lean, and when he offered us his protection we all breathed a prayer of thanks. The Fascists were establishing themselves in the area, protecting the people who remained loyal to the cause, keeping relations with the Nazis good. We might yet have had a very different war, had it not been for the rise of the dreaded *partigiani*. The delinquents, the trouble-makers, the bringers of destruction.

Fiorlindo brought us bread, jam, *salame*. We ate well for the first time in years; the pleasure of eating something other than *castagne* was so sweet. As our friendship grew he would bring me treats, a piece of chocolate, a biscuit. I believe he admired me, and I blushed to hear his honeyed words. He never crossed the line of decency, for he knew I was a married woman and he assured me he would never put my honour at risk. It was clear he enjoyed the company of a good Christian woman after so many years of doing his duty and working hard, and I was thrilled to find a friend who was so brave. When he kissed my hand, his dark eyes gazing into mine, I admit my heart would flutter in my chest. When he asked me if I would be his ears and eyes in the valley, I was honoured. If I could help our country in some small way, I would do it willingly. In truth, I would have done anything for him.

The day he told me he suspected that Matteo had returned to the mountains and was involved with the partisans, I was horrified beyond belief. My own brother-in-law an outlaw? My disbelief quickly gave way to the realisation that it could be true. I recalled his weak nature, how easily he could be led astray as a child. If the rebels had got to him first he could indeed be hiding out in the mountains. Fiorlindo told me these partisans were mainly academics from the city, playing at freedom fighters. Stupid kids daring to poke the Nazi hive, unleashing their fury onto our innocent civilians. Communists, most of them, he told me, filling me with fear. Fiorlindo suspected that Matteo would sooner or later make contact with his mother at Stazzana, and that if he did I knew where my duty lay.

"I do," I told him, mesmerised by his dreamy eyes. "With you, Fiorlindo." He smiled, stroking my cheek, looking at me with such affection it quite turned my head. "And our country, of course," I added, blushing, unable to tear my gaze from his face. His visits became the highlight of my dull life, and I often sat in my room watching the track, hoping to spot him coming towards the house in his fine uniform.

I had grown used to shunning the gossip of the womenfolk in the evenings around the fire, preferring to read my Bible in peace. But mindful of the task Fiorlindo had set me I took to joining them, listening out for snippets of information that might be useful. Fiorlindo's mother and sisters were living there, as well as two other families who were *sfollati*, displaced by bombings and Nazi raids. There were few means of gaining information in those days, but through our trips up to the neighbouring farm to buy bread we occasionally learnt of developments. My suspicion about Matteo's return was accidentally confirmed by his mother, when one day I came upon her carrying some bread into the woods to the north of the house. I am an honest soul, deceit does not come naturally to me, but on this occasion I knew the means would justify the end. She looked wary, and I knew this was my chance to determine if Matteo were indeed back.

"Give him my love," I whispered, and her face broke into a smile of relief.

"Who told you?" she asked, glancing around to check no-one else was listening. "Was it Giuliana?" I nodded quickly, and put my finger to my lips, before turning my back and returning to the house, not trusting myself to conceal the shock of the revelation. For days I wrestled with this new-found knowledge, my duty to Fiorlindo conflicting with the fact that this wasn't any old traitor but Giovanni's brother, his flesh, my family. I loved Benedetta, had seen her lose her husband and one son, and I couldn't bear the thought of her losing another, no matter what his crimes were.

I was still trapped in my moral dilemma when Fiorlindo came to see me. It was March 1945, and it felt as though the war had rumbled on forever. I was a young woman in my prime when it began, but by 1945 I felt like an old lady. Thin, wan, exhausted by working and waiting. Giulia ushered him in to the sitting room, offering him the seat closest to the fire. I noticed his skin was tinged with grey, and dark shadows circled his eyes. He lacked his usual good cheer which we so looked forward to. He had bad news to share, I realised, and my heart went out to him. His head was bent low, and when he finally raised his head he sought me out and beckoned me to his side. I obeyed, trembling, and my first thought was of Giovanni. *He brings me news of his death*, I thought, but then I saw Benedetta standing anxiously by, and knew that she would have been the first to have been told. Fiorlindo took my hand and proceeded to tell me of a reprisal in Castelnuovo that had happened the previous evening. Following a landslide attributed to the partisans that had killed several senior German officers, one hundred civilians had been rounded up and taken to the cemetery. The local priests had intervened, begging for mercy, and eventually fifty people had been released. The remaining fifty had been shot there in the cemetery and left for the local people to bury where they could. Even before he told me who had been among the fifty victims, my heart was already screaming what I knew to be the truth. My brother Luca, my sweet fifteen-year-old brother. A boy with his whole life ahead of him. I uttered not a sound as Benedetta and the other women gathered around me, sobbing and sharing my grief.

Fiorlindo helped them escort me to my room and laid me gently down on the bed. I was silent, dry-eyed, vacant. But on the inside every cell of my body was distorting with pain, shrieking against the injustice of it. Yelling for my brother to come back to me, riling against fate, the Germans, the war, the man who shot the bullet that killed my brother. In the end my blame came to rest on the partisans who had forced the Germans to enact this punishment. They with their childish war games, their ignorant conviction that they could take on the might of the Reich, the erroneous belief that they were on the side of good. The cowards who rained destruction down on the Germans, only to retreat and hide in the woods. Leaving innocent citizens to pay the price in blood. How I hated them, how I prayed to God for their punishment.

When Fiorlindo came to knock on my door to say farewell, I knew what I must do. Matteo and his partisan friends had not thought of my family when they set off that landslide, and to my mind he was no longer family. I pushed thoughts of Benedetta and Giovanni from my mind, and saw only the lifeless body of my brother. I told him what I had learnt from Benedetta, that Matteo was indeed back in the mountains, and that he was based somewhere north of Stazzana. That way lay the villages of Sassi and Eglio, and above them Sant'Antonio sull'Alpe. He listened to me grimly, his jaw twitching with rage. A black cloud of hatred seemed to emanate from his being and I drew back in fear. He no longer resembled the charming friend I had entertained these last months, our knight in shining armour. He was someone I could not recognise, swollen with anger, coiled with latent violence. Even then I wished I could take back my words, afraid of what I had set in motion. He departed with barely a goodbye, leaving me cold and alone. I watched him march down the track, fuelled by something that I knew was more than duty. For some reason this was personal, and I shivered with premonition. In one day I had lost my brother and my friend, and I feared what lay ahead for all of us. I knew that this decision, born of grief and anger, would bear consequences that would change my life, but I had no idea how many other lives would be thrown off course.

26

Emma

2018

We flew back to Pisa in mid-January, rejuvenated from our holiday in Scotland. I felt my anticipation mounting as we headed north from the airport towards the mountains, the pull of Stazzana growing stronger by the mile. Again there was that feeling of emerging into a brighter, bolder world. The air was crisp and the sky overhead completely clear, a powdery blue. I noticed how clean the air felt in my lungs, how dry it was. The view across the mountains stretched much further in the chill winter air than under the hazy summer sun, and I marvelled at how far I could see. Little villages in the Apennines stood out in such detail I could practically see each sheet fluttering in the breeze on the villagers' balconies.

As we drove uphill from Gallicano we reached the snow line and the landscape was transformed from the dull brown of the woods to a kingdom of pure white. I was glad that Sam had put the winter tyres on in October, obligatory in mountainous areas from October to April. As we drove into Montaltissimo there was a sense of homecoming that I think we all shared. The girls pointed out their school, still festooned with fairy lights, and a couple of our neighbours out working on their land, bent over collecting bundles of firewood. They waved energetically and carried on their work; there is no retirement here in the mountains. It must be what keeps people so fit and living well into their nineties. Pietro and his wife were waiting at the house to welcome us back with kisses and greetings, and there was a selection of gifts for us on our kitchen table. Creamy milk from the cows down the road, potato bread from our next-door neighbour Marisa and two bottles of Pietro's best wine. There were chocolates for the girls and a bag of oranges from the South of Italy that another neighbour had dropped by. The stove was already lit and we were grateful for that since the temperature was well below zero. The fire crackled away merrily, welcoming us back home, and we warmed our hands and set the little kettle on it for tea.

We settled back into the cottage and the girls enjoyed playing with their new Christmas toys by the fire, while Sam and I unpacked and put together some dinner. Already I could feel the tug of Stazzana; it was hard being so close and yet not able to see her, but we were all weary from our travels and decided to stay put that evening and head down there in the morning. Sam was already wondering if the storms had brought down any more trees, and whether the cold and snow had done any further damage to the house. When we talk about the house Sam and I make an effort to stay detached, to convince ourselves that our concerns are practical. But I know that Stazzana already means much more to us than that. It's that kind of a place, one that touches your heart and calls to your soul. A place where the old magic still reigns, where anything can happen.

The next morning dawns bright, the brilliance of the low sun on the snow blinding us as we emerge onto the balcony to marvel at the view. After a breakfast of milky coffee and toast with home-made fig jam we are ready to explore. We wrap the girls in bright woollen hats and scarves, and all head off hand in hand down to Stazzana. The girls chatter away like songbirds, pointing out familiar features of the landscape that now look completely different in their winter attire. We crunch through the snow in our boots and the girls stamp joyfully on frozen puddles, giggling as cracks squeak and spread across the surface. They clutch on to Sam as they slip and pretend to ice skate across the surfaces of the larger ones, and their laughter floats across the fields, breaking the silence of the snowy morning.

I can feel the spell of Stazzana as we descend the valley following the stream, and a hush falls upon us as we enter what the girls call 'the forever winter' part of the land. The valley bottom, where the track crosses the river, remains in shadow all day during the cold months. The frost never thaws, and there are icicles all along the stretch of rock where the freezing water cascades over it. We jump between stepping stones, holding on to the girls' hands as we do so. We look up and there is Stazzana, waiting for us. The sun's weak winter rays have just reached her, and she sits basking in the light, her stones glowing warmly. A smile comes unbidden to my lips and an absurd urge to wave, to greet her. I feel her welcome reach out to us, enveloping us. The thought comes to me that this house has the power to bring the past to the present, to stretch across centuries to connect families, friends, loved ones. I find myself picturing my grandfather and his brothers as children sledging down this hill, their high-pitched shrieks piercing the silence of the valley. I see smoke rising from the chimney stack, a sign of life within. Inside three red-cheeked boys warm their hands by the fire in the main room as they venture in, sitting down to a plate of steaming pasta *fatta a casa* by their mother. I sense that all of this still exists within the walls of Stazzana, caught in the very fabric of the building. Laughter in her old chestnut beams echoing through time, love engrained in the stones that hold her up.

Screams of delight end my reverie, piercing my link to the past, and I realise that Sam and the girls are ahead of me, further along the track. I catch up with them, treading carefully around the icy puddles, and find them all bent over examining the ground. Aria grabs my hand and points eagerly at some tracks, clearly visible in the snow.

"Look, Mama! Paw prints!" I see them now, large paw prints, about the size of my own hand.

"Wow!" I enthuse. "That's a big dog, darling!"

She shakes her head, frustrated, and I see Luna looking at me, waiting for the light to dawn. "Tell her, Daddy!" Aria begs, turning to Sam, and he smiles over at me, his excitement as great as theirs.

"I don't think that's a dog, Emma. It's a long way for a local dog to roam, and it's much bigger than most of the hunting dogs. The pad is wider, and see how the claws dig into the snow, making more of a mark than a dog's would? I really think we're looking at wolf tracks!"

"Yes, Mama!" Aria bursts in. "And look, there's more than one!" The girls whizz around us in the snow, finding more tracks, and I gaze in amazement. A real wolf pack, making its way across Stazzana! I picture them out there, wild-eyed, travelling across the vast swathes of chestnut woods. Hunting wild boar and deer, raising their pups, howling at the moon. I wonder when it was they crossed and find myself scanning the woods, but I know they would be long gone with our noisy arrival.

We start to follow the tracks across the lower field where they head down to the river, following the path that leads to the chestnut house. I wonder if Luciano ever saw a wolf the winter he lived there. I know local people are very anti-wolf, since they occasionally take a sheep or a goat, and we decide not to tell anyone about our discovery. The tracks across the field are linear, another reason to think they are wolves, not dogs. Dogs tend to zig-zag, following scents and going where they please, whereas wolves head straight for where they are going, in this case probably the cover of the woods. Under the bare chestnut and oak trees the snow is patchier, and it becomes harder to follow the tracks. By now we think we are following a large male and two smaller wolves, perhaps females. We find some hair caught on a section of old fencing, grey and soft, with a pungent, musty scent. Luna tucks it in her pocket, keeping it safe. Just past the chestnut house the tracks head directly up the steep hillside, and we cannot follow.

Happy with our discovery and blessing the snow which revealed the wolves' presence to us, we head home. As we approach Luciano and Maria's farm Luna tugs my hand and looks towards the farmhouse, where the grey whirl of smoke in the sky tells us someone is home.

"Shall we go and say ciao?" I ask her, and she nods and leads the way. Maria is thrilled to see us, and with loud exclamations of joy she ushers us to the fire, asking how our holidays were and welcoming us back. She has baked a batch of biscotti and puts a new pot of coffee on the stove to brew. We help the girls to strip off their layers of warm clothing, and we put our boots and gloves to dry by the fire. She calls out to Luciano, who is down in the cantina making cheese, and within minutes he is with us. He lights up when he sees us, the lines around his eyes deepening in delight. With relief I notice his spirits have returned; the depression of last year's end seems to have dissipated. He grips Sam's hand and shakes it vigorously, telling him they have much work to do pruning the vines and trees before spring. He drops to the ground on his knees, at eye level with the girls, and soon they are telling him all about the wolves, jumping up and down like little jumping beans. They know we didn't mean Luciano when we agreed not to tell anyone. He produces a chunk of cheese from each pocket and they take it, grinning, pleased their playmate is back. Finally his eyes meet mine, and they are full of emotion.

"Emma," he murmurs, and embraces me with a kiss on each cheek. "It was my greatest fear you would not return." While Maria fusses about the children and Sam, Luciano leads me to the kitchen where another fire burns, a cooking pot hanging over it. We sit down at the kitchen table, the aroma of bubbling stew and woodsmoke filling the air, invoking a sense of nostalgia in me, though I am not sure for what.

"How was your Christmas?" I ask, politely, and we both laugh at my British small talk. I know it will have passed as years gone by have done, with good food and some wine, and the usual farming tasks to be done. I fish about in my pocket and pull out an envelope with one of the postcards from 'G' that I found at my parents' house. I show it to Luciano, and he puts on his reading glasses and reads it, his brow creasing in concentration. He nods and puts it gently back on the table.

"Who is G?" I ask, leaning forwards, sensing I am finally about to find out.

"I did not know she kept in touch with your grandparents," he says simply, his expression distant. Lost in his thoughts, or perhaps memories. "G is Giuliana, my sister." My mind reels at this revelation, and I try to take it in. Luciano's older sister, who lived at the chestnut house with him that last year of the war. The one who left shortly afterwards, never to return. Just like my grandparents. What is the thread that connects them? Luciano is now pulling a letter of his own from his pocket, and he tells me, "I have a letter for you. From Giuliana." It's one thing to seek answers about the past, to research from a safe distance. But without warning the past has stretched its dusty hands out to grasp me in the present, and I am dumbfounded.

"For me?" I ask, stupidly, and Luciano nods and takes my hand in his own.

"Please read it, Emma. I will stay with you while you do, if you wish?" I do, and I take the envelope and pull out the letter, written in the same sloping black handwriting I recognise immediately from the postcards to my grandparents. At the top there is the same address in New York, and the date is mid-December.

Dear Emma,

There is so much to say and I fear I have little time left to say it. I know I am asking a great deal of you, but I beg you to find a way to visit me here in America soon. I enclose open tickets for yourself and Luciano, and I pray you will come and see me before it is too late. There is much I need to tell you, Emma. I have felt the urgency building for some time, but it was not until I received a letter from Luciano with news of your dear parents' deaths that I knew what I needed to do. It is my last wish to see you, and I hope that telling you the truth will help you and your family.

With love and kind regards,

Giuliana

I read and re-read the letter, and when I have finished I look up at Luciano. He is anxiously twisting a button on his jacket, a muscle in his jaw twitching. I realise what a huge thing this is to ask him to do, to fly halfway across the world at eighty-six when in your whole life you have never ventured out of Tuscany.

"Would you go?" I ask him softly, and I know he has been asking himself this question ever since his own letter arrived. Fear and doubt still flicker in his eyes, but he is brave, and I see something is driving him, some reason of his own.

"*Sì,*" he replies. "And you? Will you come?" I think of Sam and the girls, but I already know what my husband will say, that he will urge me to take this chance. Even if it should prove to be a wild goose chase to visit a crazy old lady. I worry briefly about Luciano, and whether he will be up to the long journey, but I know he will be furious if I voice this concern. It occurs to me that Luciano cannot have a passport; how will he possibly be able to fly in time? He reads my thoughts and grins, his face full of pride as he pulls a shiny new passport from his pocket.

"Elena helped me," he tells me. "She's been wonderful." He glances to the door and furtively pushes it back in his pocket. "I haven't told Maria yet," he whispers. "I didn't want to risk the fire before I knew whether you would come." I can only imagine what her reaction will be and how much trouble Luciano will be in when he reveals his furtive preparations. He's watching me nervously now, and I see how much this trip means to him. The same resolve that brought me to Italy, the same desire to solve the mystery surrounding Stazzana urges me on, and I know what my answer will be.

"Yes." I nod, smiling at him. Joy spreads across his face and he clutches my other hand, pulling me to my feet, doing an impromptu dance across the kitchen floor.

That was the day I decided to fly to New York with an eighty-six-year-old man from a tiny Tuscan village, who had never even seen a plane up close let alone been on one, to visit a ninety-year-old lady who he hadn't seen in over seven decades. We liaise with Giuliana's nurse about our dates and accommodation, and gather from our communications that Giuliana is seriously ill and close to the end. I am terrified we will not make it in time, but somehow Luciano and I manage to arrange everything for the following week. Maria's protests can be heard from the piazza, and I know Luciano will need all of his courage to go ahead with this mad plan. But he has me to look after him, and I find myself being incredibly grateful that I have him too. He's more than a friend, I realise, or a neighbour. I feel like he is family. I have no idea what awaits us in America, and I will miss the girls and Sam terribly, but I have a sense of expectancy and a wild hope that something wonderful might happen.

27

Luciano

2017

I've led a small life, a simple life. I never felt the call to travel, to explore the world. Never even cared to venture as far as Lucca really. I was lured away on occasion, to the coast for my son's wedding, to Florence once for an art exhibition my daughter was involved with. I dressed up, admired the fine buildings, but I was always relieved to return home to the mountains.

"Don't you ever want to get out?" my daughter used to ask me, as she grew frustrated with our valley, the time it took to get 'anywhere good'.

"Where would I go?" I'd reply, shrugging my shoulders. "Everything I want is right here on this mountain." She'd smile indulgently, but she didn't understand. She left, of course, as soon as she was able to. As all the young have left. I wasn't being completely honest, anyway. I didn't have everything I wanted: there was a hole where my sister should have been. Along with the husband and children that should have been. A day never passed without me thinking about her, wondering where she was and what she was doing. Whether she was happy. And these thoughts always brought on the prickling of guilt, the sinking feeling in my stomach as I remembered why it was she had left.

When her letter arrives I take it out to the barn, wanting to read it in peace, away from Maria and the thousands of questions that she will bombard me with. My hands shake, and I pull the letter from the envelope, where there is also a letter addressed to Emma. Her writing is looser, harder to read than it used to be, but immediately recognisable. She gets straight to the point, as she always did. There is no reproach for the time I waited before contacting her, just an invitation to go and see her as soon as we can. She is ill; she fears she does not have long to live, and the journey to Italy would be impossible for her. The urgency in her letter tells me she also believes the time has come for Emma to know the truth. I sit with the letter in my hand, my heart beating as fast as the engine of my old tractor. *Come to New York*, she says. *As soon as you can.* I've never even left Tuscany, and the thought of getting to America is impossible. It's another world, another language, and I cannot see a way forward – where would I even start? Maria will be no help; I know she will oppose the idea with all her might. I can hear her voice already: "*An old fool like you, flying to New York!*" It's a week until Christmas and Emma will not be back until the New Year, so I cannot ask her. My daughter Elena springs to mind, my intelligent, resourceful daughter. She lives in Florence where she works for an art gallery, and she often travels for work. I wait until Maria has gone to do the shopping the following day, and then I call Elena on the mobile number I find written in Maria's telephone book.

"*Papa? Che c'è?*" she asks in alarm, assuming something must be terribly wrong. *How sad*, I reflect. *Have I really never called her just to talk?*

"Everything's fine," I tell her, uncomfortable on the telephone. I mistrust it, this disconnected voice. I like to look a person in the eyes when I talk to them. But needs must, and I must overcome my discomfort. "I need your help, Elena," I tell her. "Can we meet somewhere, please?" I'm still not ready to tell Maria my plan, afraid she will convince me I can't do it. She's probably right, but I know I need to try. For Emma's sake, and for my own. The thought of seeing Giuliana again after all these years is both terrifying and wonderful.

"It's a week 'til Christmas, Papa," she protests, "what's the hurry? I've got a to-do list as long as my arm!"

"Please, Elena, it's important," I reply, and she pauses, intrigued I imagine by my out-of-character request.

"*Va bene*," she acquiesces. "I'll meet you at Gallicano in the bar on Saturday." I'm out of my comfort zone already, just driving down to Gallicano to meet my daughter. How could I possibly fly all the way to New York? Perhaps ten years ago it would have been possible, but I'm too old now, too weary. *What have you got to lose?* the voice sneers, and it gives me the kick I need to carry on. I see Elena straight away at the bar, her glossy hair tied back, her fancy outfit marking her a city girl. She's in her fifties now, a curator at a gallery in Florence and mother to two teenage boys. She embraces me with the customary two kisses, and we take a seat at a small table. She has already ordered two coffees and tells me she only has an hour. It's a three-hour round trip to Florence, and I'll have taken up most of her day. Unsure of how to start, I show her the letter from Giuliana. She's fascinated, of course, and full of questions about this sister I've never mentioned until now. I tell her a little of what I know about her life since she left the mountains, her work as a nurse, her travels to Africa and Asia, her apartment in New York.

"She sounds amazing, Papa!" Elena exclaims. "Why have we never met her? Did you not get on as children?" I sigh, for there are so many questions, and the answers are so complicated.

"I loved my sister more than life itself, *cara*. When she left I was so sad I could never bring myself to talk about her. I always got on well with your *Zia* Margherita and *Zia* Rosa, but Giuliana was my best friend, the light in my life. I have missed her every day since she left. I should not have left it this late, but now I need to see her while I still can. Will you help me?" She is looking at me differently already, seeing a side of me she never imagined existed. I can already imagine the phone call she will make later to her brother, their debate about whether Papa is finally going crazy, getting a passport and flying to America at his age. She smiles at me, and for a second I see the child she was, full of wonder and joy. Before she joined the adult world and forgot about us.

"*Certo, Papa,*" she replies. "I'll start the paperwork for your passport application today. We can get some photos taken now. I don't know how long it will take, especially with Christmas coming up." Her expression becomes curious and she asks, "When are you going to tell Mama?" I shrug sheepishly and tell her I will wait until Emma returns, to see if she agrees to go to New York. I can see Elena wants to know much more, why my sister wants to see Emma, this foreigner whom I have been spending so much time with, and why I must go with her, but for the moment she needs to get back to Florence. Over the next few weeks she helps me with my secret mission, even going as far as taking me shopping to Castelnuovo, declaring that my old farmer's clothes will not do for New York. The time we spend together is special, and having common ground to meet on we find a way to communicate, to laugh together, to tentatively build what feels like a real relationship. At the farm I always let Maria take centre stage when they visit, fussing and feeding them. I usually absent myself, awkward amidst their happy chatter. But on neutral ground I find that despite our differences Elena and I get on well. We find to our surprise that we both share a dry sense of humour, a sceptical outlook on life. She provides me with not only a passport but a new wallet replete with my first-ever credit card and instructions how to use it. I have a new suit hidden away in my wardrobe, and she manages to put my passport through as an urgent matter and it arrives in the second week of January, the day before Emma, Sam and the children return from Scotland.

The excitement that has surrounded my preparations turns to fear as I wait for Emma's return, terrified that perhaps they will have decided to stay in Scotland. When I see them walking up to the farmhouse I send up a prayer of thanks, the words rusty on my tongue through neglect. Emma shows me the postcards that Giuliana sent to her grandparents every year, and I hand her the letter from my sister. I can see she is confused, but finally here is the chance to get those answers she has been seeking ever since she arrived.

The following weeks fly by in a blur as Emma books our flights and liaises with Ada, Giuliana's nurse. By the end of January we are ready to fly, and Maria is declaring to everyone she is ready to divorce me, that the old fool has finally lost his marbles. I try to explain to her why I need to go, but it is hard. It takes every ounce of my resolve not to back out and stay put on the farm. But this is my last chance to tell the truth, and God knows I have waited long enough.

The journey to America was tiring, and had I not had Emma by my side I don't know how I would have managed. I will never forget the feeling of power beneath us, the sheer improbability of it all, when the plane roared along the runway and suddenly lifted up into the sky. How we soared through the clouds, how I clutched Emma's hand for dear life and gazed amazed through the little window. I saw our mountains from the vantage point of the eagle, higher even, and it quite took my breath away. This was the world from the viewpoint of the angels, up in the clouds.

We landed safely in New York, somehow, and took a cab to our lodgings, a hotel not too far from where Giuliana's apartment is. I think New York must be about as different to Montaltissimo as it is possible to be, not that I have seen many places in the world. Instead of mountains rising around you there are huge grey tower blocks, and instead of twisty lanes there are enormous freeways. The air is thick with grime and fumes, and my lungs already long for the clean mountain air. There are people everywhere here, far too many to recognise and greet, and this has led to a strange indifference between even neighbours that strikes me as odd. What a place for my sister to end up, worlds away from her roots. I try to block out the strange words all around me, the unfamiliar sights, sounds, sensations. There is almost nothing I recognise here, not even the earth beneath my feet.

Emma is my guide, my friend, my saviour. She takes us effortlessly from airport to hotel, out to dinner and back to our rooms, in a way that makes it easier for me. I take it step by step and find to my surprise that I am doing it, surviving this strange new world. I even manage to enjoy some parts of it. I find some of the courage that brought my sister to this place, and as I think of seeing her the next day I feel as excited as a young man. I'm reminded of the boy I was, running wild in the mountains with his sister, feeling the confidence she always gave me. She has brought me a long way, and though I fear the confession I must make, for the moment the joy she inspires is stronger.

28

Giuliana

2018

I look around my apartment and find I barely recognise it these days. There are tokens of places I have lived, people I have known, but even these seem to be fading away now that I have allowed the past back into my life. I thought I did a good job of moving on, never looking back, over the years. I was so busy for decades, a hurricane of action, never daring to pause.

Only once did someone see past the mask. I was in in South Africa, working with orphans. Long days filled with colour and heartache, trying to bring some hope to these beautiful, fragile children. I remember the red dust of the earth, the acrid smoke that filled the streets, the starchy taste of plantain eaten at the side of the road. I was on my way back from the orphanage one night, back to the little hut I shared with a local family, when I noticed a tent set up by the wayside that was not usually there. I was drawn in by the mysterious glow that emanated from its doorway and a voice singing a hypnotic melody. A Nguni tribal woman, strung with coloured beads and shells, was sat on a stool, apparently expecting me. She wore bright cloth around her head and draped across her body, and she was smiling at me, as though we had met before. Her eyes were kind and slightly irreverent, and she cocked her head at me questioningly. I noticed she was unmarried, lacking the traditional *isigolwani* neck-hoop made with grass and beads. So, another free spirit. Unusual in this society, perhaps in every society. I sat down in front of her, and she held my hands. I hadn't been looking for guidance; I was always of the opinion that we make our own destiny. That was how I had lived since I'd left my home, my country. Yet there I was, in a tent with a wise woman, a fortune teller. She greeted me in fluent English, with a cheerful African accent. Her expression grew serious, and she shook her head slightly.

"You been running a long time, lady. Running from the end that was also a beginning. Running from your blood." She closed her eyes and started to hum, a low rumbling that resonated throughout the tent and through my being. Images started to mass behind my eyes, sparks of light dancing in the darkness. Faces I had blocked out, images of what might have been. The pain of remembering started to stab at my insides, the visions gathering force, coming for me. With a supreme effort I wrenched myself free of the trance I was falling into, snatched my hands from the wise woman and staggered out of the tent. Had I been looking for that? To seek some kind of resolution, to start some sort of healing process? Everything could yet have been very different, but that night I chose to run. Away from the possibility of sharing my grief with this wise woman in the depths of Africa. Away from letting her hold me in that safe space, while I faced the darkness I had left behind. After that I strengthened my guard, determined to never let anyone slip past again.

I never stayed longer than two years in a country, always moving on when my attachments grew too strong. When a man started to talk about love, a future together, that was my cue to leave. When a child started to rely on me, when my own heart started to melt when I looked into their eyes. I had my rules, and my rules were my life. I thought I was brave, sticking to my plan. I realise now it was all cowardice, a lifetime of running away from anything that mattered in life. This brilliant gift that is life, full of its colours and joys. This gift that was denied to so many, that I wasted so resolutely.

God must be merciful, for this old woman has been given one last chance. One opportunity to tell the truth, to ask for forgiveness. Every day the past strengthens its grip on me, and the present becomes a little less real. I can hear the voices calling me, asking me to join them. It would be so easy to let go of this body. It takes all of my resolve to stay anchored here, but stay I must.

My nurse Ada has been liaising with Luciano and Emma, and I gather she has tactfully told them about my situation, for they arrange their travels most promptly. The day of their arrival I find I am as nervous as a young girl waiting for a date, and I laugh at myself. Ada helps me get ready, and she kindly pulls a comb through my snow-white hair and pats some powder onto my fissured old face. Years in the African sun and ninety years on the Earth have turned my face into a map of the world; I marvel at its complexity. I try to remember myself as Luciano would have last seen me; will he find some trace of that girl in this worn-out shell?

When he arrives I realise I have still been thinking of him as a gangly youth, but into the room walks an old man. Thick grey hair brushed back, his face a map to mirror mine. Skin brushed bronze from toil under the Italian sun, smartly dressed for his travels in a new suit. His gait is sprightly for an old man, and I imagine he still works the land. He has become a man, a father and a grandfather, and I have missed it all. And yet when I look beneath the surface, beyond the changes, I see the same sweet boy. The same nervous expression, waiting for me to take the lead. *Mio fratellino.* My little brother. We embrace, and I feel tears filling my eyes as the years slip away and we are children again, back in Montaltissimo. We pull back and stare a moment longer, both surprised to discover we have grown old.

"*Ma sei un vecchietto!*" I tell him. "You're an old man now!" and the laughter bursts forth from him, dispersing the tension.

"*E te, Giuliana?*" he retorts, still laughing heartily. "*Non sei un giovincello!*" "You're no spring chicken yourself!" I take his arm, and already I feel a warmth that I haven't felt since I was a girl; I am in the presence of my kin once more. My Italian is rusty, I haven't spoken it for years, and there is much of the local dialect Luciano speaks that I have forgotten. I turn my attention to the young lady who has been chatting with Ada, and who is now approaching me. At a distance I would think her Scandinavian, perhaps Dutch, with her fair hair and translucent skin. Tall and slim, she has a beauty that expresses itself through her every move, how she walks, moves her hands, glances over at us. I note how she checks on Luciano, and, satisfied he seems well, focusses her attention on me. She is close now, and as her eyes meet mine I feel my heart pause in my aged chest. Deep pools of forest green, alive with light. She bends down to kiss me, a kiss dropped on papery skin, and I am speechless. For a minute I take her in, this young woman I have thought about so often over the years. The baby, the little girl, the young woman she has become. She is smiling at me, polite, interested. I wonder how she will see me once she knows the whole story. Once she knows all that I have done. I see the pain behind her smile still and remember the trauma she suffered last year. It haunts me still, the thought of that accident. And worse, the fact that I was not told, that I gave up the right to share in the grieving, to attend the funeral. I must focus: I will need all my energy to tell this story. There has been enough loss; now I must see if a story can save us.

With an effort I pull myself together to smile at my guests, and offer tea and cake. I compliment Emma on her beautiful family and ask Luciano for news of his own. How Maria is, how his children and grandchildren are. Once we have finished both our tea and our small talk I know I must begin or I will not be up to the task ahead.

"I must thank you for coming, Emma and Luciano. It's a long way to travel, and I'm sure it must have been hard to leave the children. I wish to tell you my story, and much of it has been shrouded in darkness and lies for over seventy years. I had thought to die with these secrets, but I believe the time has now come. I hope that the truth may help you, dear Emma, with your own journey." Over the next hour I recount my story, as I remember it, from childhood through to the outbreak of war, and the difficult years that followed. I speak partly in Italian, for Luciano, and partly in English, when Emma seems to be struggling. Luciano nods, smiles and weeps at various points, but he never interrupts, and Emma listens attentively the whole time. I speak of my love for Matteo, how he left for war and how we lost our home when the village was invaded in 1944. I describe the cold, the hunger, the roar of falling bombs. The constant stream of bad news that dripped into our lives through neighbours and acquaintances. Cousins that were bombed while they slept, sons sent to Germany, friends rounded up and shot as part of the *rappresaglie*, the reprisals. I recount my joy at Matteo's return to the mountains, and how our love affair grew stronger with each passing month. How I became involved with the partisans, became a *staffetta* crossing the front line on several occasions. I tell them of my friendship with Benjamin from the Buffalo division, of his kindness to me, of how we would play cards and talk about America once I had learnt enough English from Don Franco to be able to converse. How he opened my mind to the realities of race, politics and prejudice, how for the first time in my life I imagined far-away countries, different cultures and languages. I spoke of the freedom I felt for the first time in my life, having meaningful work to do away from the domestic chores of the household. How I began to dream of a future where I could work, earn an income, be more than just a wife and a mother. I knew it would be hard for Emma to imagine how radical that was at the time. It was another world. But a rapidly changing world, and the change was brought by these outsiders who came to our valley.

"We were so close to having it all," I tell them, my voice weakening as my spirit ebbs. "A brave new world. Victory. And it came, in a way. The Allies won, and the partisans were immortalised. The brave martyrs of the resistance. But by then it was too late for me. The dream had died."

Ada steps in, her brows knitted with concern. "Time for a break," she declares, and Emma and Luciano acquiesce quietly and head off to the kitchen. Ada fusses around me, taking my blood pressure, and I realise how drained I am. She brings me my pills and some tea, and I doze for half an hour, regaining some strength. She suggests our guests return the following day, but I don't want to take any chances. I am acutely aware of time slipping through my fingers, the last few silken grains.

"Just a rest," I tell her. "I'll be fine."

The light is fading on the New York streets, this place that has become home to me over the years. Ada turns on the lamps, and my audience returns. They both look tired, and I can see the journey both to New York and to our shared past has taken its toll on Luciano. I let my mind drift back to the early spring of 1945 and continue my story. The fear of reliving those last months looms large ahead of me, but it is time to face it. I take a deep breath and enter the battlefield.

"For months we waged our secret war with the Germans and the fascists, hiding in the woods we knew so well. Our childhood playground. Despite the hardships and the danger we knew we were winning, partly by the vast numbers of Fascist soldiers defecting. Young boys most of them, far from their families, caught up on the wrong side of a war they didn't believe in."

Memories of one particular Fascist come flashing back to me, and waves of hatred take me by surprise. I had told Emma and Luciano of my escape from the Germans at the hands of Fiorlindo, but no more. I hadn't told them how he continued to visit me at the chestnut house, how I saw his suspicion and frustration growing with each visit.

"The war, for me, ended one night in March 1945, only a month before peace was declared and the bells rang throughout the mountains. One of our safe houses was discovered, and Matteo and many of our *banda* were killed. Shot in cold blood." I hear my voice falter and push myself to continue. "With Matteo gone, I lost myself. I had no reason to live, nothing. Just pain and darkness, loss. Loss of my love, my friend. Loss of our future together, of any happiness in the future. He was so young, so full of life. In one night, it was all taken from us. I gave up my work with the OSS – none of it meant anything anymore. Victory and peace came to the mountains, and we left the chestnut house and returned to what was left of our home in Montaltissimo. It all passed me by. Many times I wished I had been killed that night, but it was not meant to be. It was not long after the end of the war that I realised I did have a reason to continue living, that I was carrying Matteo's baby. Through all the destruction something wonderful had been created. I was only sixteen, but I had lived through a war and lost the love of my life. I knew this baby was important, that he or she would be the way Matteo could live on, for him to be carried forward into a brighter future. I know these days it's acceptable to be a single mother, an unmarried mother. I regret to say in Italy in those days, indeed in most of the world, it was not. I was not a married woman, and the father was dead. I was barely a woman at all, only sixteen. My mother and Benedetta hatched the plan for Matteo's brother Giovanni and his wife to take the baby, and they in turn decided they would emigrate to Scotland, to make a new life. There would have been rumours, speculation, however careful we had all been, and they wanted a fresh start. Like many young people who left, having somehow survived the war. For me, once the baby was taken from me, there was nothing left to live for. The mountains were a daily reminder of Matteo and all we had lost, and their beauty turned to torment for me. For years I ran, seeking to forget my sorrows, to drown myself in other faces, sensations, languages, adventures. I kept in touch, once a year, with Giovanni and Assunta, and heard how baby Giovanna was getting on. That was my only contact with the past, the only luxury I permitted myself. Any more and I felt I would unravel, lose the person I had built up from the ashes."

I pause, trying to find the words to express myself properly. "I want you to know, Emma, that I never regretted having your mother. In fact, it was the only thing in my life I was proud of. It might sound strange, but I never regretted giving her to your grandparents either. I always knew they would make wonderful parents, and they did. They were a stable, loving family, and I was a sixteen-year-old mess. Too wild and impulsive to be a good mother. Too unsure of my place in the world. Too unaccepting of the place I would have been given in the world, which for my child's sake I could not have resisted. No, it was all for the best, and though you have not known it, the thought of you has given me great joy ever since I first saw your photo in 1982. I only wish I could have known you better, have known your mother, that I could meet your little girls."

I break down now, to my shame, exhaustion and emotion washing away all my defences. I weep, tears flowing down the riverbeds of my face. Suddenly I am not alone: Emma's arms are around me, and her own body is racked with sobs. We cry together, and for the first time in years I know the comfort of a friend. When we finally pull apart I look at Emma's tear-stained face and ask her the question that haunts me. "Can you forgive me?"

Her eyes are lighter now, washed clean with tears, a spring green. I see myself, and I fancy I see a little of Matteo in the curve of her mouth.

"Yes," she says, taking my old hands in hers and squeezing them gently. "There is nothing to forgive. My mother would have said the same. She had a great life, a loving childhood, she was happy. I only wish you could have known her." She leans in to me again, I hold her as she cries and we both think of Giovanna. My child, who should still be here in this world, who should never have died before me. My beautiful dark-haired baby, who never cried in my arms but gazed into my eyes, whom I have missed every single day since the day I lost her. My daughter, taken before her time, who will miss out on seeing her grandchildren grow, all those precious moments of childhood. As we weep the air around us grows a little lighter, the voice in my head retreats into the distance and disappears into silence. I have waited a long time, but I find I am somehow being a grandmother, holding my granddaughter in my arms.

29

Luciano

2018

When we greet, after so many years, it's hard to hide the shock at how time has changed us. Having not seen the interim years, the onset of wrinkles, the first grey hair, it's hard to reconcile the crumpled old bodies with the memory of the bold young ones. Giuliana was such a beauty, with her shining black locks, her flashing green eyes. Unusual, in our part of the world, green eyes. *Witches' eyes*, her opponents would mutter, when she bested them at some sport, or some test at school. Her eyes are what let me know it's still her. They have lightened with time, and the lashes that frame them are now white, but they still have the same spirit, the same life force. We laugh at ourselves, at how time has changed us, and I feel the same dynamic, the same joy at being with her. *Mia sorella*. I listen to her story, and I am amazed at what she achieved during the war. I had no idea what she was doing, that she crossed the front line so many times. That she had been captured by the Germans and rescued by Fiorlindo. His name sours the air around us when it is mentioned, and I shiver involuntarily.

It takes all of Giuliana's strength to tell her story, and Emma and I listen as the words fall around us. She paints pictures of that time that are familiar to me but different, from another perspective. It strikes me how relative life is, how many different stories are out there in the world. My heart is heavy as I listen; I know the time is drawing closer when I must make my own confession, tell my own terrible tale. I dread the possibility that having just found my sister again I will lose her, this time forever. How will she look at me when she knows the enemy lay much closer to hand than she ever imagined? And Emma, my friend, my family, how will she see me? When she knows that all this time I have been telling her half-truths, lying to her.

When Giuliana finishes her story we are all in tears, and I watch them embrace as grandmother and granddaughter. What was lost is now found, and Emma is no longer without family in this world. I too am elevated to the role of family, to that of the great-uncle. I have known all along, of course. I knew the instant I saw her green eyes that day in the field. How I longed to tell Emma the truth of her heritage, but it was not my secret to tell. At this point they imagine the truth is now out, set free. Giuliana believes she was the only one to carry a secret all these years, to live a double life. To nearly drown in the ocean of nothingness between the two worlds that she inhabited. She does not suspect that her *fratellino* would be capable of having such a deadly secret.

Giuliana is exhausted after her efforts, and under orders from Nurse Ada Emma and I retreat back to our hotel, where we have a quiet dinner and go to bed early. Each lost in our thoughts, hearing her story playing itself over and over in our minds. The next day we return to find Giuliana tired and a little pale after the exertions of the previous day, but otherwise refreshed. She greets us with pleasure and she seems lighter, younger. She stands strong in her truth, and I find that I envy her. I think of her actions during the war as a *staffetta*, the close calls she had, and I try to find some of that courage for myself. Emma has already noticed my gloom this morning, I can see the worry on her face. Giuliana also senses the tension in me, the strain. Ada fusses kindly about us, bringing us fresh coffee and donuts. Once we are settled and she is satisfied Giuliana is well, she heads off out to the shops.

"*Che c'è Luci?*" Giuliana gets straight to the point, as blunt as she always was. "Are you not well? Are you homesick for the mountains?" I shake my head, and take a deep, ragged breath.

"Yesterday you told your story, Giuliana, and today I must tell mine. I too have a secret I have kept too long." I falter, wishing I had thought more about what to say, how to say it. I haven't the way with words my sister has, and my head is murky, muddled with fear. "You had a reason for staying quiet: you made a deal. It was the right choice, and you were strong. I'm ashamed to say I have no such excuse. I should have told you the night it happened, but I was scared. I've lived my whole life being afraid, hiding in the shadows." I catch Emma's eyes, and I lower mine in shame. "I must tell you both, though my greatest fear is that I will lose you. You will despise me." Emma starts to protest, but I stop her. "Hear me out first," I beg, "and then you can decide.

"It was March 1945, only a month from the end of the war. The night you described yesterday, sister, the terrible night that Matteo was killed. I was thirteen by then, and the whole war had passed me by. I was of no use to anyone, and so many men had already sacrificed themselves for our country. My father, my cousins, my friends. Even you, Giu, you were busy with your partisan friends. I didn't know what you were doing, despite how often I begged you to tell me. I realise now that you were protecting me, keeping me safe, but I wasn't grateful at the time. I missed you being with us at home – you were my hero, my role model. Our mother and sisters treated me like a baby, keeping me in the dark, keeping me out of the way all the time. I wasn't even allowed to go fetch the bread in case I was taken as part of a *rastrellamento*, a round-up operation. By the end of the war I was bored out of my mind, desperate for some action, some *life*. I'm not trying to make excuses, only to explain why I did what I did.

"That night I knew you were going back up the mountain to meet your friends. I'd seen the look in your eye, the excitement, the anticipation. I'd watched you sharpen your knife and wrap yourself up warm in those men's clothes you always wore, expecting a long night out in the cold. You slipped out into the dark of the woods as you had so many times previously, but this time I decided to follow you. There was a storm brewing that night; low clouds were already threatening more snow overhead. The wind was rising and my heart raced with fear as I followed you up the hillside, taking care to stay out of sight. I was downwind, and I think that also helped me to stay out of earshot. The direction you took led me to realise you were heading to the Lost Barn, a hay barn we had been to together on a couple of occasions as children, before the war began. I wondered if you were meeting Matteo there, or some other partisans. My plan was to catch up with you and beg you to take me with you on whatever mission was planned for that night, and I was hoping against hope that you wouldn't just send me home alone. I was counting on the fact that if there wasn't time to accompany me back then you would be forced to take me with you. However angry I knew you would be, at least I would have lived a little. In my naivety I even told myself I could protect you if anything happened, I had brought along my machete after all. All these scenarios were playing through my head when I realised too late that the hunter had become the hunted, and I felt the cold hard barrel of a gun pushed into my back. I can still remember the shock of it today, the paralysing terror that gripped me.

"Hands up," a voice hissed in the darkness, and, petrified, I complied. I was just processing the fact that my attackers were speaking Italian, not German, when a light was shone upon my face, and my name spoken.

"Luciano," a voice chuckled, low and mirthless. "I wouldn't have thought you had it in you. Does Mama know you're not at home in bed?" It was Matteo's cousin Fiorlindo, along with another soldier, and as he glanced up the hill I knew the terrible truth. That I had all but led them to the Lost Barn, that they would discover you and your friends. I tried to shout out a warning, and a bird roosting nearby shot out of the trees with a high-pitched shriek. That was the last I knew as the gun butt came down upon my head and I collapsed onto the snow. I woke at dawn, bloodied and frozen, my head thumping. I ran to the barn, fearing what I might find. It was deserted, but there was the dark stain of blood on the mud floor, matted with dried hay. Sick with dread I staggered home to the chestnut house, cleaning myself up in the river on the way, and to my eternal relief, there you were, safe. I thought you were asleep – you were lying motionless on the bed, curled into a ball. Our sisters and mother slept quietly next to you. I passed out, thanking whatever angels had brought you safely home, and vowing I would never seek adventure out again.

"I awoke from dreams into a different nightmare. Your body was there, but your spirit was gone. Matteo had indeed been killed that night at the Lost Barn, and he had taken you with him. You spoke not a word; you were far from us all. Mother and our sisters were so worried – they crowded around you, trying to determine whether you were ill or whether something terrible had happened. You were completely still, until Mother asked you if Matteo was the cause of your distress and your face contorted into a mask of agony. You screamed, a wail of pain that broke my heart every time it replayed in my memory. I ran out of the house, along the stream deep into the woods, unable to bear the sound of your grief. Tears flooded down my cheeks as the realisation flooded through me that I was responsible, that I had led the soldiers right to you, that they had caught you unawares. That Matteo was now dead, and that it was my fault. I should have told you straight away; I should have gone back to the chestnut house and shared your pain, allowed you to hate me, to beat me. Prayed that one day you would forgive me. But I was a coward then, and I have remained thus every day until now, when it is too late. How could I have hoped for forgiveness, when I lived and he died?"

I turn to face Giuliana, whose face is drawn tight; her eyes have all but disappeared into the deep lines that track her face. Is she angry, disappointed, vengeful? I swallow, my throat dry and scratchy, and bow my head to her.

"I know it is too little too late, but I ask your forgiveness, Giuliana. For the wrong I did you all those years ago, for the great wrong I did to Matteo." I turn to Emma, who is as pale as her cotton shirt, her cheeks shiny with tears. "Emma, I must also ask your forgiveness. On behalf of your mother, Giovanna, yourself and your children." The thought of all these generations who have suffered from my mistake, the weight of it finally breaks me, and all I can do is sob the words, "I'm sorry, I'm sorry," over and over. I had hoped to feel unburdened, lighter, but instead a weight is spreading across my chest. I struggle to breathe, and my head starts to spin. I am aware of the darkness sweeping in from the sides, slowly sucking me under, and I yield, grateful for a rest, a reprieve. The pain and guilt slip away into a sort of peace, and the last face I see before my eyes close is the golden-haired angel who came for me in that field all those months ago.

30

Giuliana

2018

I see my little brother collapse in front of me, a man broken by
a lifetime of guilt. I watch, a useless old woman, as Ada snaps
into action, dialling 911 and administering aspirin. Emma
is terrified, calling out to him, clutching his hand, and I want
to stop time. To go back, to make everything different. It was
not supposed to end like this, before we had a chance to make
amends. To finish the story. All these decades I thought I was
the only one with a secret, with a past to hide. How selfish my
life has been, though I passed it off as a life spent in service to
others. At the end of it all the love we give to those who love us
is the only true currency, and I am out of time to pay my debts.

Emma leaves with Luciano in the ambulance, and all I can
do is sit and wait, praying for his recovery. I am a hypocrite, of
course, praying to a God I turned my back on long ago. I pray
not for myself, but for Luciano, and I am sure the angels will
look kindly on him. *Please save him*, I whisper into the silence,
looking up at the pearly sky out of my window. *Please let him*

live, so that he may know the truth and let go of the guilt that has weighed upon him for so long. I am still shocked at his revelation, at what he has believed all these years. If I had not exiled myself so thoroughly he might have had a chance to lay aside this burden sooner. Now it may be too late, and he may die not only believing a lie but also that he has lost my love.

Ada tries to reassure me, but I brush her off. I do not deserve any such comfort. I sit alone in the fading light, waiting for the telephone to ring. When it does its shrill tone startles me and I strain to hear what Ada is saying in the kitchen. When she comes to find me, beaming, I know there is good news and I exhale, sinking down into my chair. I feel the tension evaporating, my jaw relaxing, my shoulders slumping. The words *thank you* form within me and emanate outwards from every cell in my body. Luciano did not have a heart attack but a panic attack, brought on by stress. Emma is with him now, and he is sleeping. I have been given another chance. Not just to tell the truth, but the whole truth.

"Thank you, Ada," I say humbly, remembering my rudeness earlier. "Now I need to ask you a favour. I wish to visit Luciano in hospital." She is resistant, of course, worried whether I am strong enough to manage the trip. "It's to the hospital," I joke, trying to win her round. "If anything happens I'll be in the right place!" Eventually she agrees – I can still be persuasive when I put my mind to it. I know this must be done, that there is no time to wait. Ada prepares a bag with my pills and some supplies, and calls a cab.

I have not left the apartment in months now, and the world outside my door takes me by surprise. The bite of the frosty air, the growl of rush-hour traffic. Exhaust fumes blend with frying donuts, cologne from a passing young man follows a whiff of sewers. I breathe in the familiar sensations, the heart of life that is so raw here. Our cab ducks and dives through the evening traffic, and my head spins with all the movement, all the lights. At the hospital Ada guides me from the car to a hospital wheelchair and proficiently manoeuvres me to the ward where Luciano is recovering. Thank goodness he has Emma with him, to translate. What a terrifying experience it must all have been for him. When I arrive in the private room I note with relief that he looks well, sitting up in bed with a cup of tea and a biscuit on his tray. Emma is by his side, holding his hand, and they really look like family.

"Giuliana!" they both exclaim in unison, and Emma rushes to my side, an action that touches my old heart more than she knows. Her affection is given willingly, without reserve, and I am grateful for it. Ada pushes me up to Luciano's bed and goes through his notes with another nurse, reassuring us that all his tests are as they should be. She excuses herself to give us some time to ourselves.

"I thought you were going to beat me to it back there!" I tease him, and his face creases into a smile. The smile fades as memories of the afternoon's events return, and he takes my hand.

"Giu, you should have stayed at home. I'll be out of here tomorrow. I don't want to put you at risk." I shake my head, wondering where to begin. Hoping my confession won't upset him or bring on another attack. The room is warm and peaceful, shades of blue on the walls and the bedding. It feels like a safe place to tell the last chapter in my story. Emma sat on one side of his bed, me on the other, our little triangle complete.

"Luciano, Emma, we need to return to the night at the Lost Barn. I need to tell you what really happened. The beginning and the end you had right, Luci, but not the middle. In the middle lies all the death and destruction, all the actions that sent so many lives off course. That night has haunted me so often over the years, despite all my attempts to put it behind me. What I never suspected was that you were there with me, Luci, haunted just as I was. If only we could have shared our grief, shone a light on that darkness. I came here tonight because there is no time to waste; I could not leave you one more night believing yourself responsible.

"As you say I did indeed set off for the Lost Barn that evening, after night had fallen. There was a storm brewing; milky clouds full of snow raced overhead, obscuring the higher mountains. The wind was growing stronger and whistled around my head as I walked, deafening me to your footsteps following me. I imagined no patrols would be out on such a night, fool that I was. I should have read the signs, sensed the danger, but my mind was full of Matteo and the joyful anticipation of seeing him again after a week's absence.

"He was waiting for me in the Lost Barn and we clung together, sharing our news and laughing in between embraces. The bliss I felt in his arms, the power, the joy, still lingers on in my memory even now. He was perfect that night, the full expression of his talents and beliefs. Physically he was strong from his constant trekking across our mountainous terrain, and despite the meagre rations we lived on he was in his prime. His hair had grown long and fell around his face, unruly black curls that I loved to run my fingers through. His beard had also grown, giving him a swarthy look, making him seem older than his nineteen years. His eyes burned with passion when he spoke of their successes, and it seemed the angels were truly with them as their missions went exactly to plan time after time, with no casualties on their side. He told me of landslides, never an exact science, that crashed their furious vengeance down on enemy convoys perfectly, as if nature herself was fighting with them. He recounted raids on the Todt factories and fortifications where by chance they found only light defence, quickly overwhelmed. He told me how by now hundreds of young Fascist soldiers had crossed No Man's Land to lay down their arms and be led back across to occupied territory, to be returned safely to their families. There was always a moment of danger with these encounters when the partisans were at great risk, unsure whether it was a trap or a genuine group of disillusioned young Italians ready to stop fighting with the Germans. There were other partisans who preferred not to take the risk, who saw them as traitors and executed them without mercy. This was not the way for Matteo and the rest of our group; they always gave the benefit of the doubt, and so far their empathy had been rewarded.

"His news shared, Matteo would always listen attentively to mine, his jaw tightening as I recounted the more dangerous parts, his eyes shining with pride as I brought news of another successful operation. I knew the safe houses of the area well now and counted many of those who ran them as friends. By this point I could converse well in English, and my friendship with Benjamin had blossomed during our brief encounters at the OSS. The news I brought back, not only my official orders from the authorities but also the word on the street from the soldiers themselves, was valuable to us, and I believe our little group of freedom fighters had earned the respect of the Allies. I knew they were particularly keen to avoid supporting groups of a communist bent that might seize power after the war. Officer Mark Anderson, whom I met with on my first trip across the river and who remained one of my principal contacts had already referred to my post-war future, indicating that I would have a part to play if I so wished. For a sixteen-year-old girl from a tiny mountain village this was incredible news indeed. I gave it little thought, though. The war was still to be won and the Germans were like a cornered, wounded animal: increasingly desperate. We couldn't afford to take our eyes off the game.

"Matteo and I had been meeting at the Lost Barn for months now; perhaps we had become a little less vigilant. With our work we were scrupulously careful, but when it came to our love story we were blind. When we kissed, when we lost ourselves in our passion; all else ceased to exist. All we needed was each other, and it made us both invincible and terrifyingly vulnerable. That night our embrace was interrupted by the warning call of a buzzard – your warning, I now realise, brother – and at once I knew something was terribly wrong. The storm outside was building, and we were lucky to hear the bird in between the rumblings of thunder that were drawing closer. The air around us crackled with danger and we froze, aware that our safe haven, the scene of so much happiness, had been discovered.

"There was only one entrance to the Lost Barn, and as we headed for it we could already hear footsteps approaching; we were trapped. Matteo raised his rifle, and I drew my knife from my belt. How many were there? A whole patrol of Germans? Who had given us away? All we could do was react instinctively, like animals, as we waited to find out. I stubbed out our sole candle with my foot, plunging us into darkness.

"'Hands up!' a voice barked out in Italian, and the wooden barn door was kicked to the ground. The wind came rushing in, sending dry leaves and hay flying towards us, the timbers of the barn moaning in the gale. 'Lay down your weapons!' the voice yelled, struggling to be heard over the storm. 'You are surrounded!' I felt Matteo squeeze my hand in the inky darkness, and a strange peace descended on me. The storm was almost upon us, and amidst the chaos engulfing us I felt calm, aware of a point of power deep within me. I knew Matteo wished me to answer, thinking they would feel a woman was less of a threat. We may yet come across as a pair of lovers, and not be shot as partisans. We lowered our weapons gently to the ground.

"'Our weapons are down,' I replied, my voice strong and clear. Two figures appeared silhouetted against the pale snow and entered the barn, shining torches in our faces, blinding us. We could not see them as we squinted into the light, but the voice when it spoke was familiar, and with a sinking feeling I knew he had come after me. *Fiorlindo.* His tone was soft, dangerous.

"'Cousin Matteo,' he purred, 'so the rumours are true. Let me guess, our brave hero is fighting for freedom in the woods.' I felt his focus move to me, and the torch moved from my face down to my trousers. 'I see you are recruiting women now to do your dirty work. Little Giuliana, how disappointed I am to discover you chose the wrong side. The wrong man.' He paused, spitting on the ground. I sensed his anger rising, the whirl of red thickening around him. I suppose that's what I always liked about you. *The challenge.* How much sweeter your kiss will taste when I have had to break you for it.' I could feel Matteo's own rage next to me, gathering momentum. I pressed his hand, trying to soothe him, to stop him from being goaded into making a mistake. Fiorlindo was stepping closer to us now, enjoying every moment he could taunt us. I could sense his excitement growing by the second. He would finally rid himself of Matteo and claim me for his own. 'I would have offered marriage, done it all properly,' he said quietly, wistfully even, directing his words at me. He noticed my hand gripping Matteo's and his tone changed. 'But now I see you are a partisan's whore I will treat you as such.' His hand shot out and grabbed my hair, hurling me down to the ground, away from Matteo. In slow motion I saw him raise his revolver towards Matteo's head and I screamed, the sound shattering the tension and waking the giants of the sky as my scream became a crash of thunder, deafeningly close. A flash of lightning illuminated the second Matteo's arm rose to thrust the gun from Fiorlindo's grip and I heard the clatter of the gun crashing to the floor, followed by the writhing mass of the two men's bodies, locked in a deadly wrestle in the darkness.

"My attention was drawn to the soldier in the doorway who was standing, gun raised, ready to shoot Matteo when the opportunity presented itself. I myself was cast in shadow now, the soldier's gaze and torch fixed on the fighting men. In between flashes of lightning I groped around for where the revolver had fallen, and when the next lightning bolt struck I took aim and fired. The gun exploded into action and the soldier crumpled to the ground, like a puppet whose strings have been dropped.

228

My strength vanished and I collapsed to the ground, shocked at how easily I had taken a life. There was silence, and in the sooty darkness my head swam with confusion, unsure of what my new reality was. Was I alone in the darkness with Fiorlindo? Had he killed Matteo? I heard a groan, and the thud of a body as someone rolled a corpse off themselves.

"'Giuliana,' a voice groaned, and with joy I realised it was Matteo; he was alive. We found each other in the dark, and for some minutes clung to each other, still incredulous that we were alive. In the confusion immediately following the gunshot Matteo had stabbed Fiorlindo with his knife, right through the heart. His coat was now soaked with blood, as was mine, pressed up against him. The storm had passed on down the valley, grumbling away into the distance. The barn had survived the storm, lightning striking several trees all around it, and against all the odds, so had we.

"We lit a candle and surveyed the corpses in the flickering light, aware already of the need to make them disappear, of the danger of reprisals against our families were they to be found. The stain of blood spread across the dirt floor of the Lost Barn, and I felt a deep sadness that our special place had been desecrated. In death Fiorlindo held no threat, though I still shivered to look upon his face. A cruel sneer lingered on, as if he knew something we didn't. I felt no remorse, only relief that Matteo was safe and that we were still together. We dragged the bodies to a ditch near the barn, where we buried them under the snow as best we could. The storm had passed but the freezing sleet continued, and as we worked we felt cleansed, purified. It was a little after midnight, judging from the stars, when we finally went our separate ways. Matteo up to the *capanna*, myself back home to the chestnut house. I cleaned myself up in the stream, hid my bloody clothing and collapsed into the family bed. I thought we had changed our fate that night; I believed we had avoided tragedy.

"I slept deeply, only to be awoken at dawn by Dino. He was wounded and limping, his face etched with pain and dirt. He motioned silently for me to follow him, and I left my sleeping family and found him outside by the river. Gently, painfully, he told me how the *capanna* had been attacked just before dawn by a German patrol. How they had put up a good fight but that they were overwhelmed, outnumbered, and everyone save Dino had been killed. Raffaello, Ottaviano, Silvano, Canzio, my Matteo. He had seen them die, take their last breaths with him by their side, as one by one they were shot, trapped in the barn with nowhere to escape. Canzio, who had been on guard that night, had been the first to fall, taken out by a sniper while the others slept. Matteo had survived the battle of the Lost Barn only to walk straight into another one: a premeditated attack. Dino had escaped in the smoke of the gunfire, slipping away down the hillside to come and warn me not to return there, that it was now in enemy hands. The Germans had set fire to all the surrounding houses and barns, the villagers having already fled with the gunfire. The smoke was visible on the horizon; I will never forget the sight. That was the last time I saw Dino. I cannot remember saying goodbye, but I do remember how he held me when I fell to the ground, unable to bear the news. How he rocked me, like a small child, as my useless tears fell onto the forest floor, as my heart split into a thousand pieces."

I find I am weeping again, reliving that moment. Through my blurry vision I realise Luciano and Emma are also crying, and I am not alone this time. We weep for Matteo, my love, killed only a month before the end of the war, and for all the life he has missed. We weep for ourselves, who have lived without him all this time. For the family we have lost, and for the family we have now found.

31

Emma

2018

We've been in New York three days now, and it feels like weeks. I'm far from home in this city and I miss Sam and the girls terribly, but I feel closer to my roots than I've done since my parents passed away, maybe even further back than that. Perhaps there was always this gap, this mystery, this part of my heritage that was missing. I wonder if my mother ever felt it, if she ever suspected her parents were not her biological parents.

The stories I've heard, from Giuliana and then from Luciano, are incredible. Shocking tales from a war-torn country, a very different Italy than the one we've come to love over the past few months. Sometimes revelations like these take time to sink in, to become part of our reality. The news of my parents' accident took me weeks to accept; even at the funeral part of me was telling myself it was a terrible mistake. That any time now they would be back in my life, that everything would return to as it was before. But Giuliana and Luciano's stories are not like that. It was less like being told a new story and more like remembering something from a very long time ago. Missing pieces of the puzzle finally being returned and slotted into place.

I loved my grandparents, and I will always love and remember them fondly. They worked so hard to create a life in Scotland, a good life, and to give my mother a safe and happy childhood. But seeing Giuliana and getting to know her brings me closer to my mother; in some small way I feel part of her has been given back to me. In Giuliana's sparkling eyes, the curve of her cheekbones, the strength of her character, I see my mother. Her descriptions of Matteo, of the courageous young man that he was, bring him close to me and I feel proud that his blood flows in my veins and those of my daughters. For the first time in my life I know exactly who my ancestors are, and I feel a sort of peace inside, a knowledge that deepens my awareness of who I am. I have become familiar with loss and its power to reduce, to empty. The stories are filled with loss and death, and yet that is not the feeling I am left with. Instead I feel *full*, complete, like I understand my place in the world, and I know where I belong. *At Stazzana.* The words come unbidden, whispering themselves in my mind. Where it all began. I realise that I belong to Stazzana as much as she belongs to me. Where my grandfather was born, where both my grandfathers were born in fact, I reflect with a small smile. Giovanni and Matteo. I wonder fleetingly if they were close, if Giovanni thought about Matteo much over the years. How sad they could not talk to my mother about the past, about the family they had left behind. Some dead, some living. The secret they had carried to their deaths. It would have remained buried forever had that terrible accident not occurred and sent me looking for answers. Sent me back to the source, back to Stazzana, to disturb the ghosts of the past.

I look at Luciano in his hospital bed, holding hands with Giuliana, reunited after so long. I see how much younger he seems, unburdened of the guilt of Matteo's death after so many decades believing he was responsible. My great-uncle. He really is family now, and I feel a wave of love wash over me for this little old man I came across in a field. What a shock he must have had to be confronted with me, the past bursting into his present just like that, with a sprained ankle and a suitcase of grief. Ready to stir all the pain of the past back up for him.

None of us want to end this moment, sat together in the blue warmth of the hospital room, finally basking in the relief that the stories have all been told, the past has been laid to rest. We are giddy, joyful, like schoolchildren released for their summer holidays. When Ada returns to tell us it is time we went home Giuliana and I reluctantly leave, and I promise to be back in the morning, when Luciano should be released to come home. Giuliana asks if we will stay at her apartment for the rest of our trip and we happily accept her invitation.

I spend the evening back at my hotel room, giving Giuliana an evening to relax and get some rest before our arrival the next day. I call Maria to let her know Luciano is safe, and then I call Sam. His voice fills me with the urge to fly home immediately, to be back in his strong arms. He tells me their news, how Aria has lost another tooth and is excited about the tooth fairy's visit, how Luna has been making snow angels. The girls are asleep now, he tells me, curled up in bed with their arms around each other. He messages me a photo, and my heart aches as I gaze at them, searching their little faces for any changes I have missed. I can picture Sam there too, sat by the fire, his long legs up on the sofa. I miss them fiercely and I know my place is there with them, but for the moment I need to stay a little longer. I recount the stories Giuliana and Luciano both told, and Sam whistles in amazement when he hears what really happened on the night Matteo died.

"Thank goodness you went, Em," he says, softly. "Not only for your sake, and for Giuliana, but for Luciano to finally discover the truth." We end the phone call with loving words and agree to talk again the next day. I hang up and look at the phone, my throat suddenly dry as I think of my mother, and I desperately wish I could phone her. Tell her everything that has happened this year, bring her to Montaltissimo, to share our new family with her. I think of the thousands of phone calls over the years: phone calls to share news, to cry down the phone after a break-up, to hear her shrieks of delight after good exam results. To tell her a funny story, to ask her advice. Phone calls for big reasons, but most for no other reason than to hear her voice, to let her know I was thinking about her. I send up a silent prayer to her and my father, wherever they may be, letting them know I'm still thinking of them.

The next morning I go the hospital where Luciano is discharged, and he seems much stronger. We take a cab to Giuliana's apartment and Ada helps us settle into the guest rooms. I admire some African artefacts hanging on the walls and wonder if Giuliana will have the strength to tell us about her time there during the rest of our stay.

The days that follow are precious, days I will always remember as a sort of sweet dream. With snowstorms battering the city outside we mostly stay warm inside the apartment, drinking tea and chatting. Ada tells me that Giuliana's vital signs are strong, that she has really rallied since our arrival. Out in the kitchen together, in a quiet voice, she tells me this can happen in the last stages of cancer, and that we should not expect she will live far beyond our stay. I nod, the bitter taste of disappointment filling my mouth, knowing it to be the truth. I had been fooling myself, wondering whether I could get Sam and the girls out here to meet her, dreaming of us all celebrating Easter together. It's cruel, to find my grandmother only to lose her so soon, but in a way it makes the time we have more special, knowing it is finite.

One afternoon I show Giuliana the postcards I found at my parents' house, her annual correspondence with them over the many years that they kept in touch. She handles them gingerly, squinting at each faded postcard through her reading glasses. I try to imagine the younger Giuliana writing the postcards every December. The postcards are so brief; so much was left unspoken. The empty spaces between the words, the questions silently hovering around the polite enquiries.

"I so longed for news," Giuliana admits with a sigh, "and yet I dreaded it as well, for it always undid all the work I had done that year. The life I tried so hard to create to replace the life I should have been living. I kept moving so fast that I thought the past would never catch up with me. Foolish girl that I was. I see now that it was with me all the time; I could no more outrun it than I could outrun myself. I took my pain with me everywhere I went – there was no country in the world that had the power to take it away. The power lay within me, all the time. Perhaps I knew it but did not believe I deserved forgiveness. A happy ending. Perhaps by remaining trapped in that half-world, between life and death, the past and the present, I was trying to stay close to Matteo. If he was not alive then neither would I be. I sought out danger, death, war. I ran so many risks; I showed such disrespect to this gift that is life. I threw myself into adventure, challenge, travel. New people, new countries, new words, new faces. In the beginning I would be seduced, excited to learn a new language, to lose myself in a new lover. I would be passionate about the cause of some displaced people, some war waged between countries where the victims, as always, were the innocents. I wrote myself a new story each year, trying to make myself believe it would be enough. But each December the postcard would arrive, and I would see my life for the sham that it was. The smokescreen distracting me from what I had lost. One small postcard and the smoke would clear, disappear into the ether. I would remember the baby I once held in my arms, those tiny fingers curled around my own, and it would all come flooding back. I would spend hours staring at the latest photograph that Giovanni and Assunta would include, marvelling at the changes that had occurred in the space of a year. I would search for Matteo in the little girl's eyes, for traces of him in her face, in the jut of her chin, in her smile." Giuliana breaks off, aware, perhaps, that she is talking more to herself than to me. "Forgive me," she smiles at me, squeezing my hand. "The ramblings of an old lady. Would you like to see the postcards, the ones your grandparents sent to me?" I would, very much, and Giuliana tells me where to find them.

I leave her to take a rest on Nurse Ada's orders and take the box to the quiet of the dining room. I take each postcard from its envelope and lay them down carefully on her table, the perfume of the past mingling faintly with the scent of beeswax. With my forefinger I softly stroke the ink of my grandmother's handwriting, imagining her as a young woman newly arrived in Scotland. The earliest postcards are in black and white, switching to colour a few years later. Some are of the mountains, some of the lochs. One is of Edinburgh, another Aberdeen. Did they create an impression, for Giuliana? Did she study them, trying to visualise her daughter growing up in the land she knew so little about? My grandmother's tone is friendly and warm, but there is little detail that can be provided in a postcard. She always wrote an update about my mother, and included a photo. I wonder why she never wrote a letter, never went into greater depth. Was this an unspoken agreement, a line not be crossed in their correspondence? Did my grandparents ever worry about Giuliana coming back into their lives, wanting to reclaim her daughter? Did they live in fear that one day she would learn the truth, and would want to find her mother? These are questions I will never find answers to, and I can accept that. I am keen to steer my conversations with Giuliana onto happier subjects, for us to enjoy our time together. When I rejoin her for afternoon tea I guess that she does not especially wish to discuss the postcards – what is there really left to say?

"Keep them," she says, pushing the box towards me. "Please.

I don't need them anymore. I have something much more precious now – I have the real thing." She smiles and reaches her hand out to softly touch my cheek, as if to check that I am real.

The following day we sit in the living room, Giuliana, Luciano and I, and with my help she shows us some photographs from her time in Africa, along with various artefacts she has kept from those years. I am intrigued to see this vibrant young woman, with her jet-black hair and such life in her green eyes. I see her as a nurse, newly qualified, just arrived in Kenya to work with a local Mission. She is surrounded by children, radiant dark-eyed children, their faces shiny from the sun's heat. There are photos from all over the world, parts of Asia, America and many different African countries. She seems to have spent several years in Sudan, and then Uganda. She reminisces about the appalling living conditions, the lack of food and water, the dearth of medical equipment. But she also paints a picture of a community, a spirit, an appreciation for life even in the most dire of circumstances. Even in the refugee camps, living with desperate people who had lost everything, she describes people she became friends with, who were able to retain their humanity, their dignity, even in the face of such horrific loss. My admiration for my grandmother grows with each passing hour, and I believe she has crammed several lifetimes into one. Such energy, such devotion. I think of all the lives she has saved, all the people she has helped, all with no thought of personal gain. I notice she has slumped down low in her chair, clearly exhausted from her travels to the past. I watch with concern as her energy drops, her life force seems to fade before our eyes.

"Time for a break," Ada interludes, and Luciano and I creep away, leaving Giuliana to rest and have her afternoon nap. We make ourselves lunch in Giuliana's kitchen, and sit at her breakfast bar, thinking about what she has shared with us that morning.

"I always knew she was special," Luciano tells me, gazing out of the window at a grey tower block opposite. "I think she would always have outgrown us, in some way. If Matteo had lived, if they had raised a family at Stazzana, perhaps she would have been happy. But perhaps she would still have wanted more. A life beyond the mountains." He pauses, lost in his thoughts. Very quietly, so softly I have to lean closer not to miss his words he says, "Perhaps in the end, everything was exactly as it was supposed to be. Perhaps we are too small to understand it, but maybe the things we see as endings are really just beginnings. Perhaps everything is in the right place, after all." He does not seem to require a reply, and I sit with him and stare out of the window also, not seeing New York in 2018 but Stazzana in 1945, Giuliana as a wife and mother, an alternate reality. I try to imagine a world where my parents are still here, and I realise I would never have travelled to Italy, never have met Giuliana or Luciano. My hazy image of Stazzana in the past comes into focus, and I see a young couple outside the house, by the front door. With a shock I realise it is Sam and me, and playing in the meadow, surrounded by wildflowers, are Aria and Luna. I look at the house and note that the roof is new, I see the varnished chestnut eaves overhanging freshly rendered walls, red geraniums lining the stone walls descending to the cantina. The overgrown patios have been laid with traditional stone slabs, and I notice chickens pecking around in the yard. As I watch the vision fades, and I am back in New York, sitting on my own. Luciano has also wandered off for his own afternoon siesta. I wonder where the vision came from, whether it has shown me the future or whether I just became confused, thoughts of the family that never was merging with my own.

The next day is our last, and whilst I am longing to see Sam and the girls again, I am full of sadness to be leaving Giuliana. My grandmother, whom I have known for just a week. One week in a lifetime, so little, and yet we came close to it never happening at all. In such a short space of time we have to come to know each other, to form a bond, to become family. I've loved watching Giuliana and Luciano together again after so long, and in their friendly sibling banter I see shades of the children that they were, that they still are at heart. Children running wild in the meadows of Stazzana, exploring the chestnut woods and the mountains. I know the time has come for us to return to Montaltissimo and to Stazzana, and I suspect Giuliana will not be far behind us. I have seen her shrinking a little with each day, her colours fading, and I can see the effort it takes her to stay with us.

When we part I hold her tight, close my eyes, and try to fill her with my love, surrounding her like a golden light. "I love you, Nonna," I whisper to her, and I feel her tears against my cheek. "I love you, *mia carissima Emma*," she murmurs back, and I wonder again if we should stay longer, stay with her to the end. She pulls back and meets my gaze, and her green eyes are radiant with love. She shakes her head slightly, and I know she wishes to part like this, that our last memories will be of her smiling and waving us off, as if she were seeing her brother and granddaughter off on a holiday. As our cab pulls away I look up at her window and see her face, small and white, looking down at us. One hand flutters a goodbye, and I blow a kiss up through the softly falling snow to my grandmother.

32

Luciano

2018

I am an old man, and I had thought life held no more surprises for me. How wrong I was. Since the day Emma appeared in my field my small life has been turned on its head, and I have had to grow into the man my sister always believed I could be. That which was missing all those years dropped in from the sky and changed everything. A pair of green eyes, and a desire to know the truth. I had become so heavy, so tired of life. Disillusioned, bitter, I was halfway to the grave already. I had lost my contact with the land, my appreciation for the beauty of this place we are blessed to live in. Emma, Sam, Aria and Luna, they awakened the part of me that lay sleeping, the part I had forgotten. I was so terrified I would lose them when they knew the truth. It never occurred to me, all these long years, that what I believed to be the truth was in fact not so – that I had made assumptions that proved to be false. The end result was tragically still the same, but I know now that it was not my fault; I was not the reason Matteo died that night. It could have easily been the case: I am not completely innocent. I still led danger to their door. I wonder if the attack was coordinated, the Fascists taking the Lost Barn at midnight, the Germans the *capanna* at dawn. The whole *banda* in one go. Were they betrayed? Had Fiorlindo suspected Giuliana ever since the night he had saved her? I think of the young man who, in the usual course of life, would have found employment, married, had children. He was never one for the family farm, I remember; perhaps he would have moved away to a town, maybe even abroad. Off to seek his fortune in America, maybe. I imagine he would have prospered; he had a cunning about him, even as a child. His brother Mario came home from the war and lived out the rest of his life in Eglio with his wife and children. His other brother was killed in Russia, like so many. One of his sisters, Rosina, remained in Eglio, caring for their mother, missing her own opportunity for a family. She may still be alive as far as I know; I have not ventured far from the farm for many years now. His youngest sister Antonietta died during the war, from a childhood illness, as I recall. *How sad*, I think, *that it all ended for him in the hills where we used to play as children.* His body was never found; his file was marked missing in action. I don't know if they ever looked for him, his fellow soldiers, or if by that point in the war it was too late: the war was as good as lost and surviving the surrender was at the forefront of their thoughts. Had he even told anyone where he was going that night or was it a private mission, a risk he ran based more on desire for my sister than on orders?

We will never know now, but it strikes me that when we return to Montaltissimo I should alert the authorities, see that he finally has a proper Christian burial. Perhaps we will head up there, Emma, Sam and I, see if the barn still stands. I am aware of the harm he tried to inflict on my sister and Matteo, but seventy-four years later I do not wish to carry any ill feeling. I have had enough bitterness and guilt for this lifetime, and now, through some stroke of grace, I have been absolved. I have another chance, and I intend to take it.

Saying goodbye to Giuliana, so soon after finding her again, is more than I can bear. As usual, she is the strong one. The one to make the decision, to tell us the time has come to leave.

"I am a contented old woman," she tells me, our last day. "I am the happiest I have ever been. To have shared this time with you, and to get to know Emma. It is a blessing I did not expect, and I shall treasure it, hold it close. I want you to remember me like this, while I am still myself." I feel my eyes fill with tears, as I realise what she is saying. She will die shortly, alone save for her faithful Nurse Ada. With no family by her side, no-one who will tend to her grave once she has gone. She squeezes my hand; her grip is weak, but her spirit is still strong. "I am not afraid of death, Luci." She smiles at me. "I have lived long enough, and now I have done what I needed to do. This body is tired, used up. I am ready to return now." Days later I remember her words and muse on her meaning. To return to Montaltissimo, to Matteo? To whatever state we come from before birth? I loved my sister, all my life, but huge parts of her life will always remain a mystery to me.

Emma and I fly home to Pisa, where Sam is waiting for us at the airport. As we drive north towards the mountains, I feel a strange sense of disconnection. For once I am the traveller, not the one waiting at home. I have flown across the ocean, visited the strange land of New York, spent time with my long-lost sister. Things I never dreamt of doing. I think of Maria waiting at home for me, and I find I am excited to see her, to share my experiences. I feel less like an old man of eighty-six and more like a young man off to court his lady. I think of Elena, and how we grew closer as she helped me prepare for my visit. I wonder when we can see her again, how I can get to know her and the children better. My son Antonio springs to mind, and I see how I have focused on what is missing for far too long. I looked at him and saw his lack of interest in the farm, when right before my eyes was a healthy young man that any father should be proud of. How we can bridge this gap I can't think, but I have come this far; I have to believe there is a way. I think of other relations I've not seen in decades and decide I must visit them soon. I haven't been to the market in Castelnuovo for years. As a boy I would always accompany my father on a Thursday. Market day was a sacred ritual, an appointment not to be missed. I wonder if the menfolk still gather in the piazza drinking their *caffè corretto* and putting the world to rights. I know Emma often buys her fruit and vegetables at the market; I will ask her for a lift, see if I can be one of those old men in the square for however many years I have left. I make a silent promise to myself as I watch the villages fly by from the back seat of the car, to make the most of my new lease of life. To enjoy each day, and to attempt to bring some joy to those I love.

We've been home for two weeks before Emma, Sam and I are able to make the journey up to the Lost Barn. It's only February, but spring has come early, even if I suspect that March and April will bring some late winter weather. Catkins hang on the walnut trees, snowdrops are pushing up through the forest floor and bright splashes of purple crocuses illuminate the meadows where they are springing up by the day. The snow has melted everywhere but the highest mountaintops, the grass has started growing and there is even some blossom on the cherry trees. The chestnut trees are still bare, which will help us find the barn. I wonder what state it will be in, if I will remember the way after all these years.

Emma has brought her black and white maps of Stazzana which show a building at the northern edge of the *terreno*, the terrain, but the maps don't show the ravines and rivers so they are little use. The land has been neglected for many years now, and I imagine we will have to cut our way through overgrown brambles and undergrowth. It will be easier now than it would be in the summer. I've brought my machete, and I see Sam has as well. He has taken to our ways like a natural; he has a feel for the countryside and a respect for the land that I love to see. Rare in young people today. We trek uphill from Stazzana, venturing deep into the forest that clothes the slopes of the hill leading up to the village of Sassi. Some of the climb is very steep, with little to hold on to except the trees, and I see Emma glance nervously at me from time to time. Her concern is unfounded: I am at home in the woods, as sure-footed as when I was a boy.

Once we are well within the forest it is hard to know where we are exactly, hard to gain perspective when all we can see are the trees, but I keep heading north, leading us around the steeper ravines. Twice we cross the smaller tributaries of the river, the streams that run fast in the winter and in the spring with meltwater from the snows above, only to dry up completely in the summer months. I see Sam checking his compass and marking the map, and I smile to myself. We never had gadgets in the past. We navigated the mountains by the sun and the moon, the stars above. We knew the trees like friends; every hill had some story we were told by our elders, some adventure recounted from friends. In the absence of technology, video games, even books, as most folk were still illiterate in those days, the land was our storybook. Each season a new page, each generation a new chapter to be written.

I think of myself making this same journey all those years ago, that night in March. So young, so foolish. Desperate to join in the game, to be part of the action. I shiver to think of the figures that were lurking in the shadows, stalking me. From my farm I overlook these hills below Sassi, and in winter I can sometimes pick out the roof of the Lost Barn, its russet roof tiles contrasting with the bare branches and decaying leaves of the exposed forest floor. For years I would avoid looking at it, glad when spring came and the new leaves would once more hide it from sight. I always thought of it as the site of Matteo's death, but now I know it was not thus. It sits strangely with me, the truth, after a lifetime believing otherwise.

As we approach the barn we find that brambles have grown up around it, monsters that tower over us, even Sam. They are bare and have died back a little with winter, but they remain formidable foes. I search for a chink in their armour and find a place that seems less dense, and start to hack through with my machete. We all emerge from the brambles scratched and bleeding; they seem to be protecting the Lost Barn, ensuring no living soul ventures there. Or could they be protecting outsiders from what lies within? We stand side by side, Emma, Sam and I, and stare ahead, as out of the wilderness rises the Lost Barn. The woods around us fall silent and I remember feeling a drop in the temperature, a chill in the air that was perhaps due to the nearby stream, perhaps something more sinister. The barn puts me in mind of a witches' hut in the woods; there is something dark and foreboding about it. It's hard to believe Giuliana and Matteo spent so many happy times here.

I glance over at Emma and can see that she feels it too, a shift in the energy around us. The sense that we are trespassing, that we are not welcome here. Sam seems to be oblivious to it and presses ahead, approaching the barn and entering through the doorway, the door itself rotting on the ground. I feel waves of anger rolling over us, the very air seems to thicken and I feel the urge to flee overtaking me. I see Emma fighting the same instincts, but instead of turning she runs towards the barn, shouting Sam's name. I watch, helpless, as she disappears into the darkness, and I hear a terrible groan, a cracking of ancient timbers as the main beam of the barn collapses, and the roof starts to crash to the floor. Emma and Sam emerge from the crumbling building followed by a cloud of dust rolling after them, and they run to me, shaking. Sam is in shock, I think, saved by a second, by Emma's intuition. He is covered in rust-red powder from the roof tiles, fired over a century ago. He drinks shakily from the bottle we brought, the water dribbling down his chin, running rivulets through the dust.

I try to talk to Emma, to ask her how she knew, but she is looking towards the ditch behind the barn. Distracted by something, unable to hear me. Her green eyes are shining, her pupils dilated, as if they are looking into a great light. I shiver and look towards the ditch, but I see nothing. Only motes of dust hanging in the weak sunlight breaking through the trees. Emma walks towards the light, her hair gleaming white. Somehow she avoids the dust and dirt of ages, and appears brighter, lit from within. I think of little Luna and her other worldliness, and realise it comes from Emma, and through her Giuliana. They have some gift, some ability that I cannot comprehend. Emma reaches the ditch and kneels on the earth, her back to us. Sam moves to join her, concerned, and I put out an arm to stop him. It is hard for me to hold back too, aware as I am that Emma has entered the eye of the storm, the centre of the darkness that I still sense all around us, crackling with resentment. Emma leans forwards to retrieve something from the mud, and sits, cradling it to her chest, muttering words I cannot distinguish, again and again.

I could not say how long we remained thus, but gradually I become aware of birdsong in the trees, the babbling of the brook and I recognise the woods around us for the friends I once knew them to be. The air feels as fresh as it does straight after a summer storm. What power Emma had to forgive, to bring to an end the bad blood between her family and his, I will never know. Eventually I summon the courage to approach her and she startles, momentarily confused. The object she is cradling in her arms is mud-stained, but where she has held it the white purity of bone shows through. It takes me a moment to recognise it for a skull, shockingly human. I have seen many animal skulls, but never a human one before. The image is a bizarre one. Giuliana's granddaughter, a twenty-first-century girl, lost in the mountains, rocking the skull of a Fascist who died during the Second World War.

Emma looks drained, but she is calm, and she lays it down again on the ground with infinite care. I help her to her feet, and ask her, "Fiorlindo?" She nods gently, looking back down at the skull, and where I imagine some of the rest of his skeleton must be. Without a proper burial I would expect wolves and foxes to have scavenged the body, but the bones would probably remain in the vicinity. We will arrange for the authorities to come, organise a proper burial, after all this time. For Fiorlindo and the other soldier. The sun is starting her descent, a gibbous moon already climbing the silvery sky, and it is time for us to leave. An owl hoots, announcing the approaching dusk, and we start to wend our way home. Sam and I each take one of Emma's arms, as we turn back to our gateway through the brambles. Emma takes one final look at their resting place.

"*Dormi bene*," she murmurs, almost under her breath, as we leave. *Sleep well.*

33

Emma

2018

The funeral is held in late April, and Sam, Luciano and I attend
while Maria watches the girls. The police removed the remains
of his body the week after our visit, and confirmed his identity,
along with the other soldier who was shot that night at the Lost
Barn. The church of San Frediano in Sassi is located inside a
vast rock fortress, and until now I have only ever seen it across
the valley. For a village church it is imposing, and it adds to
the solemnity of the occasion. I look back across towards
Montaltissimo and marvel at how small it looks, with its tiny
church and the few stone houses scattered across the ridge.
Between our two villages lies Stazzana, down in the valley,
hidden from view.

I enjoy the service, the scent of incense, the coolness of
the church, the history that we are now a part of. It is a fitting
resting place for a soldier, I think, as the words of the Catholic
liturgy echo around the nearly empty church. As they often do
my thoughts fly to Giuliana, and I try to feel her presence, to

send her my love. She passed away a week after we left New York, with Nurse Ada by her side. Her body will not rest here in the Garfagnana, but I believe her soul will have returned home. Back to where she was happiest, where Matteo also rests. She is closer to me now, and I think of her every day.

When we emerge back into daylight to follow the coffin to the mausoleum the light is blinding after the darkness of the church. Our duties done we linger in front of the church, admiring the view towards the coast and over the Vagli lake and the mysterious village of Isola Santa. We make polite conversation with the handful of mourners and discover that most are distant relatives. Luciano chats away with them all, until a lady on the edge of the group draws his attention.

"Rosina," he breathes, and I only just hear him. Fiorlindo's sister, his only living sibling. Once she has greeted the other mourners Rosina makes her way slowly over to us, and I see a little mouse of a lady, shrunken and wizened with age, but with a sparkle in her eyes that I suspect is the cause of her longevity. She greets Luciano first and the two exchange pleasantries, trying to work out when they last saw one another. He introduces her to Sam and me, and she grips our hands, her dark eyes curious. I realise that we must be relations of a sort, if she was Matteo's cousin. She is interested to hear about our children, and how we travelled from Scotland to visit Stazzana.

"I haven't been there in years," she reminisces, "not since the end of the war. They were hard years there, a house of women and children all alone in the middle of the fighting. We kept ourselves busy as best we could, but it wasn't much fun to grow up in, I can tell you that." She studies me, her gaze steady and disquieting. "We always wondered what happened to him," she says, nodding back towards the mausoleum. "My brother. We figured he met his end at the hands of the Allies, somehow. I never thought all these years he was there, within sight of my house. He was a brave boy. Never had much time for us younger ones, but that was the way of things. He used to visit us at Stazzana, brought us food. We relied on him and the protection he offered, stopping the Germans stealing our animals and our produce. He kept us all safe, and our mother so looked forward to his visits." She looks at me, apprising me with those sharp eyes.

"You don't take after your grandmother, that's for sure. I was sorry to hear of her death. We got to know each other well, those years we all lived at Stazzana together." I wait for more, fascinated to discover a living person who had known my grandmother in the war years. "She blamed herself, you know, for what happened to Fiorlindo."

"Pardon?" I ask, confused. "She knew what had happened to him? How was that possible?"

"No, no," Rosina replies, "she never knew what happened exactly, none of us did. But we knew when he didn't return to Stazzana that something terrible had befallen him. He wouldn't have abandoned us like that, with no message. Assunta was a religious girl, always at her prayers. On that last visit he made to us she said she told him something, something she always regretted. It was the day she heard about her poor brother Luca's death; she was distraught. It made her tell him something she later believed she shouldn't have."

"Do you know what it was?" I persist, but she shakes her head, tired from standing for so long, perhaps.

"No, cara mia. The war was full of regrets. We were all so keen to move on, to bury the past, that many secrets were buried too. I must go home and rest now, but come and visit me – it's the last cottage before you leave the village. Bring those children of yours." She smiles at Sam and me, and clutches our hands. "And grazie, for bringing him home."

As I watch her make her way down the hill, assisted by the priest, what she has told me floats around my mind, and as the words settle they arrange themselves into what I realise with a sickening dread is the truth. The sun is suddenly unbearable beating down on me, and I grasp Sam's arm, feeling weak.

"Emma? Are you OK?" he asks, frowning in concern as he guides me to a bench in the shade of the fortress wall. "What is it?" Luciano has followed us, sitting heavily down next to me.

I struggle to breathe, let alone find the words to tell Sam what I have finally understood. The last piece of the jigsaw. *She told him*, I tell myself, afraid to voice the truth, aware of how hideous it is. *She told him about Matteo, about the partisans, where their barn at Sant'Antonio was. It was he who organised for the German patrol to attack it; it was he who followed Giuliana, knowing she would lead him to Matteo.* My grandmother, the woman who cared for me throughout my childhood, who raised my mother, was responsible for the death of my true grandfather. Her own husband's brother. Giuliana gave her baby, my mother, away to the woman who had brought about her grief. The woman who took away not only the love of her life but also the child of that union. Raised it as her own.

It's too much, and I run and vomit in the bushes, aware of Sam's hand on my back, of his soothing words. I turn and bury my face in his chest, crying hot tears of anger and betrayal. I blurt out my discovery to Sam, who is as shocked as I am. He knew her as a sweet, religious old lady. Reconciling this knowledge with the lady we knew will be difficult. We walk back over to Luciano, and I see from his expression that he has also apprehended the terrible truth. He says nothing, but when I sit next to him he takes my hand.

"I always wondered whether the attacks were coordinated," he says quietly. "The partisans were not popular among the locals: people were scared of reprisals. I always suspected someone might have betrayed their location. Not to the *nazisti*, but perhaps to the *fascisti*. They were our countrymen, after all. But I never imagined it could have been Assunta." There is a silence, while we all try to understand what made her do it. It's easy to see how she could have learnt of Matteo's return, living with his mother. The execution of her brother must have turned her mind, made her want to strike out, to hold someone responsible for his death.

"My mother never knew," I whisper hoarsely, thinking of my beautiful mother. "She never knew her real mother, her real father. How he died fighting for what he believed in. How he died because of *her* betrayal." The tears sting my eyes, my throat tightens with pain and nausea threatens again. "My mother could have known Giuliana; they could all have come back home to Italy together. If only she had known the truth." I think suddenly of my grandfather and whether he ever learnt that it was his own wife who'd betrayed his brother. He left behind everything, his family farm, his mother, his friends, all because of his wife's betrayal. I know instantly that he never knew, that it would have been beyond his comprehension, beyond forgiveness. My grandmother must have lived alone with the knowledge her whole life. I see with retrospect how her religious devotion must have been an attempt to make amends, to pay penance for the wrong she had done our family.

We return to Montaltissimo, and the grey cloud of our revelation follows us. Luciano bids us farewell, and I can read the pain on his face. He is thinking of Giuliana, his beloved sister, and what she was deprived of. Now she will never know, but perhaps that is for the best. What good could come of it now? I wish I myself did not know, that my memories of my grandmother and my childhood had not been tainted. The peace I felt following the day at the Lost Barn and the satisfaction that my quest was complete are shattered, and I am restless and bad-tempered. I find myself looking back through family photos, staring at my grandmother and questioning who she really was.

With terrible clarity I now understand the reason for the deathbed promise that my mother would never go to Italy, her terror that she would one day discover the truth. Her attempts to sell Stazzana, to delete it from our family history forever. Her refusal to remember the past, the place they came from. How she forbade my grandfather to talk about it, even to his own family. I miss my mother like a physical pain in my chest, and I so wish I could tell her everything, ask her advice like I always did. It strikes me that I am now the matriarch, the oldest mother in the family, and I feel unequipped for the role. I yearn to lie in my mother's lap, to feel her stroke my hair and tell me everything will be OK. Luna seems to understand, for she stays close to me, cuddling in to my heart and calming me with her presence. I am aware of the role reversal, a three-year-old comforting her mother, but she is no ordinary child. There is such wisdom in her green eyes, my little angel.

April passes in a blur, a spell of mist and rain enveloping the village for most of the month. It suits my mood, and I closet myself away with my memories, while Sam works at Stazzana and the girls go to school. When Sam tells me the forecast for the first of May is sunny and we should spend the festa down at Stazzana I do not resist; I know the girls will enjoy it. It is Labour Day, the *festa dei lavoratori*, and the whole country will be on holiday.

The day dawns bright with the promise of the first really hot day of the year. As we walk down the track we notice primroses growing and the girls delight in eating one golden head each, believing it will help them to see the fairies. The track is dressed in its springtime finery, with acacia blossoms forming a white mist above our heads and elderflowers filling the air with their sweet, tart perfume. As we cross the river and emerge onto the fields below the house the girls grow excited, and Sam shoots me a smile as he pulls a scarf from his pocket.

"Surprise, Mama!" the girls both cheer, and I let myself be blindfolded, wondering what they are all up to. With Sam's strong arm around my waist to guide me we head uphill towards the terraced land alongside the farmhouse where a vineyard grew in the past. I guess that we turn to walk along what we call 'Pear Avenue', a small track lined with ancient pear trees covered in lichen. Eventually we stop, the girls clutch my hands in excitement, and Sam gently removes the scarf from my face.

In front of me sits a rustic wooden bower built over a large bench, with roses planted all around it. Their colours, pinks, reds, white and yellows, are splashes of colour on the verdant green hillside, and I see that with time they will grow to cover the bower. There is also sweet-smelling jasmine, and several kiwi plants. I walk towards the bench, beautifully carved by Sam, and I notice there are words engraved on it. I read my parents' names – *Duncan Graham Jamestone, Giovanna Jamestone* – and run my hand gently over them. Just beneath their names there is a grey slab of slate set into the bench, and my breath catches in my throat as their images smile out at me.

"I found a company that prints photos onto slate, for remembrance sites," Sam tells me shyly. "Do you like it?"

I turn to him in amazement and can only pull him close, at a loss how to express what this means to me. He grins with relief and lifts the girls up to sit on the bench with us, and we all look out over the view together.

"I thought it would be a place to come and talk to your parents," Sam tells me, "to feel close to them."

"This is what you've been doing down here this month," I realise, thinking of the hours he has spent creating this surprise for me.

"In amongst all the strimming work, yes." He grins. "I'm in great demand at this time of year." I gaze at this gorgeous husband of mine who has shown his love in so many ways this past year, and at the faces of our two perfect children. I think how blessed I was to have two parents who loved me, and grandparents who loved me, whatever may have happened in the past. I know I will struggle to forgive what my grandmother did, but I believe she must have paid the price many times over, a lifetime of guilt and the perpetual fear the truth would one day come out. I have spent enough time dwelling on my loss, I need to appreciate those who are here with me now and look to the future. *Our* future.

Sam produces a bottle of my favourite spumante and two champagne flutes, and pours us both a glass. He has also brought along a bottle of pink lemonade for the girls, and two tumblers.

"To Nonno and Nonna!" Aria solemnly declares, and we all clink glasses. My parents may have never travelled to Stazzana, but as we sip our wine looking out over the green hills, the perfume of roses all around us, butterflies dancing on the spring breeze, I know that they are here now.

34

Assunta

1989

Giovanna was a peaceful baby who rarely cried. As she grew into a tumbling toddler and a sweet schoolgirl, I began to believe she really was our child. Our gift, our joy, the link that made us a family. We were miles from home, in a land that was dark and cold and so different from the Garfagnana, but they were happy times. We arrived in Scotland war-torn, terrified, desperately seeking a new start, a safe place to establish our family. Like so many in the forties. As the years passed we worked hard, earned our place in the community. We learnt the language; we embraced our new culture. We forged friendships and Giovanna grew up speaking our native Italian at home and English at school, in the shop and with her friends. It was a life built on solid foundations: work, school, church, family. By day I could keep the faith, relax even, safe in parameters of our new life. But at night the fear would return, rise like the wind that could blow away all the illusions and reveal the lie that was at the heart of it all. The terror that she would be taken from us, that our lives could be swept up like dust.

I worked so hard to make amends, to pay penance for my sins. Any opportunity to volunteer with the church, any help our neighbours needed, I was always there. I tried to be the best mother I could, making sure Giovanna had everything she needed. She was never spoilt, for I always had an eye to her soul, wary of what may lie within her. But there I need not have feared. There never was a sweeter child, a purer heart. She was goodness and light, and Giovanni and I loved her more than life itself. We chose her name for her father, who was named after his own father. An attempt to tie her more closely to us, to knit her into our family? We were never blessed with more children, a fact I always saw as divine will. Punishment, perhaps. But it was one I accepted gracefully: Giovanna was always enough. She was a quiet soul, a contented child and she grew into a graceful young woman. She loved to cook, and when she wasn't studying she was always either in the garden with her father, or in the kitchen with me. Every day I would give thanks for this life we were blessed to share. Not a grand life, but it was everything I ever wanted. Our ice-cream parlour became well-known in our part of Scotland, and we saw generations of children grow up there. We worked long hours and made enough money to buy a home of our own and send Giovanna to university. The first from our family to gain a degree, we were so proud of her that day. When she met Duncan we were pleased: he was a wholesome young man and we felt sure he would take care of our daughter.

I will always remember the day we met baby Emma at the hospital in Ayr. A blanketed bundle, with wispy fair hair peeking out the top. She favoured her father, with her white rose complexion. I was holding her, admiring her tiny fingers, when she opened her eyes. I froze, my throat constricting silently, a liquid chill filling my stomach. Green eyes fixed me and I thought I would vomit, so great was my shock. I could not move; I was fixed to my hospital chair, the past sweeping across the years to assail me. My greatest fear, my well of guilt, all in a pair of green eyes. The life I had built, nurtured, come to believe in, stripped away in an instant by a newborn baby.

I recovered, of course. I am a survivor. I came to love little Emma like I did her mother, a love that was endless and uncompromising. I learnt to hide the dark chord of fear that often gripped me when her eyes met mine. I never worried that Giovanna would seek the past out; she was a good girl and I had warned her of the dangers. But since the day Emma was born, I have been fearful. The old nightmares have returned, the voice that mocks the life we built here, threatens to strip away the very foundations it rests on. Her green eyes remind me that we can never escape ourselves, our destiny, the truth. There is something of eternity in them, a timelessness that can transport me to that other time so quickly. She was a good child, like her mother was, but there was something of what the Scots call the fey about her, even from the earliest age. I look after her while her parents work now, two days per week, and if I ever need to remonstrate with her she listens attentively, and appears to have learnt the lesson, but I always have the feeling her soul is elsewhere.

She isn't physically like *her* in any other respect, only her eyes. I spent most of my life haunted by her, in one way or another. As a child I was plagued by the sin of envy; it gnawed away at me from the inside. Giuliana was everything I was not: beautiful, popular, charismatic. Intelligent too, though she never applied herself at school as she could have done. When she entered a room with that restless energy she had, she caught the attention of everyone present. She shone too brightly for our little mountain community; she overshadowed the rest of us. She would always have left at some point, I believe; it was the way she was. Never content to stay at home, never one for tradition and routine. The bitterness I felt back then has faded over the years; I know that my own sins were far greater. The guilt I have carried for a lifetime, the fear I will be discovered, is ever-present.

I dread the year end, the month of December. The month of reckonings. When another postcard arrives from somewhere around the world, and I have to squirrel it away, always terrified that Giovanna might see it. As per our agreement I write our own news and send a photograph of Giovanna and, since her arrival, also of Emma. It was our only contact, the briefest of correspondences. The cord that connects us now is slight but unbreakable. I kept to our contract out of fear that she would come back into our lives, and as I read of her exploits around the world I am ashamed to say I am always relieved to hear her plans do not include Scotland. It assuaged my conscience to some small degree to see what an unsuitable life she led for a child, how I knew with certitude that Giovanna was better off with us. *But that's not the life she would have been living,* my guilt would whisper in my ear, *were he still alive.*

I trained myself to look forwards, never backwards, to forge a life in Scotland that looked to the future. I pushed all thoughts of Stazzana and the pain they always brought far from my mind; I tried to erase our past by replacing each memory with our new experiences. But we are a composite of our past, and I was only tricking myself. When Giovanni inherited Stazzana upon the death of his mother it was emotional for both of us. I know he felt guilty he hadn't been there at the end of her life – her only living son. The journey was long and expensive in those days, and we worked long hours in the ice-cream parlour. Giovanni suggested we travel back to see his mother for a holiday several times, but it was out of the question for me. I reminded him of the dangers of such a trip, the risk that someone would say something out of turn to Giovanna. That she would want to go back again and again, and as she grew older the threat would only increase. I pointed out how hard we had worked, that we could not throw it all away. He always understood and backed down, but I know it was a great sadness for him. Of course he only knew half the story. He never suspected my real reason for never wanting to return, the guilt that was forever associated with my homeland for me. The deaths I set in motion that night. His brother and cousin, wiped out in one strike. By the time he inherited Stazzana we knew we would never return. We made attempts over the years to sell the farm, but no-one was ever interested. The house was one of many unwanted remnants of the past. Abandoned by a generation who turned their backs on the old ways, unable to go back to that way of life after the war. No matter how hard I tried to forget about her my mind would sometimes find its way back to Stazzana. The place my married life began, where I spent those lonely years of waiting and praying, the pain and grief that coloured my days there. Every hill, every tree is etched into my memory. Age has taught me it will always be a part of me.

The church teaches us that if we confess our sins, they will be forgiven. I am a believer, but I have never managed to convince myself that what I did could ever be forgiven. Every happiness we have enjoyed has been bought at the expense of others. Our time in the sun was gained through death and loss, and I know that the reckoning will come. Debts must always be paid, and the Lord knows all the secrets of our hearts. For myself I am not afraid to suffer, but I could not bear for them to know what I did. If Emma does find out one day, I can only pray I am long gone by then.

35

Emma

2018

A year has passed and June has come again, my new favourite month of the year. The month we arrived in Montaltissimo, the month I met Luciano. Tonight is midsummer, the most magical night of the year, and Stazzana is dressed in her summer finery. The hills have burst into life, the trees glorious with their new leaves, filling in the bare gaps with vibrant shades of green. The grass in the fields and meadows is impossibly bright, a buttercup-yellow green, full of sunshine and joy. The insects, the birds, the people of the mountains, we are all celebrating the arrival of summer and being alive to enjoy it. Winter had her brand of beauty, the snowscapes, the exposed curves of the hills, the wild storms, but that time has passed and we are ready to welcome *la bella stagione*. To throw the windows open once again, to bathe in the river, to picnic in the fields.

The farmhouse is festooned with fairy lights, the work of Sam and Luciano, and tiny solar lights are dotted throughout the orchard, ready to reveal themselves when night falls. The house has made it through another winter, though we fear it might be her last without a new roof. One main beam is rotting, and another ceiling has collapsed. The house is off limits tonight, the doors closed to keep the children out, but the night is warm and there is no sign of rain. We've been planning our midsummer party for weeks and have invited the whole village, as well as many other friends we've made this year. Some friends from Scotland have also flown over for the event, including my best friend Cat, and Sam's parents Daisy and Archie. They are captivated by the area, throwing themselves into sightseeing with great gusto. They love being shown around by Aria and Luna, who are keen to show off their local knowledge and their growing Italian skills. Everyone here has brought a contribution: a focaccia, a dessert, a cheese, some home-made wine. The feast is laid out on a long table stretching from the house along to the orchard, and a gentle evening breeze is making the white tablecloth dance. I have been frying zucchini blossoms in tempura on our campfire, *fior di zucca*, which a neighbour's daughter is now offering around. They are crunchy and salty, and perfect with an early evening aperitivo. The zucchini are fresh from our vegetable garden here at Stazzana, which we have worked hard on since April. It's been quite a feat keeping the vegetables safe from the wild animals that roam the land, and Sam and Luciano have built some robust fencing to surround the garden. The wild boar are powerful, and would make short work of our produce. The deer can jump so high that they have built the fencing over two metres tall, and it does rather resemble a cage. It was all worth it though, when we had our first *pomodori*. I inhaled their musty perfume and was instantly transported to my grandfather's greenhouse. They popped in our mouths, flooding them with the taste of summer and the goodness of the earth. We've grown a few varieties of vegetable and a large herb garden, from which I picked armfuls of basil this afternoon for the tomato and basil salad, and to make a pesto for my pasta dish.

I've also made a salad entirely of foraged herbs from the fields of Stazzana: dandelion leaves, plantain leaves, *rughetta selvatica*, wild arugula, all strewn with blue borage and golden calendula flowers for edible decoration. It amazes me, this incredible land of ours that offers so much more than we realise at first glance.

After a scorching day the air is warm and balmy, and I can still feel the heat on my bare arms. Sam and Luciano are standing by the pizza oven they just finished building in time, peering in as the first creation cooks. Archie and Pietro are with them, glass of wine in hand, and I smile, thinking how perhaps the pizza oven is the Italian equivalent of the British BBQ, always the gathering place of choice of the menfolk.

As I watch Luciano, I notice how much younger he seems than when I met him, hardly an old man at all but one in his prime. His transformation has also brought new life to Maria. Her arthritis doesn't bother her anymore, and she stands taller, straighter. I never hear her scolding him, or only in jest, and her laughter comes easily, gathering force until it rings through the air. Luciano has been attentive to her since his return, determined to make up for his lack of affection in the past. At first she was suspicious of these romantic gestures: the compliments, the flowers, the help around the house. She demanded what had happened in New York; had he been unfaithful to her? When would this lovestruck fool turn back into the grumpy farmer she'd lived with for over fifty years? But slowly, surely, the new Luciano won her over, and she blossomed like a spring flower. Their children, equally bemused by the change in their father started to visit more often, at first out of concern and then gradually out of genuine pleasure. Here was a father who listened to them, wanted to get to know them, cared about them. A father who kissed and hugged and told them he loved them. A grandfather who delighted in his grandchildren, who was interested in their lives. They are here tonight, Elena and Antonio, with their spouses and offspring. The grandchildren are in their twenties now, mostly studying in various cities or abroad, but tonight they are all here, playing with the children and helping take care of the smallest ones. No gadgets tonight, I note with a smile, although perhaps the lack of an internet connection has put pay to that.

As he said he would, Luciano has re-connected with relations he had long since lost contact with, and has made visiting them a regular occurrence, always laden with gifts from the farm. His famous lemons, a creamy cheese, a bottle of last year's wine. He is now a permanent fixture at the Thursday market at Castelnuovo, standing in the piazza with his friends, reminiscing about times gone by. I pick him up after I have dropped the girls off at school, and he is always waiting by the farm gate, smartly dressed in his suit and hat. I struggle to find the right words for how I feel about Luciano; I can only say that I cannot imagine life without him. He is a treasure uncovered, an unexpected blessing. Out of the ashes of my loss, my grief, has risen this new life, this friend who is both old and new. He always claims I am his angel, that I saved him, but in truth it was he who saved me. He led me to Giuliana, to the truth, even though he feared he would lose it all.

My attention is drawn north of the house, up the hill, towards Sassi. The hillside is now painted in sweeping green strokes, lush with the thick foliage of the chestnut trees. The Lost Barn is hidden from view, but I can picture it, roofless, slowly returning to the ground. The mud mortar disintegrating, the rocks falling to the forest floor, the ivy and ferns slowly covering the remnants of the barn. That chapter is now closed, but my mind drifts back to the day we walked up there. It feels like a distant dream; I struggle to remember the details. I recall the metallic taste of the air, the tension all around us. I believe Luciano was also conscious of the pressure, but Sam was oblivious to it as he went ahead to explore the old barn. I remember the screaming in my head, the warning which gave me the strength to push through the fog, to drag Sam to safety before the roof collapsed. I remember the voice calling me, familiar and yet not one person, an amalgamation of ancestors, of love. I remember knowing where to go, what to do, what was needed. It was wordless, thoughtless, as if something deeper had taken over and I was being guided. I was aware of the blood flowing through my veins, the blood that connects me to my mother and my grandmother. The blood which gave me the power to forgive, and to ask forgiveness. The energy that surrounded me was white, misting the forest around me; I saw only light and the darkness that hovered near the ditch, the resting place of he who could not rest.

With the light protecting me I allowed myself to feel the fury that lingered there, the force of the love that Fiorlindo bore for Giuliana. Unrequited, frustrated love, that had turned into impotent rage over the long years. Unable to move on he was trapped in the place where his spirit had been wrenched so violently from his body. Denied a wake, a funeral, a grave for loved ones to tend to. I don't know how long I sat there, rocking his skull. Safe with the love of Giuliana and my mother all around me, I let the healing flow until the darkness dissipated. When I opened my eyes the forest was just a forest, the birds were singing and my legs were stiff and aching beneath me. He had gone, and I prayed was now at peace.

It is general knowledge now, that I am the granddaughter of Giuliana and Matteo. Before I think many people suspected but were afraid to say anything. The reserve I sensed with many of the villagers before has now disappeared. They no longer need to watch what they say, to stay on safe ground. For the first time since we arrived here I know where I fit in this community; I know who my relations are. I feel a sense of belonging and I know that I would like to raise my children here, to grow old here. But there is Sam to consider, and I haven't broached the subject yet, afraid to hear that he is longing to go back to Scotland. To his job, our friends, our house, our former life.

Laughter floating up from the meadow below the house

returns me to the present moment, and I smile to see Aria running around the trees with the other children who have come tonight. Some neighbours' grandchildren, friends from school, Luciano's grandchildren. Her pale blue dress streams out behind her as she runs, her hair glinting in the last of the sun's light before she disappears behind La Pania. Aria is leading the little gang of children, singing a song she has learnt at school. It thrills me to hear her chatting with her friends, in a perfectly accented Italian. She flips between the two languages with ease, unaware of what a gift she has. She is so full of life, my little sun child; she shines so brightly. The other children are drawn to her and she is generous with her friendship, her ideas, her games.

I scan the meadow for Luna, and I see her sitting beneath an apple tree making a daisy chain. I see her lips moving and I know she will be playing with one of her imaginary friends. Her best friend seems to be a boy called Piero, who she tells me is often with her. She does play with the other children and with her sister, but she seems to be older than them in some ways, aware of more than they are. She loves the company of adults and spends much time with Luciano. They love working in the garden or the fields, going on walks with her little basket to collect flowers, herbs, nuts, whatever the season is offering. They remind me of the times I spent with my nonno Giovanni in the garden in Ayrshire. I do worry about her, my serious little moon girl, but she tells me not to worry even before I have voiced a concern, leaving me marvelling at this child I have created, yet who remains a mystery to me.

"*Buona sera, bellissima*," a voice murmurs in my ear, and I feel muscled arms encircling my waist, warm kisses landing on my cheek. I inhale his scent of bergamot, spice and smoke from the fire, and I nestle in closer. We gaze across the valley, at the view that has become so familiar. The fields below the house, the orchard, the terraces which we've now planted with young olive trees. The sound of laughter fills the air, and it feels good that after so many years of silence Stazzana is now buzzing with life again.

A full moon is rising in the sky to the east, over the Apennines. I think how much has changed in a year, how this community has welcomed us. I think of my parents, as always, and the stab of pain that accompanies the memory of their accident still hurts, but I realise my memories of the good times are growing stronger, the debilitating sorrow reducing. I regularly go and sit in the bower that Sam built in remembrance of them and spend time reminiscing, holding on to the happy times. I take a cup of tea and just let myself cry, smile, whatever feels right at the time. It's over a year now since the accident, and whilst I still miss them every day, I can see the way ahead. I feel their presence here with us this evening, and I send a silent prayer up into the sky for them. I think of Giuliana, who passed away a week after we left her in New York, and I pray she has now returned home and been reunited with Matteo. I think how their love story continues even today, in the lives of myself and my daughters.

Sam turns me to face him, a smile on his lips, and he gently brushes the hair away from my face.

"Let's stay," he whispers, his eyes alight with love and excitement. "Let's make Stazzana a home again, do it up, live here, maybe run a holiday business." I stare at him, speechless, a desire to laugh building inside me. "That is what you want, isn't it, Emma?" A note of anxiety has entered his voice, and he searches my face for answers. The laughter bubbles out of me, unrestrained, and I jump into his arms, kissing his face, overwhelmed with relief that this is what he wants too.

"I was so scared you wanted to go back to Scotland, that you wanted to sell Stazzana," I gasp, my vision blurred now, and he pulls me tighter, laughing too.

"I could no more do that than sell you," he murmurs, relaxing into our embrace. "It's part of our family, this place.

Even I can feel that it's special, that it wants us to stay." As I hold this husband of mine tight, thanking whatever powers might be for his love over the past year, I spot the first firefly of the year glowing right in front of my face, before disappearing back into the dusky meadow. I hear the singsong chatter of our friends and family all around us, and it joins with that of another age, another time. I feel the love of my ancestors, the people who chose this rock to build the house upon, and I know that we are home, that our place is here at Stazzana.

Epilogue

Giuliana

The pages of my life were written in many languages, in many locations, and though I did not value them at the time, they were my story too. Not my first story, not the story I would have chosen to write, but my story nonetheless. It is only at the end, looking back, that we see clearly. We see the futility of our struggles, our attempts to thwart fate. We see how blind we have been, how obsessed with our own agendas. How small we make ourselves, when in reality we are limitless. I look back and I see that every second of my time was precious, that it was filled with beauty. With grace. Now I am one with the world I understand that which I could not understand before. How I fought! Against life, against love, against happiness. Instead of facing my pain, feeling my loss, I ran towards the future, even whilst I knew it would never hold that which my heart longed for.

Liberated from my ninety-year-old shell I am light as the wind, free to follow my heart. I remember who I was, back then, the wildness that lived in my heart. The love I bore for the mountains I was raised in, the timelessness of the days I spent exploring them.

There was no distinction, then, between the two of us. Matteo was my heart and I was his soul, so he told me. I have had a long exile, believing I could never return, but now in death I have found what I lost in life.

Midsummer's Eve holds some special magic, the line between our worlds blurs, as it does at All Saints. I drift unseen over the festivities, the laughter ringing through the air, the woodsmoke from the campfire caught in the evening sun. I see Emma standing below in a white dress, looking upwards at me, and I feel the love she is sending to me and to her parents. My darling Giovanna. The breeze flutters her flaxen hair, and she closes her eyes and breathes the evening in. All is love this evening; all is peace. Up north at the Lost Barn, seat of my happiness and my despair, the storm has now passed. It is just a barn, returning to the ground.

I become aware of a pair of green eyes fixed upon me, a voice calling me down to play. My friend, my great-granddaughter, Luna. I play awhile with her beneath an apple tree, this child who has the gift. Who sees beyond this world, whose understanding already extends far beyond my own. I kiss her, my dark locks brushing against her gold head, and she smiles, knowing where I am going. Even now my heart quickens as I follow the wolf track along the river. Insects dance across the pools of water, illuminated in the last rays of evening sun, their tiny wings ablaze. I round the corner and see the chestnut house ahead of me. He is there, waiting for me under a tree. Waiting as he has done for decades, as he promised to do for all eternity.

Bibliography

La resistenza in Garfagnana – Renzo Bertolini

L'altra faccia del mito: Diario del gruppo Valanga. Garfagnana 1944 – Pietro Petrocchi and Silvano Valensi

Senza Patria – Leonardi Giancarlo

Partisan Diary: A Woman's Life in the Italian Resistance – Gobetti Ada

Memorie di guerra vissuta. Garfagnana 1940–1945 – Tommaso Terra

At War on the Gothic Line – Christian Jennings

Con la guerra negli occhi – Donne e Uomini di Garfagnana raccontano 1943–45 – collated by Oscar Guidi

With thanks to the Second World War Museum in Molazzana for its wonderful collection and helpful team of volunteers.